KHAKI
Fever

LINDSAY NORMAN

Jonathan Ball Publishers
JOHANNESBURG & CAPE TOWN

© Text: Lindsay Norman (2025)
© Published edition: Jonathan Ball Publishers (2025)

Originally published in South Africa in 2025 by
JONATHAN BALL PUBLISHERS
A division of Media24 (Pty) Ltd
PO Box 33977
Jeppestown
2043

ISBN 978-1-77619-462-9
ebook ISBN 978-1-77619-463-6

*Every effort has been made to trace the copyright
holders and to obtain their permission for the use
of copyright material. The publishers apologise for
any errors or omissions and would be grateful to be
notified of any corrections that should be
incorporated in future editions of this book.*

jonathanball.co.za
x.com/JonathanBallPub
facebook.com/JonathanBallPublishers

Cover designer and illustrator: Sean Robertson
Design and typesetting: Johan Koortzen
Printed and bound by Pinetown Printers (Pty) Ltd
Set in Sabon MT Pro 12pt on 15pt

For Jan and Sean
Thank you for always cheering me on.
And in loving memory of Roy and Hettie Norman,
always in our hearts.

1

I MANAGED A BRIGHT SMILE as a group of tourists made their way to my Land Cruiser.

'Hi! I'm Alex, and I'll be your guide for today.'

They gazed back at me, looking dubious. To be fair, I'm not exactly what people expect in a guide when they go on a safari, even when it takes place in a glorified zoo. I'm exactly five foot and two inches, and even though I never stop eating, I'm a bit on the skinny side. I have to sit on a cushion when I drive the Land Cruiser, and my rifle is almost longer than I am. It's understandable that all this doesn't exactly inspire confidence, especially since my fellow guides are all men with thighs bulging out of their shorts and have pecs that are more exciting to view than the animals.

Two women in their twenties looked wistfully at my colleague Magnus and the group he was guiding. Totally at ease because he's a people pleaser, he was doing his usual two-handed hand-shake. Personally, I don't like to touch guests because, firstly, I'm not a touchy-feely person and, secondly, you wouldn't believe the number of guests I've seen not washing their hands after they go to the loo.

Undaunted, because their reaction was, like, totally normal, I continued.

'Let's talk about a few safety instructions. Hopefully we will see lion today, but if we do, please remain seated and keep still. The reason for this is that we don't want to break our silhouette. Keep very quiet when we approach game ...' Blah blah blah, I could see I was boring the pants off them and frankly I was boring myself too.

Magnus, I noticed out of the corner of my eye, had his group enthralled. He had one hand on the bonnet of his Land Cruiser, all the better to display the muscles in his manly arm, and was casually leaning on his rifle with the other, luckily pointing it to the ground, because how he got his licence I do not know. Every now and again they broke into little gusts of laughter as he rolled out his practised quips.

'Right, if you're ready, you can hop on board, and we'll start our drive.'

After they got in, I remembered that I had to ask them their names, and it was a bit awkward as they could see it was an afterthought. The women in their twenties were Mandy and Candace from America. Then David and Joanne from Australia, and finally Inge and Jürgen from Germany. I can almost immediately see who's going to cause problems on a game drive, and in this case it was David. It turned out David was a South African who had emigrated to Australia in the 1990s and was clearly feeling pissed off about that. He was also a bit of a know-it-all and already telling some unlikely stories about his trips to the Kruger Park when he lived in Johannesburg.

'The Kruger Park is much bigger than this place, and much more authentic,' he said. 'Probably about a hundred or maybe a thousand times bigger and there are no separate encampments for the animals. It's a pity you can't all go there instead.'

'We're going to the Serengeti next week,' said Candace. 'In Tanzania, right?'

'Never heard of it,' said David. 'If you get on it right away you

2

might still be able to hire a car and get a rondavel in the Kruger.'

I made a mental note to reassure Candace and Mandy about the Serengeti and to tell them that it would be nothing like this godforsaken excuse for a reserve. The Plains is about a two-hour drive from Cape Town, making it ideal for tourists looking for a one-day excursion and what we call a Ferrari Safari. On arrival they get a dodgy buffet lunch and then they are loaded up and taken to see the animals. The Plains is not big enough for the big game to roam freely so we drive them in and out of encampments and try to pretend they're very lucky to see so much game. Some guests stay overnight at the lodge, which was what my guests were going to do, and I was already dreading having to make polite conversation over dinner.

As we entered the first encampment there was no sign of Magnus. He usually did the first one at speed, since he found the antelope and bovids boring, preferring instead to head straight to the second one, where the lions are kept.

Of course, the first antelope we saw were a herd of impala. I stopped and turned off the engine and began.

'Here we have …'

'Impala,' said David. 'And they're rutting, which means they want sex.'

'Well, no, not exactly,' I said. 'The rutting period is from April to June, but you're right that rutting is when they engage in sexual activity. This is a mixed herd of females and males, and you can tell the difference because the rams have horns, and the ewes don't.'

'I've seen a lady impala with horns,' said David.

'That's not possible,' I said as politely as I could, because I was already getting a bit irritated with him. 'Females don't have horns.'

I started up the engine again and, in the mirror, I saw him turn around and roll his eyes at the others. Other than making lewd remarks about the size of the buffalos' balls and telling a stupid joke about a zebra, he kept quiet, and I began to hope that he wasn't as bad as I thought.

I drove aimlessly around the second enclosure pretending I was looking for the lions, but I knew exactly where they were. They'd been given a couple of impalas the day before and were so full they could barely move.

'There they are,' I said in a dramatic whisper as we drove into a clearing. The lions were fast asleep under a tree and didn't even open an eye as we approached. Even though they were not exactly in the wild, I always felt a thrill of excitement when I saw them. Jürgen and Inge gave gratifying gasps, and Mandy and Candace said, 'Oh my God!' about a thousand times. Even Joanne looked animated, but not so David.

'Pity they're not doing anything,' he said. 'You wouldn't believe the number of lion kills I've seen in the Kruger.'

It was on the tip of my tongue to say that I genuinely wouldn't, but instead I launched into my talk about lions and answered questions like the pro I am. There were some good ones for a change, and we were just about to get going again when David stood up and clapped his hands.

'Wake up, pussies!' he shouted and then bent down and slapped his hand against the side of the Land Cruiser. Apart from the young males who got a fright and shot off into the bushes, the others just lifted their heads and stared at him as if he was a madman – which he was.

Joanne grabbed his arm and pulled him back down into his seat, giving me an apologetic look.

'Plug it in, David,' she said. 'You always have to show off, and spoil it for everyone!'

I felt sorry for her for being married to such a tool, so I didn't say anything to him and drove away, leaving the couple to a muttered argument, which eventually lapsed into a deathly cold silence.

Luckily David sulked for quite a bit, so the next encampment went without incident. Our final stop was to see the elephants, and by now we'd caught up with Magnus and his group. The Plains has a small herd of elephant and they're so acclimatised to the Land Cruisers there's literally not been one incident. Until this particular day.

I could immediately tell that the oldest male, Oubaas, looked a bit out of sorts. He's really harmless, but he does sometimes get a little grumpy if you drive too close. Fair play to that. Actually, to be completely honest, he had tried to push over a Land Cruiser a couple of times, but personally I wouldn't describe that as an incident. I mean, you just have to watch out for the signs and respect his space, but that fool Magnus had driven so close his guests could practically touch him.

'Now that's a ranger,' said David. 'He knows what he's doing.'

'He's not a ranger,' I said. 'He's a guide and to be honest he's much too close. You can see the elephant doesn't like it.'

Magnus eventually clocked that Oubaas was getting a bit annoyed, and drove away. It was our turn to drive up to the herd. I turned off the engine a good distance away from them.

'Can't we go closer?' said David. 'I want to take a picture where you get only its eye in.'

'Use your zoom,' I said. 'That's how most of those pictures are taken. I don't want to irritate him. He's used to us but it's best not to take chances with elephant.'

'She's scared,' I heard him mutter. 'Women shouldn't be rangers.'

And of course, that's when I decided to do something very stupid. I decided to give David a fright. Without saying anything, I drove right up to Oubaas on my and David's side and turned off the engine. I was even closer to him than Magnus had been, and I was happy to see David shift nervously in his seat.

'Turn the bloody engine back on!' he whispered.

'That would be the wrong thing to do,' I whispered back. 'They don't like the noise. Just keep very quiet.'

I admit I also felt just a little uneasy. I didn't think Oubaas was in one of his moods where he would try to overturn us or anything, but he stopped eating and stood very still, and I could see he was irritated. He moved around and faced David full on, his trunk up, and then took a step forward.

'Go!' said David, now almost in his wife's lap.

'Just sit still and shut up,' I said. 'He won't do anything.'

But he did. Oubaas stuck out his ears, reversed into a better position, tucked down his trunk and then pushed against the Land Cruiser. Not very hard, but his right tusk sort of prodded David's shoulder. I could see it was just a mild warning but that he'd do it again with a little more force if I started the engine.

Everyone screamed, especially David, who let off a high squeal of terror, and I'm afraid to say that's when I laughed.

'Go! GO!' he shrieked. 'Get out your bloody rifle! He's going to kill us!'

'For God's sake, SHUT UP and keep still!' I hissed. Thankfully he fell into a state of shock, and apart from the odd moan he kept quiet.

Oubaas stood staring at us for a while and then he slowly moved away – but stopped again. You could cut the tension with a knife as he stood still for a few seconds, as if weighing up whether he'd made the right decision. Eventually he started to eat, and I gave a small sigh of relief because this meant he had relaxed. I waited until he was a few metres away and then started the engine.

'Whoa, that was *so* cool,' said Mandy. 'I got some amazing pictures. Are you okay, David? You were so scared! I guess you were too afraid to take a picture of his eye!'

As everyone laughed, David realised what a fool he'd made of himself and he let rip at me, calling me every name under the sun and demanding I take him back to the main camp. I ignored him because I didn't see why everyone else should miss their evening drink. That was another mistake. When we got to the clearing where the drinks table had been set up, he leapt out and ran behind a bush that was unfortunately too close for us to miss the sounds of the physical manifestation of the fear he had experienced.

I'd forgotten to take a loo roll, so I gave Joanne some paper napkins and a spade to take to him. When he eventually emerged, his face was set like stone, and he got back into the Land Cruiser without saying a word. The rest of us finished our drinks, but it wasn't exactly convivial.

I could feel David's eyes boring into the back of my head as we drove back to the main camp, and I knew that trouble was coming.

Barend, the owner of The Plains, was waiting for us as we arrived, his chubby, kind face wreathed in a smile.

'Did you have a good drive?' he said.

Everyone responded with enthusiasm, even Joanne, and for a minute I thought I was going to get away with it. But no such luck. David waited for a pause in the chatter.

'It was the worst experience I've had in my life, and I want my money back.'

Barend looked startled and gave me an enquiring look. I shrugged and looked away.

'Jinne, I'm sorry to hear that,' he said. 'Why do you say so?'

'Thanks to your ranger, I nearly got killed by an elephant and all she did was laugh,' said David. 'She's irresponsible, drove right up to the bloody thing, and it charged us.'

'It did *not* charge us,' I said, turning to Barend. 'He was whining about getting closer to take a picture of Oubaas' eye, and you should have seen how he behaved around the lions.'

'She told me to shut up after nearly getting me killed,' continued David, 'and she knows nothing about animals, besides being bloody rude and surly. Stuff-all people skills. You must be off your head letting her take guests on game drives.'

'It's the first time someone has complained about Alex,' Barend lied.

'Well, frankly, I don't believe you. She's a ranger's arse,' said David.

'For the last time, I'm *not* a ranger, I'm a guide, you stupid idiot,' I said. 'And if anyone is anything's arse then it's you. In fact, you're the biggest arsehole I've ever met, and that's saying something because I've come across a few, believe me.'

'You see?' said David. 'I rest my case. I want my money back and to get the hell out of here, and then I'm going to write a review on Tripadvisor.'

He couldn't have said anything worse. Barend adored Tripadvisor, even though he sometimes got mediocre reviews on account of the animals being in camps, but he always countered them with made-up ones from his friends.

'Alex will apologise,' he said, giving me a pleading look. 'And I'll give you your money back and a free night at the lodge, or even two. Premium cabin, drinks on the house. Whatever you want.'

David looked at me expectantly. I looked back at his mean, smug face.

'I'll burn in hell before I apologise to a moronic bully,' I said.

Boom. Nail in coffin.

Barend took the whole group off for free drinks and vouchers, and I went back to the staff quarters. From the look on the other guides' faces I could see that Magnus the legendary eavesdropper had already filled them in on my latest disastrous encounter with guests. Actually, there hadn't been *that* many, but I suppose I'm not really a people person. Some of them couldn't hide that they were pleased about the drama, because I'm not exactly popular.

Inevitably I was summoned to the office less than an hour later.

Barend's wife, Antoinette, runs the show. She's quite nice, but she's the one with the business head and so she's a bit harder on the staff than Barend. I think she'd rather be running a nice B&B in Milnerton or Blaauwberg, but The Plains is Barend's dream, and it's quite sweet how mad about him she is, and I think she'd do anything for him. Antoinette works very hard and does try to fit in with the whole safari thing, but it doesn't really work because she loves faux fur, and basically everything in her wardrobe is some sort of animal pattern. She also goes for a very glamorous look and wears a ton of make-up but it's more in the blue-eyeshadow and permed-hair line, if you know what I mean, and so sometimes her vibe is a bit startling.

Antoinette was the only one in the office, which was not a good sign, because Barend always disappears when someone's in trouble.

He's a big softie and I once saw him cry when Antoinette fired a chef.

She had my employee file out and was tapping her long red nails on her desk when I entered. Also a bad sign. She gestured for me to sit and then sighed.

'Alex,' she said. 'I mean, wat de fok? Barend is so the bladdy moer in with you.'

She held up her hand as I opened my mouth to speak and looked at my file.

'You've only been with us for just under three months and there have been six complaints about you. And this latest one makes seven.'

I must say I was a bit surprised. I didn't think there had been so many. I could see that she was going to go through each one, though, so I said nothing and tried not to look sulky.

'So, one group said you made them feel stupid when they asked questions. I quote: "When I asked her where hippos lay their eggs, she said under a termite mound. I looked it up afterwards, but she didn't have to be sarcastic just because I didn't know hippos don't lay eggs. A respectful answer would have been appreciated." Then a group complained because, and again I quote, "our guide told our five-year-old that if he didn't stop singing, she'd tell an ostrich to peck out his eye". Fokken hell, Alex.'

'He was ruining the drive for all the other guests,' I said. 'He literally would not stop screeching "The Wheels on the Bus" at the top of his voice, and his parents did *nothing*.'

'But you can't say something like that to a child, man. And then this other one when you told that lady she had blood on her bourgeois hands when you saw her ivory bracelet.'

'Yes, but that was *true*, Antoinette,' I said. 'I mean, she should have known that it's disgusting to wear ivory. And I suppose another complaint about me was that man who told me he was going hunting in Namibia.'

'Ja,' she agreed. 'It was a shit show and he nearly sued us. Barend had to buy him a whole case of brandy and give him all his money back. Not to mention the other guests on the drive.'

She stared at me for a few moments and then sighed.

'Your qualifications and everything are excellent, so it's not like you act like this because you're just bladdy stupid.'

'Antoinette, we must have *principles*,' I said. 'There's no point in knowing something is wrong and then you don't say or do anything about it. This is meant to be a game reserve, for God's sake, even though it's more like a zoo to be honest, but we're meant to be about conservation and everything. I actually don't regret any of those incidents at *all*.'

She gave me this sort of death stare.

'I'm now seriously on my last nerve with you,' she said. 'I'm sorry but you're a liability, my girl. Your contract has a three-month probation clause and I'm going to have to let you go.'

I could see by the look on her face that there was nothing I could say to change her mind. And me being me, I was too proud to try anyway.

'Sure, no problem,' I said as flippantly as I could. 'When do you want me to leave?'

'Tomorrow morning,' Antoinette replied. And then, because I hadn't been technically fired, she handed me an employee evaluation form to fill out. I stuffed it in my pocket and walked out. I could have gone back to my room, but I decided that the least I could do was to join my group for supper. Besides, I was absolutely starving, even though I had eaten most of the snacks when we'd had drinks earlier, and I couldn't face any questions from my colleagues at this stage.

As I made my way towards the dining room, I wondered for the umpteenth time why guests were made to eat indoors. It was a beautiful balmy evening at the beginning of November and the cloudless Karoo skies were stuffed full of dusty stars and the hazy band of the Milky Way. Instead, they had to have their dinner in this massive, cavernous space with the air-conditioning set so high they all had their jackets on.

Antoinette is seriously into artificial flowers and plastic

tablecloths and so the dining room looks a bit like something you'd expect in a cheap resort in Miami. She's definitely not into lighting and ambience, though, and the fluorescent lights with exposed tubes make everyone look a bit green, like they've got stomach flu, which to be honest is totally not unusual at The Plains.

I could feel the curious stares of the other guides as I joined my guests, who were seated in the furthest corner of the dining room. They'd already been at the buffet for their starters and, judging from the amount of food left on their plates, they weren't impressed. Antoinette is very sentimental about the food her granny made in the 1970s, and she forces the chefs to make these aspic moulds filled with leftover vegetables from the night before.

Luckily, David the loser was at the end of the table, and I took a seat next to Joanne, who had chosen to sit as far away from her husband as possible.

'I'm so sorry about this afternoon,' she said. 'David can be such a prick. I'm not speaking to him right now, but he's actually got a good heart. He's just got a lot of baggage.'

I always cry when people are kind and so I quickly looked away.

'It's okay,' I mumbled.

She put her hand on my arm.

'You look a bit upset? I hope you didn't get into trouble? I'll speak to Barend and tell him it wasn't your fault.'

'No, it's fine,' I said. 'Honestly, it's all fine. Are you ready for your main course?'

I ignored all the meat dishes because I'm a vegetarian, but I loaded my plate with roasted potatoes and the vegetable bake, and I also added some of the mushroom pasta, the macaroni cheese, lentil curry and some garlic bread. Antoinette always told me not to overload my plate because it was embarrassing and not cost-effective, but it was my last night, so I didn't care. I also didn't bother to make conversation with any of my guests

11

because that's the part of being a guide that I really didn't like and wasn't good at. Basically, I couldn't ever think of what to say, plus it seemed pointless talking to people you're never going to see again.

Barend kept the free wine flowing and so they all got quite drunk. David was in a better mood at the end and started telling Australian jokes, which were actually quite funny, to be honest. I didn't laugh on principle, though, and concentrated on the trifle.

When dinner was over, Jürgen and Inge asked for my WhatsApp number so they could stay in touch. I suppose I looked a bit surprised, but Inge said they had been on lots of game drives all over Africa and hadn't ever laughed so much. Joanne also asked for my number – when David wasn't looking – and of course I gave it to her because she was so sweet. Mandy and Candace took a whole lot of selfies with me, which I absolutely hate, but I also gave them my WhatsApp. Guests often ask for your number, but you usually don't hear from them again, which is a bit of a relief, to be honest.

When everyone had gone to bed, I went and sat by myself outside and looked at the stars. It was quiet and peaceful, and I steered my thoughts far away from everything that had happened that day. In the distance I could hear the lions roaring and, not for the first time, I wondered what it would take for The Plains to become a proper game reserve.

Eventually the lights went out in the guides' accommodation block. I waited another half an hour to make sure they were all asleep and then I went to my room. The guides have to get up really early for the morning drive, so I set my alarm for half past three so I could leave before they all woke up. I had a shower and then put on my jeans and a hoodie so I wouldn't have to bother getting dressed in the morning, and then I got into bed. I couldn't sleep, though, because my heart was racing, and I felt a bit sick. Then I remembered the employee form, so I got out of bed again and read through it.

It had all these questions about how I would rate my experience as an employee. I had nothing to lose, really, so I decided to be very honest, and I wrote tons of extra stuff about how I would improve things at The Plains. I wrote so much that I ran out of room on the form and had to staple a few more pages to it. My alarm went off just as I was finishing, and by this time I had such a bad headache I could hardly see.

My car was parked near the office, where I'd left it nearly three months ago. In my off time, I didn't go to Calitzdorp (the closest town to The Plains) with the others because I preferred going out into the bush on my own – and they didn't invite me anyway. It was covered in dust and leaves, and even under the lights its glossy blackness looked dull.

My car is a brand-new Cherokee Jeep that my parents gave me for my birthday, and I hate it. All the other staff drive beaten-up old cars, and so when I rocked up at The Plains in my Jeep, I could see immediately that I was labelled as some spoilt rich kid, which was true, to be fair. I don't *act* spoilt, though, and I had really wanted a second-hand bakkie with a canopy.

As I unlocked the door I nearly jumped out of my skin when I heard Magnus whisper my name.

'Alex? What are you doing?' he said.

'What do you think?' I replied, slinging my bag into the boot. 'I'm leaving.'

He looked around nervously. 'Do Barend and Antoinette know?'

'No, I've just raided the safe and stolen all their money, so don't say anything, okay?'

He looked so horrified that I nearly smiled.

'I got fired, you idiot,' I said. 'That's why I'm leaving.'

He looked even more horrified, if that was possible. Magnus is a prototype head boy.

'Was it because of yesterday?' he said.

'What do you think?' I slammed the boot shut and reached for the car door.

'Jeez, I'm sorry,' he said, quickly coming forward to hold it open for me. 'I … we'll miss you, Alex.'

'Yeah, right,' I said and started the engine. I gave him a little wave and drove away.

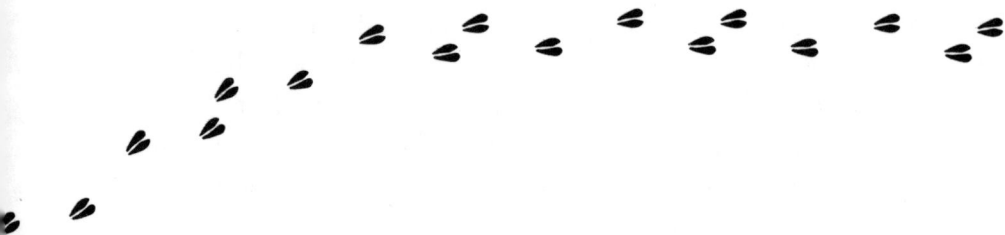

2

It was only a five-hour drive home from The Plains, but I wished it were closer because all these thoughts were racing through my mind. Basically, I was panicking because I'd failed. Again.

This psychologist I once saw said that I lived too much in my head and this made me watch other people having important life experiences while I didn't properly engage. He said I was like a bystander in life and couldn't face up to things that upset me and that's why I struggled to have relationships with people and said stuff to push them away. I didn't go back after that because he was getting dangerously close to the truth.

Driving home I felt that was how I had behaved at The Plains, and then I started thinking that everything in my whole entire life was my fault and I needed a filter, except I didn't know how to get one. Maybe it started at birth. My mother said I was a very belligerent baby and it only got worse as I got older.

My family is seriously wealthy. My father is a property developer and a lawyer – enough said – and my mother does interior design for anyone who can afford her. I'm the youngest of four children. My brothers, Charles and Richard, came first and they're extremely good-looking identical twins. After university they were ramp models for male underwear in Milan and Paris for a few years and made an absolute fortune. When they came back to Cape Town two years ago, they started building padel courts with majorly overpriced coffee shops and they're making a killing. It also helps that they're very charming and the whole of the southern suburbs is totally in love with them, including the men.

My sister, Jessica, is five years older than me and married to Roger, whose parents own a couple of exclusive boutique hotels in Plett and Mauritius. It's never been very clear to me what Roger does, but he goes on lots of business trips. I'm not mad about him (huge understatement) because he flirts a lot with other women, and I can see that it hurts Jessica's feelings. Also, I suspect that he's a bully. Jessica is a *very* kind and gentle person, and although she's so beautiful she's also quite insecure because she doesn't think she's clever. When she left college, my dad bought her a spa in Camps Bay which is really successful because she's so innovative and also incredibly nice to her clients and staff. I really love Jessica even though we haven't got anything in common. As I got closer to Cape Town, I started getting excited to see Jessica and I hoped that she hadn't gone on holiday or something.

And then I was back in the city, but it didn't feel like a city for long because we live in Constantia on a sort of tiny farm, I suppose. There was a new security guard at the gate, and I had to show him my ID.

So, I also tend to worry about stuff, and I actually *look* for it. On the way up to the house I worried about the hydrangeas in the driveway because the south-easter was so strong and the flowers were too young for the wind. And then I saw that the gate to the pool area was open even though it's always meant to be shut because the dogs like to drink from the pool and if they fall in they could drown, and everyone *knows* that. I stopped the car to see if they were at the bottom of the pool. They weren't. But they definitely *could* have been.

Sindi was hoovering the Persian carpets in the hallway and

swearing at our German shepherds, Tulip and Clive, who were attacking the machine when I walked through the front door.

'Hamba, fok off!' she was saying, and then looked up and gave me a huge smile.

'Hello, my lover,' she said, switching off the hoover and coming over to give me a hug. In a way, Sindi is also my mother. After I was born, my mother's business really started to take off and so Sindi took over. Apparently when I began talking, I used to call my mother 'madam', after which she insisted that Sindi call her Liesbet, which is her actual name. So I ended up also calling her Liesbet, and it stuck. But don't get me wrong. Obviously, I love my mother even though she's not exactly maternal, and it's never been clear to me why she had so many children. Maybe she was bored or something before she discovered interior design.

The dogs were going mad, so I sat on the floor and rolled around with them for a bit. Then I checked their ears and teeth and felt for any lumps because I'm actually a bit paranoid about something happening to them.

Liesbet came out of her studio and gave me this vague look as if she were trying to remember who I was.

'Alexandra? Aren't you meant to be up the West Coast at that resort?'

'Karoo,' I said. 'Game reserve. I'm a guide, remember.'

She looked hurt and irritated at the same time and I felt bad that I had only been in the house for literally five minutes and I had already got scratchy with her.

'What are you doing back home? Are you on leave?'

'I decided to resign,' I replied. 'Actually, it was just a temporary job to get experience. I'm going to apply to get a job in a reserve in Mpumalanga.'

'Oh,' she said. 'Well, that will be nice for you. I'll tell Dad to put some money in your account to tide you over.'

It was on the tip of my tongue to say I didn't need money, but The Plains didn't exactly pay very well, and the week before I'd been scrolling through Instagram and saw this really thin and abused dog that an animal rescue organisation was trying to save. It was so terrible that I cried and then on impulse I donated all the money I had in my account.

I had actually been worrying about finances, but I totally didn't regret the donation and I knew Liesbet would freak out if I told her what I'd done. So I just felt awkward and didn't say anything at all in the end, but I knew I should have at least said thank you.

'Roger and Jess are coming for a braai tonight,' continued Liesbet. 'So that's good timing. Jess will be so excited to see you. I'm just going to pop down to the shops to get a few things. Do you want to come with me?'

She looked sort of hopeful and I found myself wanting to go because I actually liked doing stuff with Liesbet sometimes when it was just the two of us, because she was my mother and everything and she has this way of making things fun. But I declined because I didn't want to risk any questions about The Plains. The dogs were also looking hopefully at me, and when I went to get their leashes, it was obvious they hadn't been walked in ages because, one, the leashes were still in the exact same place I left them and, two, I had tied them together before I left for The Plains so I could check if they'd been walked when I got back.

I took them to the greenbelt near us and it was a disaster. Clive is massive and looks scary even though he's not. He tends to chase small dogs for fun and Tulip always joins in. After a while they found this little Jack Russell and chased it about three times around the meadow before I managed to catch them. The Jack Russell owner went insane and unfortunately recognised me because she was on the committee for the Friends of the Greenbelt and so was my dad. She went even more crazy when I suggested that she socialise her dog and pointed out that she wasn't carrying a poo bag. There's no reason to stay around when people start shouting so I sort of jogged off with her shrieky voice reverberating in my ears.

I spent the rest of the afternoon searching for guiding jobs and Liesbet came into my room at about six.

'No dogs on the bed,' she said automatically but without conviction. 'Jess and Roger have just arrived, and Dad has started the fire.'

I went to the patio after taking a quick shower and paused at the French doors before I joined them. It all looked homely and safe. The wisteria had started to bloom on the pergola and fairy lights twinkled through the leaves. The lawn stretched out beyond the patio, glowing golden green. Jess and Liesbet sat at the table chatting and drinking wine and my dad and Roger stood next to the fire. The wind had finally died down and the sky had gone pink, and it was all perfect really, but I felt a lump in my throat as if I were homesick, but as I was actually *at* home, I couldn't think why.

Jess saw me and her face lit up.

'Baby sis!' she said and got up to hug me. 'What a lovely surprise that you're home!'

'Yes, wonderful to have you home, darling,' said my dad, pouring me a huge glass of wine even though he knew that I didn't drink, but he was always trying to get me to because he thought it might take the edge off me or something.

Luckily Roger didn't try to hug me, and that was definitely because he disliked me as much as I disliked him. I'd always thought he was a loser, right from way back when he started dating Jess. He raised his glass in a kind of ironic salute.

'Welcome, prodigal daughter,' he said.

'Roger,' said Jess, 'you mustn't call her that!'

'For God's sake, Jess!' he replied. 'I was only joking. Stop making such a big deal out of everything I say. Jesus. I should just keep my mouth shut around your family.'

'I'm only joking.' A classic way to say nasty things and get away with it.

Liesbet stepped easily into the breach, saying, 'Edward, you know Alex doesn't drink! Pour her a lemonade.' She offered Roger a bowl of nuts and he took a huge handful and shoved them into his mouth. He's a bit of a pig around food, and I looked away to avoid seeing him spewing nuts down his chin. Jess had also looked away from him and her face was pinched and tense, so I went and sat next to her and asked her about the spa.

She told me about a client who wanted his back waxed but couldn't take the pain, so he tried to leave with only half done. It was funny, really, but Jess was so worried about him that she lit aromatherapy candles, put on music and gave him a gin and tonic, and then did it herself, really slowly and gently, and he was so grateful.

'He was probably hoping for a happy ending, the poor fucker,' said Roger with his disgusting nasal laugh.

Raising his eyebrows, this time it was my dad who stepped into the breach, but unfortunately he deflected the attention towards me.

'By the way, Alex,' he said, splashing whisky into his glass, 'I just got a WhatsApp from that bloody officious woman who thinks she owns the greenbelt. She said Clive attacked her Jack Russell and that you were rude to her.'

'I wasn't rude,' I said. 'And the dogs didn't attack it, actually. They were just very overexcited because they haven't been walked since I left, so you can't blame them. If you had walked them every day like you both *said* you would then it probably wouldn't have happened. It's very cruel not to walk dogs, even if they do live in a big space.'

'That's absolute rubbish,' said my dad, looking a bit annoyed.

'Alex, please don't start stirring the minute you get back home,' added Liesbet with an exaggerated sigh. 'Let's just have a nice peaceful time together for a change.'

I said nothing and then Jess asked me if I'd like to come to the spa for some treatments. It was sweet of her and everything because she was trying to change the subject, but honestly, going to a spa was my worst nightmare. All that touching and prodding and patting and you always leave looking greasy and shiny and far worse than when you went in. But I agreed because she'd been begging me for ages. Jess looked so happy that I felt bad, and then Liesbet got all excited and asked Jess to make sure that she included my eyebrows. I asked Liesbet what was wrong with my eyebrows, and she got all irritated again and said it took the tiniest thing to set me off.

My dad took the meat off the braai and Liesbet gave him some plant-based burgers to put on the grill for me, which was very thoughtful really. While we ate, Roger kept on checking his phone and then giving a sly smirk when he read his messages. Jess was trying to pretend that she wasn't noticing, but every time he took out his phone, she looked anxious.

'Are you doing deals, Roger?' I asked, when literally for the fifth time he looked at his phone.

'No, why?' He looked defensive.

'I was just wondering what could be so important,' I said. 'I don't want to be rude or anything but actually you're being quite disrespectful.'

'Alex!' said Jess and Liesbet simultaneously. And Roger looked furious.

'Well, he is,' I said before he could say anything. 'All of us turn off our phones when we have dinner so why shouldn't he?' I gave my dad a sideways look and I could see he was trying not to laugh but he shook his head slightly at me.

'Who's ready for dessert?' he said. 'Alex, can you get the ice-cream?'

Jess followed me to the kitchen to help with the bowls. She looked upset and eventually said, 'Alex, why do you *do* that?'

'Do what?' But I knew she was talking about what I had said to Roger.

'It doesn't help when you get all confrontational, it only makes everything worse, and now I just know Roger is going to pick a fight with me on the way home, and I can't *deal* with it.' Her voice broke and a heavy tear trickled down her cheek.

'Jess!' I said, horrified. 'Why are you crying? Is he ... I mean, does he ever hurt you?'

'No, of course not, don't be silly!' She brushed the tear away. 'It's just that it's not always easy being married, and I hate fighting because he twists everything I say and then he takes days to forgive me.'

'Forgive *you*? But if he picks the fight then he must know that, and then he should apologise, Jess.'

She stared at me as if I didn't quite get it. I did though. I had plenty of experience with Roger's type.

'Let's just leave it, okay?' She put the tub of ice-cream and pudding bowls on a tray, and I saw that her hands were shaking.

'I'm sorry, I shouldn't have said anything. But Jess, I know he's a bully.'

'It's fine,' she said, not looking at me and heading out of the kitchen. 'And he's *not* a bully. Don't call him that! Just ... just please don't say anything more to provoke him.'

Aware that on my very first day home I was well on my way to ruining the dinner for everyone, I decided not to go back out to the patio and to have an early night instead. Just before I got into bed, I took two antihistamines and fell asleep with Tulip and Clive heavy on my legs. I was dimly aware that Liesbet and Jess came into my room at some stage and called my name and that Clive barked at them. But almost immediately I drifted back into an uneasy sleep and my dreams were ruthless.

The next morning, my dad and Liesbet didn't say anything at breakfast about me disappearing during dinner. They did try to ask me how it was working at The Plains, though, and the questions were definitely leading up to why I had resigned. I told them little bits, but their phones kept ringing because the cellphone rule doesn't apply at breakfast, so the conversation didn't go anywhere. Which was good because my replies were seriously edited and my dad, being a lawyer, can get quite persistent.

After breakfast, my best friend (only friend, actually) Saskia phoned me. Without sounding too dramatic about it, Saskia saved my life at high school, but that's something we don't ever talk about since there's no point really. I felt guilty that I hadn't let her know I was back in Cape Town. Of the two of us she's the better friend and she doesn't allow me to drift away from her.

She was excited when I told her I was back, and we decided to meet for lunch.

Saskia works for the absolute top restaurant in Cape Town. It has a Michelin star and a three-month waiting list, and you practically have to be a millionaire to eat there. She always says she was very lucky to get the job, but that's because she's so humble – I personally definitely know she got the job because she's such a brilliant chef. We met at a little restaurant near the forest that makes these amazing toasted sandwiches because Saskia said she was tired of complicated food.

We ordered quickly so we could get on with the talking. Saskia got straight to the point. 'Tell me about The Plains,' she said. 'How come it didn't work out?'

I told her everything in the tiniest detail. And that's the thing about Saskia. She knows me so well that I don't even think about being cagey. We'd nearly finished our lunch by the time I stopped talking, and I felt a bit flat. Thinking about all your mistakes is one thing, but listing them out loud, one by one, is quite another.

Saskia didn't say anything immediately, and that's another thing that's good about her. She takes her time to consider stuff.

'So, it's sort of the same thing that happened when you went on that work experience at the game lodge in KwaZulu-Natal?'

'Yes,' I agreed, 'although this time, as you've probably realised, it was a lot worse.'

Saskia nodded. 'It's funny, because you know exactly what you do wrong but maybe only afterwards?'

'Yes,' I said again. 'And I totally don't blame Antoinette for firing me. She and Barend are really nice people, and they didn't deserve someone like me. I don't know how to explain it exactly, but I say and do stuff and then when I think about it, I wonder why I did it. It's like my instincts are all completely wrong and my brain isn't working properly. And then when everything goes pear-shaped all I want to do is run away.'

I told her about the walk on the greenbelt with the dogs and the braai with Roger and Jess the night before.

Saskia fiddled with her napkin, looking as if she was unsure about what she was about to say. 'Alex, do you think that maybe what happened at school … you know, maybe you should talk to someone about it because it was really bad. It's just that I think it's still affecting you and that's why this stuff keeps on happening. I mean, *we* can talk about it if you want?'

I stared at her in panic. It was like she'd broken some unspoken secret pact. We had *never* talked about it. I had to grip the arms of my chair to stop myself from getting up and walking away.

'Oh God, I'm so sorry,' she said. 'I shouldn't have said that. I'm so stupid.'

'No, no, you're not Sas,' I said. 'But you don't ever speak to anyone else about it do you?'

'Of *course* not,' she replied heatedly. 'I would *never* do that, Alex.'

'Yes, yes I do know,' I said relaxing a bit. 'But tell me about your job now, Sas. We've talked only about me this whole time.'

She gave me another worried look, which I returned with a pleading one. She sighed and then we were out of danger.

'I love it,' she said. 'Honestly, Alex, you wouldn't believe how much I've learnt, and it's really exciting because the menus change every three days, and I get to cook with ingredients I'd never even heard of. But the only thing is, I'm not sure that fine dining experiences are for me, you know? We have to make these super complicated things and foams and reductions and all that, but sometimes I wish I was making tomato bredie and koeksisters.'

I told her about the weird food at The Plains and she laughed and then looked wistful.

'You know what, working somewhere like that would be my dream job,' she said. 'Local food and local ingredients and tra-ditional cooking, and *generous*, and tourists love that kind of thing. I've got tons of recipes from my ouma, some really old ones that nobody cooks now, but it's such good food.'

'I bet you'll have your own restaurant soon,' I said. 'That would be amazing, Sas.'

'Well, I've been researching it and saving like mad,' she said, her cheeks turning a little pink. 'It would cost a fortune, but maybe one day.'

Saskia's parents aren't wealthy, and I knew that my dad would lend her the money to start a restaurant because my parents really love her and her work ethic, but luckily some of my filter was working so I didn't say anything as she's really proud and I know she wouldn't let my dad help her. Plus, I think she would worry that it might offend her parents.

'What are you going to do now?' she asked.

'I'm going to apply for guiding jobs in Mpumalanga,' I said. 'It's going to be really hard, though. I don't have any references, so I'm not sure who's going to want to employ me.'

'Well, surely there's no harm in asking Barend and Antoinette for a reference,' said Saskia. 'Maybe if you tell them you've thought about everything and you really regret it, and that you're going to change and try to make a fresh start in a new job?'

I smiled and shook my head. 'I think I pretty much blew it. I don't think they would give me a reference, especially after what I wrote on the employee feedback. But I agree about the fresh start. Sometimes I wish I could have an earphone in my ear with someone telling me what to do and say.'

Saskia laughed and then looked excited. 'Alex, let's make a deal! What if every time there's a problem or if you think you're going to do something weird then you phone me? Even if it's every single day? And then we can talk about it. And sometimes I also need that, you know. Kind of like a support and protection programme with just us two, and we tell each other *everything*. Like a dedicated group that's *only* for support.'

'But you don't need support,' I said. 'You're not mad, like me.'

'Well, I do actually,' she said. 'I haven't told you this yet, but my mom and dad are probably getting a divorce and … and it's really hard because they're treating me like some sort of mediator, and they tell me these really awful things about each other. And Ouma isn't coping because she thinks they're committing a mortal sin and

25

won't get into heaven, and she keeps on emailing the entire church to pray for them. And sometimes she even puts it on Facebook.'

She gave a watery laugh. 'So, you see, I do need your support. There's nobody else but you that I can tell stuff like that to.'

I stared at her in dismay. Saskia's parents were the last people I thought would get divorced. I'd spent a lot of time at their house during school and university holidays, and they always seemed so normal and dependable. Whenever I went there it was the same routines, nothing unexpected and always predictable, but in a good way. Like, there was always macaroni cheese for supper on Mondays and pickled fish on Fridays and on Saturday mornings we all went to the Mitchells Plain mall. I said this to Saskia. 'I know,' she agreed, 'but maybe that wasn't such a good thing because I think they're bored with each other now. I mean, now my mom wants to go on holidays and weekends away, but my dad says that kind of thing is overrated, and they can rather save money by watching the Travel Channel. And *he's* upset because my mom won't go with him to the badminton club anymore.'

'I'm truly sorry. I hope they don't end up getting divorced,' I said, wishing that my reply was deeper, but I couldn't find the right words. I felt a fierce pride that I could also be the supportive one. Up until now it had always been Saskia picking up *my* pieces. 'Yes, let's have a support group, just us two. And I want you to know that if it wasn't for you, Saskia, I don't think … all that happened, I wouldn't have got through it. I really wouldn't.'

She got out her phone and seconds later mine pinged, and I looked at the screen. *Saskia has invited you to join The Mutual Protection Society on WhatsApp.* I pressed accept and we grinned at each other.

'Only us for now,' she said. 'But maybe we'll pick up others along the way. You never know.'

3

AFTER LUNCH I WENT TO visit Richard and Charles at their padel
courts. The parking lot was stuffed with expensive cars and massive
4x4s and, judging by the noise, the padel courts were full. So was
the terrace with the café, and I could see that Liesbet had done
the decorating because it was really stylish with polypropylene
black and white mats, wicker chairs painted white and huge pots of
succulents. And her signature lighting: strings of fairy lights with
huge bulbs that stay on all day.

There were about four baristas at a coffee station, and some
people were drinking wine as well. The whole thing looked
fantastic, and it was hard to believe that they built it so quickly,
because when I left it was just a bare patch of land. My dad
found the land for them. It's in a really good position right
behind a high-end shopping centre, and I think he called in a
favour because *everyone* wanted that stand.

Charles and Richard were sitting at a table with two very pretty
girls. The one who was a bit more glamorous gave me a slitty-eyed
look as I approached and then took her time to scan me up and
down, taking in my baggy shorts and even more baggy T-shirt.
I was about to ask her why she was staring at me when Charles

27

saw me and got up to swing me around, and then passed me to Richard, who did the same. I managed to give them both a good kick, but I grinned at them when they let me go because they've never got out of the habit of treating me like a toy or something. When I was little, they were always carrying me around in their backpacks or putting me on the back of their quad bikes. It used to freak out Sindi and also Liesbet when she noticed.

The girls became enthusiastic towards me when they learnt I was the twins' sister, especially the less glamorous one with dark hair, who I could immediately tell really liked Charles.

'It's *so* lovely to meet you! The boys' little sister, and I've heard you're a guide. Wow!' she said. 'Maybe you'd like to hang out with me and Charles sometime while you're in Cape Town?'

Charles mouthed *no* at me, but I don't like it when people are mean, and that was quite a mean thing to do, actually. She could easily have seen him and that would have been really hurtful.

'Yes, sure,' I said. 'Definitely. When shall we hang out? Besides that we're actually doing it now, I mean.'

She looked a bit taken aback and sort of panicked and said, 'Well, um, whenever you want?'

'I'm free on Wednesday night,' I said. 'Do you like pizza? We can go to Bella Italia.'

She looked pleased and confused at the same time and gave Charles an apprehensive look.

'Yeah, okay,' he replied but he didn't sound exactly keen and that wasn't very nice either. Then he remembered to introduce the girls properly. The brunette girl was Sarah and the glamorous blonde one was Claire. Claire looked meaningfully at Richard, but he pretended not to notice.

'You should come too, Claire,' I said, not wanting to leave her out. 'And Richard, of course.'

'Maybe. I'll have to check if I'm available,' she said, 'and I'll let Richard know.' Richard rolled his eyes at me, but that was fairly justified.

'So, when did you get a liquor licence?' I said.

Richard grinned. 'We don't have one. But we get around it.' He winked at Charles.

'But that's breaking the law,' I said. 'You could both go to jail, and if you go to jail that's totally the end of your life because some inmate might stab you and kill you. Plus, Liesbet and Dad and Sindi would be so stressed they might have a mental breakdown and Dad could even have a heart attack because he eats so much red meat and then it would be all your fault and you'd never get over it because everyone would remember that about you forever and ever.'

They all stared at me and there was a bit of an awkward pause.

'Shit, you know how to go from zero to catastrophe, Lexi,' said Richard and burst out laughing. 'It's just a bit of booze under the table.'

Charles smiled at me because, of my two brothers, he kind of gets me the most.

'Do you want to have a go at padel?' he asked.

'Not dressed for it.' I pointed to my slipslops.

'That's okay,' he said. 'I'll get you a pair of shoes from the shop.'

Charles came back with a pair of trainers that had a R4 999 price tag on them, which is actually ridiculous, but he wouldn't take no for an answer.

It was me against both Richard and Charles and I sent them all over the court. Although to be fair they had probably each drunk half a bottle of wine.

'Jeez, Lexi-Loo,' panted Richard as I played the ball off the back wall with a cross-court backhand. 'You're a superstar!'

'She was first-team tennis when she was in Grade 10, remember?' said Charles. 'Why'd you stop playing, kiddo? I remember you stopped just before the Western Province selection. You would've nailed it!'

To avoid answering I aimed the ball straight at his thigh on my next shot, and he almost fell over laughing.

After a while I pretended that I'd had enough because a lot of people were watching us. Sarah was laughing and applauding but Claire looked sour and superior.

As I left, I heard Claire say to Richard, 'Oh my God, so what's up with your *sister*? She doesn't come across as exactly normal.' I sped up because I didn't want to hear his reply.

In the evening I walked Clive and Tulip in our vineyards, and it was much less stressful than the greenbelt although I did worry about baboons and snakes. The vineyards are on a steep slope, and I walked right to the top, where I could see False Bay stretching out in the distance. Actually, I didn't really go up for the view. I wanted to check the fire break and it was fine. The south-easter had stopped blowing completely, and there was just a little breeze. I sat on a rock with my arms around Tulip and Clive and thought about stuff.

My dad and Liesbet were having drinks on the patio when I got back.

'Do you want to join us for dinner tonight?' said Liesbet. 'We're going to a new Thai place in Rondebosch with Magda and Bernie. I know they'd love to see you.'

'No thanks,' I said. 'I'm a bit tired so I'll stay at home rather.'

'It won't be stressful for you,' she said. 'And I think it'll do you good.'

'Why?' I asked.

'Well, it's just an opportunity to talk to other people because sometimes I think you're a little socially awkward, Alex, and ...'

'She's not going to learn anything about socialising from old farts like Bernie and Magda, for Christ's sake,' said my dad.

'It's a chance to practise how to make *small talk*, Edward.' Liesbet sounded tetchy. 'I honestly sometimes think she shouldn't have gone to boarding school, because the boys and Jess always socialised with us and our friends, and Alex didn't get that opportunity. And say what you like, it's a learnt skill and we overlooked that.'

'She's fine.' My dad got up and rattled his keys. 'Let's go or we'll be late.'

As they went to the car, I could hear them arguing and Liesbet slammed her door hard, and my dad revved the engine too loudly as they drove away. I thought about how quickly things can go wrong.

Sindi and I watched *The Queen* on DStv. As I watched I realised that I could understand a lot of words without the subtitles, and that was good because I'd taken Zulu as a subject at school and I'd been trying to keep up with it in case I ever got to Mpumalanga. Sindi is from the Eastern Cape, but she also speaks Zulu, and she taught me some swearwords which she said I must never use but rolled around laughing when I said them.

Later I sat on my bed and started looking on my iPad for guiding jobs in Mpumalanga. There were quite a few I could apply for, but then I saw one that I really wanted. It was for a junior guide position at Yamihle Private Game Reserve, which is the absolute top game reserve in South Africa. Their head guide is Kwanele Chamane, and he's really well known in guiding circles. I watched a YouTube video where an elephant in musth tried to charge his group on a walking tour – and honestly, it was incredible. He made his group stand behind him and he didn't even raise his rifle. He literally just stood there for ages, and the elephant kept on coming for him, but all Kwanele did was shout and wave his arms. He was so calm and brave, but also, he knew *exactly* what he was doing because he could read every single sign. After a really long time the elephant eventually backed off and his guests were in a high state of nerves, but Kwanele looked as if he did that type of thing every day. I've probably watched that video about fifty times.

Plus, Yamihle is owned by this guy Len Fletcher who everyone calls Legend. Apparently he's very eccentric and has dreadlocks and loads of tattoos and everything, but he's totally on the same level as Kwanele Chamane, who I've read is his best friend. Without exaggerating, every single guide I know wants to work at Yamihle. They have this amazing training programme for the guides they employ and it's kind of a whole new level. I saved the application along with some others, even though I knew there was no chance I'd get the job, especially without references.

The next day at breakfast my dad said he'd like to join me on my walk with Clive and Tulip. It's not unusual for us to walk together but I could see he was preoccupied with something. After a while he cleared his throat and said, 'I hope you know you can speak to me and your mother about anything, Alex.' He didn't look at me while he asked the question but gazed into the distance looking awkward.

'The thing is, your mother and I had a talk last night and we agreed that perhaps we made a mistake by sending you to boarding school. But then again, it seemed to us that it was unavoidable because we were both travelling so much for work at that time. Those were your formative years, however, and it may not have been the best choice for you.'

'I could have stayed at home with Sindi instead of going away to school,' I said, and immediately wish I hadn't.

'The amount of time we were away didn't make that feasible.' He gave me a searching look. 'We considered it but there was too much logistics around leaving you at home. Didn't you like the school? It seemed like a good place, but I'm afraid we never asked you if you were happy there.'

I shrugged and picked up a stick to throw for Tulip. This was totally not a conversation I wanted to have. Ever.

'It was fine,' I said. 'And it was a *really* long time ago. Don't worry.'

Tulip brought the stick back and I threw it for her again. But this time I ran after her. After that I mostly played with the dogs while we walked, and I led us to the short cut home.

My dad and Liesbet went to a seventieth birthday lunch. Luckily, it was a formal occasion, and they couldn't just rock up with me in tow, so they didn't invite me to come too. With the house to myself, I set about starting my applications.

My qualifications are good, so there was no problem there.

I did a zoology degree at Wits followed by honours in animal, plant and environmental science, and that was all cum laude. Then I studied to be a guide. It was the getting-on-with-people part of me that I felt worried about.

My surname, Carnell-Ellis, is quite well known, to be honest, because my dad and Liesbet are so successful. Plus, my dad is a bit controversial on account of being a very tough lawyer and businessman on the property development side of things. Luckily, he's very environmentally conscious, but once I read this article about him in the *Business Day* that described him as a man that goes straight for the jugular. Even Barend and Antoinette recognised my surname when I started at The Plains. Actually, not Barend, but Antoinette knew *exactly* who my parents were.

My background was definitely a disadvantage, so the best thing to do would be to go undercover. I mean, I wasn't thinking of dying my hair or getting a fake ID or anything, but I started by dropping the last part of my surname. Alexandra Carnell. Then I decided to spell it with a K and one L just to be totally sure. Alexandra Karnel. Perfect.

But then something else started to worry me. I wondered if game lodges prefer employing male guides on account of khaki fever, because in my experience the ratio of male to female guides was not equal. I'm not a raging feminist or anything but that would definitely be another disadvantage. I decided to leave my gender flexible and not use my full first name. Actually no one used my full name anyway, except Liesbet sometimes. So, I became Alex Karnel and my hobbies were watching rugby and taking part in braai competitions.

I sent in the applications and wished I had references to go with them but there was nothing I could do about that. Well, I suppose there was, but you have to draw the line somewhere.

***

I wanted to reassure Liesbet that I wasn't socially feral, so I invited her and my dad to the pizza evening. And then of course

I asked Jess too and I couldn't help thinking how nice it would be if Roger couldn't make it.

Charles and Sarah and Richard were already at the restaurant when I arrived with Liesbet and my dad, and Charles looked completely haunted because I hadn't told him they were coming too, and until that point he had literally never introduced any girls to them. Richard packed up laughing and tried to give me a high five. I ignored it and frowned at him.

'Where's Claire?'

Richard said she couldn't make it and I totally knew that was a lie. But I felt relieved. I wasn't sure if she was very nice actually.

Liesbet made a beeline for the chair next to Sarah, who introduced herself enthusiastically and then blushed when my dad leant across the table to shake her hand. Even though I was standing behind him I knew he was giving her the penetrating look he gives people he meets for the first time. I suppose it was also because he's very good-looking in a patrician sort of way.

Liesbet started asking Sarah a thousand questions and even asked her what her parents did and where they lived. In between answering, Sarah nervously took huge slugs of wine, so I passed her the ice bucket. We were almost ready to order when Jess and Roger arrived. Even from a distance I could see that Jess' face looked tense, and even though she was wearing a really stunning sundress she didn't look quite as glowing as she normally does.

Charles gave me a wild look when he saw Jess and Roger coming towards our table.

'Lexi,' he said to me in an undertone, 'I mean … what the hell? I'm not even *dating* Sarah.'

'Well, well, Charlie boy,' said Roger looking all excited but totally in the wrong way when Liesbet introduced Sarah as Charles' girlfriend. 'You're a lucky man, you bastard.'

'So are you, you tosser,' said Richard pretending to be jovial so that Roger couldn't take offence. Jess gave both boys an imploring look and I thought that maybe I'd made a mistake by inviting Jess and Roger because my brothers also can't stand Roger.

The waitress came to take our order, but Roger held up his hand right in her face, literally almost touching her nose, because he was in the middle of telling us how he screwed a car salesman over on a BMW he bought. But my dad smiled at the waitress and gestured for Liesbet to order and then we all did. It was great because after the orders were in my dad started talking about something else and Roger looked sulky.

When our pizzas arrived, Jess tried to turn the conversation back to Roger's car, but he muttered, 'For God's sake, Jess, don't patronise me.'

It was obvious that he'd descended into a mood, and even though I wasn't the one married to him I found myself getting anxious. Not really on account of how he was going to behave, but about how I'd behave if he started being nasty to Jess.

'Steady on at the trough, darling,' said Roger as Jess took a bite of literally only her third slice of pizza. 'Those chubby thighs are getting a bit out of hand.'

Jess looked embarrassed but she gave a little laugh.

'Roger thinks I'm getting fat,' she said. 'And he's right! I really shouldn't eat carbs.'

'Balls,' said Charles. 'It's Rodge the podge who could shed a load.'

'Oh my *word*,' said Sarah, 'we can't talk about weight or carbs when we're eating pizza! Jess, tell me about your spa. Charles says it's totally amazing.'

Charles gave her a small smile of approval and Jess gave her a grateful one. But it didn't seem right that Roger's comment got glossed over and I felt that someone should say something to Roger in case he didn't realise how mean he was being, and that maybe I should be the one. I waited for a pause in the conversation, but then instead I took my phone out my bag and slipped it in my pocket and went to the cloakroom. I sent a WhatsApp to The Mutual Protection Society.

We're having a family dinner at a restaurant and Roger's being horrible to Jess. He's just told her she's getting fat!!! In front of everyone!! Should I tell him it's disgusting to body shame and especially to do it to his wife?

Saskia must have put some kind of alert on the group because she replied immediately.

Tricky. But I don't think Jess would want you to have a go at him during a family dinner. It'll be so awkward. Probably cause a huge fight. Timing not good for that ... Filter xx

Saskia was right, and especially about Jess. I sent her a thumbs up and went back to the table.

It didn't feel right not to say anything, though.

We all had gelato for dessert, except Jess. My dad paid the bill and wouldn't let Charles and Richard chip in. Roger didn't offer because another thing about him is that he's very stingy when it comes to spending money on other people. Plus, he didn't even say thank you. Both of those things can tell you a lot about a person.

Before we left Jess gave me an appointment card at the spa for Friday. It was going to be terrible because it was for three hours. She then invited Sarah to come too, and I literally thought Sarah was going to faint she got so excited.

I couldn't bear the thought of Jess going home with Roger and I started to wonder what kind of things he said to her when it was just the two of them. I felt so anxious I could hardly breathe, and once I was in the car with Liesbet and my dad I said, 'Why don't you say anything when Roger is mean to Jess?'

There was a long pause.

'We can't interfere,' said Liesbet finally. 'And sometimes I don't think he's conscious of being mean. It's just his way.'

'But you agree that he's often not very nice to her? In fact, most of the time.'

'No, what I *said*, Alex, is that I'm not sure he *means* it. He says things without realising that it might be hurtful.'

'Or maybe he's a passive-aggressive and cowardly bully who says horrible things but if he smiles while he does it then no one can take offence.'

'Don't cause trouble,' she said, 'and particularly about things that you don't understand.'

'Actually, I think I do,' I said, and my dad gave me a quick glance through the rear-view mirror.

We drove the rest of the way home in silence.

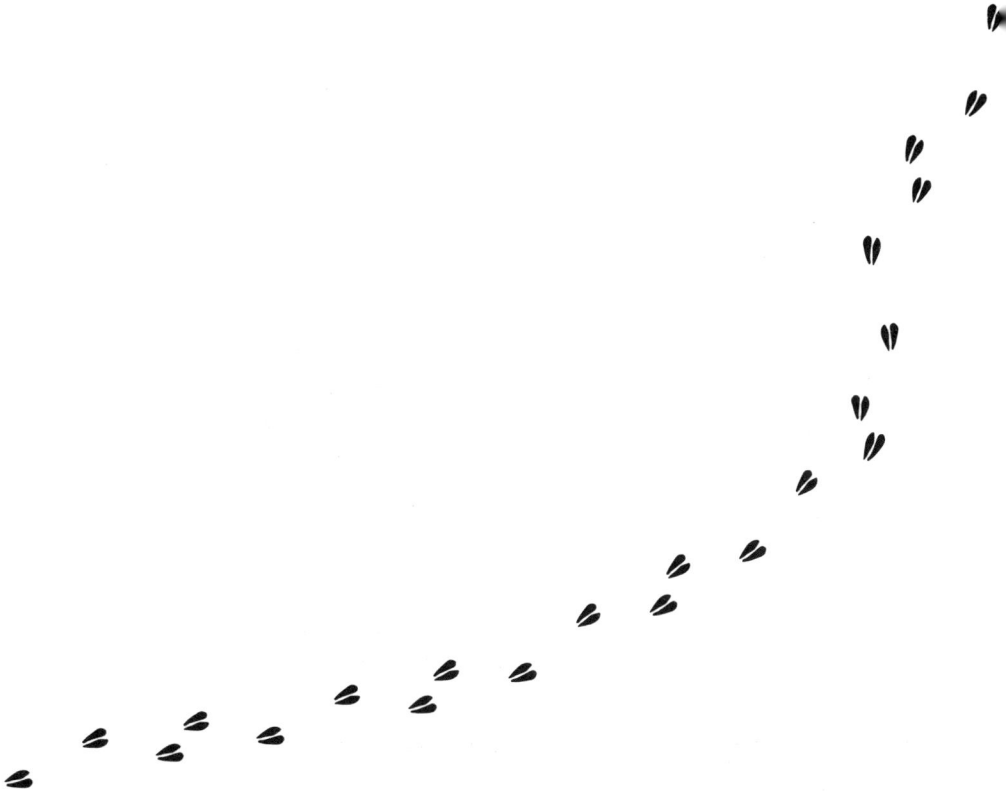

4

Sarah insisted on picking me up so that we could go to the spa together, but I knew it was really because she wanted to see where Charles' family lived.

She looked a bit daunted as I met her at the front door. I think Liesbet was lying in wait because she suddenly appeared in the hallway and insisted on showing Sarah around. Liesbet is very proud of our house because it was built by Sir Herbert somebody or other, who was apparently quite famous a long time ago. He did a great job to be fair, as although it's huge it has a lot of charm and character.

Liesbet and I had an altercation before we left because I'd decided to take Clive to the spa too. I'm not sure why I wanted to take him. I just did. But luckily it didn't spiral, because Sarah was there, and so we all tried to squash him into Sarah's Mini Cooper. She couldn't see out the back window, though, so we ended up taking my Jeep instead.

Jess was waiting for us, and she looked a bit taken aback to see Clive, but she didn't say anything. Sarah went for a massage and Jess took me off for a facial. It wasn't a success because Clive kept on trying to get on the bed and I started to get claustrophobic with all the stuff on my face, and I couldn't keep still. After a while Jess laughed and said, 'This isn't working for you, is it?'

'No,' I mumbled.

'I know!' she said, quickly wiping everything off. 'Let's give Clive a makeover instead.'

We took Clive to the yard at the back of the salon and Jess got this shampoo that's actually meant for horses, but which they use on their clients because it's so brilliant. Clive got furious and tried to run away from the hose and Jess and I got completely soaked and muddy and it was the best fun. Afterwards we met Sarah on one of the private patios and she looked at us in surprise.

'Alex and I decided Clive needed a spa treatment more than she does,' explained Jess.

'Oh *cool*!' said Sarah. 'Let's paint his nails!'

So we did and we used all the colours in rainbow order. Then Jess painted Sarah's nails to match Clive's and Sarah took a selfie with Clive and sent it to Charles. She got a reply and went all pink and happy and told us that Charles had asked her out to dinner. Jess got all excited too and she did Sarah's make-up while I watched. I asked Sarah about Claire, and she told us that Richard didn't invite her to the restaurant because he thought she wasn't as nice as he thought at first. Jess wanted to know why, and Sarah looked awkward and said that Claire can be a bit catty sometimes.

As she was putting the finishing touches to Sarah's make-up, Jess got a WhatsApp from Roger. As she read it, I saw in her face that it wasn't exactly good news. Jess told us that he'd invited *ten* people for dinner and that he must have forgotten that she had told him before she left for work that it was her turn to host book club that night. She was so stressed and upset that Sarah and I left, and I honestly wished that Roger was dead. Or maybe just that he had never existed because I remembered my filter.

Over the next few days, I got emails from all the lodges for the jobs I'd applied for, but every single one was unsuccessful. The last rejection was from Yamihle, but I had known I wouldn't get it. I still felt disappointed, though, and I did another wistful trawl through their website and watched the YouTube of Kwanele and the elephant again.

I started to feel at a bit of a loss because I wasn't sure what to do next. I told Jess about the failed applications, and she asked me if I'd like to work at reception at the spa. Almost as soon as she'd made the offer, we both started laughing because obviously I'd be completely terrible. Then she suggested that I should think about going back to university, and I started to consider doing a PhD in zoology.

I wasn't completely convinced that I wanted to do it, but my confidence was at an all-time low and I knew that at least I was good at academics.

I took a few days to consider my options at a few universities and then filled in the application at Wits. I was about to send it when I noticed an email from Yamihle in my inbox.

Alex,

Our chosen candidate is no longer in a position to work for us. Are you available to start next week? Salary 12k. Living expenses included.

Let me know.

Len Fletcher

I literally couldn't believe what I was reading, and I also couldn't believe I hadn't noticed the email. I checked the time that Len Fletcher had sent it. It was the day before at 11 am, and I felt sick at the thought that maybe he had asked someone else in the meantime. I quickly fired off an email.

Dear Len

Yes, I can. Thank you for the opportunity.

Regards

Alex

I didn't have long to wait before he replied.

Great. By the way, you forgot to include your references in your application. Can you send asap?

I WhatsApped The Mutual Protection Society. *Do you really really think I should ask A and B for a reference? Because I've just been offered a job at YAMIHLE!!!!!*

A reply came back immediately. *Yes!* 😊 😊 😊

What should I say though?

Saskia started typing and her reply took quite a long time.

How about: Dear A and B, since I left your esteemed establishment, I have deeply regretted and in fact totally mourned my shocking behaviour at The Plains and accept that you had to sadly end my contract. I would like to profoundly apologise to you both and also beg your forgiveness and ask if you would very kindly send me a reference? I would appreciate it if you don't mention the incidents but rather concentrate on the fact that I was a very good guide and have exceptional knowledge. Something like that?

It was a bit flowery, and it would probably irritate Antoinette, who was a very direct person.

I'm not sure … it's sort of asking them to lie?

I suppose. 😟 *But still think worth trying. Got to go, making dinner for Ouma. xx*

I spent about an hour composing my WhatsApp and in the end I only sent it to Antoinette because I knew Barend would give me a reference, so it didn't seem fair to include him.

Dear Antoinette, in case you have deleted my WhatsApp number, and I wouldn't blame if you have, this is Alex. I want to apologise to you for everything that happened but I want you also to know that I probably wouldn't be writing to you if I didn't want to ask you for a reference and so I also wouldn't blame you if you don't reply to this message. Or delete my number again. I have a job opportunity at Yamihle in Mpumalanga, but they need a reference. I know you may have to include the bad stuff about me because I don't want you to have to lie but if you feel you can write a reference then maybe you can also include some good things if you remember any. I'm very sorry. From Alex.

I immediately regretted it when I pressed send and after about half an hour, I felt so embarrassed by what I'd written that I decided to delete the message. But then I saw that Antoinette had blue ticked it. Plus, she was typing. Like, for a really long time. And then she wasn't typing, and I checked to see if she was still online. She wasn't. For ages. Then she was back online and typing again.

Alex. Moet dit net nie opfok nie, okay?

A short while later my phone pinged again and this time it was an email with a reference attached. And it wasn't bad, really. It included all the important stuff, but it did say that I must work on the hospitality side of guiding – but there were no actual examples. I hoped Len would just think I was a bit shy or something.

I WhatsApped Antoinette immediately.

I won't, I promise. Thank you, I really appreciate it.

Luckily Antoinette hadn't saved the reference as a PDF so I could change all the 'she' pronouns to 'Alex'. I also deleted Antoinette's cell number and email because I didn't want Len to feel encouraged to contact her to discuss me further as she suggested at the end. Actually, I deleted that bit too. I sent the reference to Len, and it must have been okay because he made no comment in his next email and just said I should be at Hoedspruit Airport by Monday morning, where someone from the lodge would meet me. He wrote it would be better if I drove to the lodge rather than flew, so I'd have a car in my off time in case I didn't want to go all the way back to Cape Town.

I decided not to tell my family that I'd got a job at Yamihle, and out of everyone I felt the worst for not telling Jess, but she has a terrible reputation in our family for not being able to keep secrets. Instead, I told them that I had enrolled on a training programme on a game reserve in Mpumalanga. Of course, they wanted to know the name so I made one up and said it was so tiny they wouldn't be able to find it on a map. Or on the internet.

The main reason I didn't want to tell them was that they knew

Yamihle. Liesbet and my dad had even stayed there a few times, and they loved it. I knew they'd be really proud and tell all their friends that I'd got a job there. The second reason, also a very good one, was that I completely didn't trust myself. If I got fired, there was no way I'd be able to pretend that I hadn't, and it would be incredibly embarrassing for them.

Luckily both my parents were distracted at the time. My dad was preparing for a business trip to buy up some land for a golf course somewhere and Liesbet was working around the clock because, besides other looming jobs, she'd been asked at short notice to redecorate a resort in Kenya and had to go and scout out the location.

I did tell Saskia, though, in case the Wi-Fi was dodgy at Yamihle. So if there was a crisis with the dogs or my family at least she knew where I was. We decided that if I managed to get through my three-month probation without getting fired then the fresh start would have been successful, and I'd have developed this amazing filter. And *then* I could tell everyone the truth and we'd figure out the details of how I suddenly popped up at Yamihle later. We had three months to think of something.

And then it all went very quickly. It's nearly two thousand kilometres to Hoedspruit and I decided to do it over three days so I could get there a bit early. Although I was excited, I had to work through the dread of leaving, and the only way I could cope with that was to become distant and uncommunicative. My psychologist called it avoidance behaviour, but I called it my survival technique.

I left early on the Friday morning before anyone was awake because I had a thing about everyone gathering around and saying goodbye. I said I was going at seven, but I left at five just as it was getting light. The road was familiar until I'd passed the exit that led to The Plains, and I felt a pang as I drove past, but then I put it out of my mind and thought about all the things that Alex Karnel, junior guide at Yamihle Private Game Reserve, was going to do in her Fresh Start.

My first stopover was Colesberg, and then the road became straight and seemingly endless as I passed through the Free State with its massive semi-desert plains. Heat shimmered ahead of me, my outside temperature gauge showing it was nearly forty degrees. There was no way I was going to stop for food in that heat, so I worked my way through a massive bag of Flings I'd bought that morning. The air became cooler and the landscape green as I crossed into Gauteng, and finally arrived in Pretoria for the night.

The next day it was just a short while before the roads descended into the wide and lush valleys of the Lowveld. Now I was in the wild heart of South Africa, and I switched off the air-conditioning and rolled down the windows to let in the balmy smell of the bushveld, tree plantations and tropical fruit farms. White River town emerged in an oasis of green, palm trees lining the streets and swathes of bougainvillea tumbling over garden walls.

By now I was starving for real food, so I found a Wimpy and I ordered the breakfast special of eggs, hash browns, baked beans and grilled tomatoes, and then I had four pieces of toast with apricot jam. Only then did I focus on my mission for White River. There was no way that Alex Karnel was going to arrive at Yamihle in a Jeep and so I needed to find a car dealership. I asked the waitress if she knew where I could find one.

'There's quite a few here,' she said. 'But I don't think any of them are open on Sundays.'

I stared at her in dismay. I hadn't thought of that.

'Maybe you could try Johan, though. He's got a dealership and he lives on the premises so there's a good chance he might be there. He's not churchgoing.'

She gave me directions and eventually I found the dealership on the outskirts of town. There was a big sign saying, 'King of the Road – Let Johan Service You'. Compared to the rest of White River, which was so lush and green, Johan's place looked desolate. Long tufts of dead grass stuck out of the cracks in the concreted forecourt and some of the windowpanes were missing from the office, which was a converted shipping container. Ancient petrol pumps that looked like they were from the 1960s stood forlornly in a row and a couple of bakkies and cars were parked under a holey green shade net. I scanned them and saw a white four-wheel-drive Nissan that had a canopy, double front seats, lots of scratches and quite a bit of damage to the body. It was perfect. I got out of the Jeep and sweat trickled down my back in minutes as the midday heat hit me.

Johan was nowhere to be seen, so I walked behind the container and found a small house. I knocked on the door and after a while a big man with a beard opened the door and came out onto the veranda.

'Middag,' he said, yawning and scratching his stomach. 'The dealership's closed today.'

'You've got a Nissan bakkie I want to buy,' I said. 'I need it today, though.'

He looked at me appraisingly. 'Wait there a minute. I'll go get the keys.'

'Can't go wrong with that Nissan,' he said, once we were walking back to the forecourt. 'She'll go around the clock three times for you. Solid as a bulldozer.'

'Do you do trade-ins?' I asked.

He shook his head sorrowfully at my Jeep. 'That thing's got a bloody serious drinking habit,' he said. 'Couldn't sell it if I tried.'

'Okay, no problem,' I said, and started to walk to my car.

'But we can talk about it.' He went up to the Jeep and kicked its tyres.

'They're brand new,' I said. 'What can you offer?'

He named a figure that was way under its value, but I was in a hurry. Plus, it was so hot that I didn't feel like negotiating too much. I countered and he whistled disbelievingly. I made as if to get into the Jeep and he gave another figure. I accepted with the provision that he put new tyres on the Nissan, and he agreed to this quite readily. I went with him to his workshop to make sure

45

that he was actually going to put on new ones, and then I said he must include an oil change as well, and a full tank of petrol. He got a bit irritated, so I left him to it and wandered off to try and find some shade.

I spotted a scraggly tree to the right of the workshop, so I went and stood under it and looked around, thinking that Johan definitely wasn't into aesthetics. I heard a deep bark and turned round to see an old boerboel chained to a kennel, panting and looking distressed. There was no shade for him other than the kennel and his bowl of dried food looked disgusting with flies buzzing in it. And no water bowl. I went towards him and put out my hand. He took a good sniff and then licked my fingers, his stumpy tail wagging. I ran my hand down his side to feel his protruding ribs and could practically put both hands around his waist. Way to go, Johan, you absolute evil bastard, I thought.

I went back to the workshop.

'Nice dog you've got there,' I said.

His head deep under the bonnet, Johan grunted as he screwed the oil cap back on. 'Useless piece of shit,' he said. 'Meant to be a guard dog. Listen, I'm finished now, so let's do the paperwork. I've got an appointment in town, and you've held me up enough, okay?'

We went to his office where he rushed through the paperwork and then tossed me the keys to the Nissan. He checked his watch and swore. 'I've got to run. Just put the Jeep keys through the window when you've transferred your luggage.'

I couldn't believe my good luck because by then I knew exactly what I was going to do. I lugged my bags to the Nissan, chucked the keys into the office through a broken pane, and headed back towards the dog. The chain was tricky to get off his collar, so I borrowed some pliers from Johan's workshop and eventually got him loose. He danced around a bit, all wobbly since he was so thin his muscles had literally atrophied. I gave him some water and then heaved him into the back seat of the Nissan. I decided it was too risky to stop to buy dog food in case I bumped into

The King of the Road. It was also too risky to go to Hoedspruit because that was the obvious place he would look for me if he even realised his dog was missing, so I decided to spend the night in Graskop, a good hour away.

After about five minutes the dog found his way onto the passenger seat and stuck his head out the window, which was soon decorated with long strings of drool.

'That's the smell of freedom,' I told him. I felt light and happy, and relieved that I was driving with him and not away from him. I decided to call him Jackson. It was only once I drove into Graskop in the late afternoon that I started to think about how I was going to explain his presence to my future employers. I pulled over and WhatsApped The Mutual Protection Society.

I stole a dog in White River.

5

Saskia doesn't lose her cool easily, but she went completely mad and phoned me instead of sending a WhatsApp.

'Alex!' she said. 'I mean, have you gone completely *insane*? You can't just steal someone's dog, and what about Yamihle? Are you even allowed to take a dog, and I bet you can't, and what happens if they catch you, and they'll never let you keep it at the lodge, and I *swear* this is the total worst thing you could have done, and it was such a brilliant chance, and ...'

She paused to take a gulp of air so I quickly said, 'Sas, listen to me, I couldn't just leave him there! He was chained up and everything and he's so old and thin and neglected. I've called him Jackson.'

She was silent for a few seconds. 'Well, who did you steal him *from*?'

'I traded in my Jeep for a Nissan bakkie,' I said, 'and I stole him from the second-hand car dealer. But he didn't want him anyway, Sas. He even said he was a useless piece of shit.'

'Oh God,' she moaned. 'That means he's got your ID number and your driver's licence, and he'll get the police to come after you. And now you're going to fuckenwell get *arrested*! You have to take him back, Alex, like right now!'

Saskia and I have literally never fought, and I didn't want this to be our first argument.

'Sas,' I said, 'please don't be angry with me. I know I shouldn't have but … actually, I should have. I couldn't leave him there. I only told you because of The Mutual Protection Society and we said we'd tell each other everything and *support* each other.'

She went silent again and I wondered if she'd put the phone down on me.

'Sas?' I said tentatively.

She sighed. 'Yes, but stealing … and you're meant to let me know *before* you do something crazy! Sorry, I just want this to work out for you so badly, but I know you can't take the dog back. Let me think about it and then I'll message you later, okay?'

I found a guesthouse quite easily and was just about to go to bed when Saskia messaged me.

So I think that you must tell Yamihle the absolute truth. Not that you stole the dog but that you found it on the side of the road or something and couldn't leave it to die an agonising and terrible death because maybe you could also say it was just about to be bitten by a snake. Like a black mamba etc.

I wouldn't have been at all unlikely to have seen a black mamba near White River, but it was very unlikely that Len Fletcher would believe I fought one off to save a dog. But Saskia was totally right about telling the truth and leaving out the stealing bit. I sent her a thumbs up and a hug emoji, and then I fell asleep on the floor with Jackson as he was too weak to get on the bed. I hardly slept. Jackson was confused and restless and my thoughts took me to places I didn't want to go.

I should have felt excited as I drove to Hoedspruit. But instead, I worked myself into a massive state of anxiety and I felt sick most of the way. It didn't help that after not checking in on me for the last couple of days Liesbet seemed to have got a guilty attack of the maternal feeling and she literally phoned me five times to check where I was and to tell me about stuff I'd left behind. Luckily the last call was to say she was about to board her flight to Kenya and that she'd be out of signal for a few days. Thank goodness for that because Jackson seemed to enjoy barking at random stuff out the window and it'd be tricky to explain the noise to Liesbet.

While I drove, I kept thinking that Saskia was right and that I'd stuffed up the best opportunity of my life. Legend would probably tell me to go straight home because, as I knew perfectly well, dogs weren't allowed at game reserves for very obvious reasons. Plus, even if he did let Jackson stay, it was likely that he was unvaccinated and then would pass on his diseases to all the animals on the entire reserve, and they would all die catastrophic deaths, and I would be to blame. I kept on going all hot and my skin went prickly with fear and I couldn't even bring myself to Google to see if unvaccinated dogs can kill wildlife with airborne diseases.

So by the time I reached Hoedspruit I was pretty near to sinking into a catatonic state that felt a little too familiar. The psychologist said I should visualise peacefulness, which is pretty stupid, really. I mean, how can you do that when you can't even think straight and when your vision of peacefulness is the very thing that you've just destroyed?

The parking lot at Hoedspruit airport was full, mostly with Land Cruisers from lodges to pick up their guests from the plane that had just landed. I remembered the first time I had been here, when I was about fourteen. The sweet and musky smell of the thatched terminal building, the air of excitement knowing that you were about to be transported into an unknown dimension, a cocoon of absorption and intensity of focus where you're protected from reality.

After about an hour all the Land Cruisers had gone and I started to panic, wondering if I'd got the date wrong. I was just about to phone the lodge when a Land Cruiser with 'Yamihle Private Game Reserve' branded on the sides entered the parking lot at speed. A girl of about my age got out and looked around expectantly. She glanced at me and smiled but went into the terminal.

'I'm Alex,' I called out to her. 'The new guide?'

She walked over to me looking surprised and then grinned.

'They told me you were a guy! Nice to meet you, I'm Marietjie. Sorry I'm late, we had staff training this morning and it overran as usual. Who's this?' She gestured to Jackson.

'His name's Jackson,' I replied. 'I rescued him on the way here.'

'Shame, man,' she said. 'Does Legend know you're bringing him to the lodge?'

'No, I guess I should have phoned to ask him, but I didn't think about it at the time. Do you ... do you think it'll be a problem?'

She looked doubtfully at Jackson.

'Um, not sure. You never know with Legend. Like, one time a guide overslept and didn't take his clients out in the morning and Legend just laughed, and then this other time someone forgot to bring the lemons for the gin and tonics on the game drive and he went totally mal.'

She bent down and patted Jackson.

'Wie's 'n oulike hond? Okay, are you ready to go? You can leave your car here. Where's your bags? I'll help you carry.'

I didn't say anything more about Jackson. We loaded up my gear, left the airport and soon turned off onto a dirt road to Yamihle.

'It'll take about an hour and a half to get there,' said Marietjie. 'We've had a lot of rain, so the roads are donners wet. I'm just gonna call the lodge while we're driving because the male guides share rooms and I think they've put you in with Petrus.' She snorted. 'Not that he'd mind, believe me. I better tell them about your uniform too. I wonder what made them think you were a man?'

'Um, maybe my name?' I said. 'Are there any female guides at Yamihle?'

'Yup,' she said, 'just me, and now you.'

I'd sort of forgotten that I'd pretended to be a guy and now it seemed a bit stupid. And definitely pointless. I hoped it wouldn't be a big deal because my arrival was going to be awkward enough with Jackson in tow.

I tried to put it all out of my mind and concentrate on my surroundings. Heavy, rain-filled clouds hung over us, with the occasional deluge stirring up the earthy smell of rain on hot sand. Now close to the end of the wet season, the bush had grown thick, and looked almost tropical it was so green.

'Tell me about Yamihle,' I said. 'What's it like to work there?'

'It's really great,' said Marietjie. 'But it doesn't exactly run like clockwork behind the scenes, so be prepared for that.'

'In what way?'

She paused to negotiate the cruiser around a large puddle.

'Well, Legend's a bit of a maverick. He doesn't have any partners so there's no one to rein him in. Kwanele, he's the head guide, does try, and Legend listens to him … but only sometimes. So you never really know what he's gonna do next. Like, if he feels like it, he'll tell the manager two hours before dinner that all the guests must have dinner in the bush about a kilometre away from the lodge. That sort of thing.'

I smiled. 'That sounds quite exciting.'

'Ja, but it's mostly a pain. And he often does the crazy things when he's been dopping. This one time he woke us all up in the middle of the night because he heard lions near the lodge, and he was convinced they were hunting. He made us wake up all the guests and take them out in their pyjamas. He was right about them hunting, of course, and the guests thought it was really cool, but he made us pack brandy as well, and everyone got so drunk, and then Legend buggered off back to the lodge to go to bed and we had to stay with them until sunrise.'

'What's Kwanele like?' I asked, trying to sound casual because, I won't lie, I had a hero-crush on him already on account of the YouTube video.

'He's actually the best part of working at Yamihle,' she replied. 'Quite tough on us, but the best teacher. And he's calm, you know? Both him and Legend are the best in the industry, but if I were in a dangerous situation, I'd pick Kwanele. Don't get me wrong, verstaan, Legend knows what he's doing, but his methods are sometimes a bit unpredictable.'

She gave a sudden chuckle. 'Shame, a lot of the female guests get a crush on Kwanele. Mind you, they also get the hots for Legend. But he's too scared of Bianca to do anything.'

'Who's Bianca?'

'His girlfriend,' she said a little gloomily. 'She's a real bitch, hey. You'll meet her at some point. She lives in Joburg, but she drives out almost every weekend to make sure that he doesn't get out of her claws.'

'And … and Kwanele? Is he single or …?'

'He doesn't have a girlfriend and he's very ordentlik. He hates it when women come on to him, so he usually disappears right after dinner when all the drinking starts. Some groups are happy to go to bed early, but jissis, sometimes you get a bunch who just want to get off their faces every night. Legend *loves* that. And then he drinks, but we can't, and we have to stay with them until they're ready to go back to their rooms.'

'So doesn't Legend do any guiding?'

'Sometimes. When he feels like it. But always evening game drives because he's mostly too hungover in the mornings.'

'What are the rest of the staff like?'

'All good. The manager, Dirk, is a bit streng, but he's only been at Yamihle for a few months so I'm not sure about him yet. Not sure if he fits in. Watch out for Petrus, though. If he gives you any kak, just give him a snotklap.'

I was about to ask why I would need to give Petrus a snotklap when Marietjie pointed out the turn-off to Yamihle. I looked down involuntarily at Jackson, who had squashed himself onto my feet. He was fast asleep and looked so sweet.

Marietjie looked at him too.

'Maybe we can hide him,' she said.

I knew then that I wanted to be friends with Marietjie. I nearly agreed, but then Saskia's horrified face literally appeared in my mind like a sort of guardian poltergeist.

'No,' I said. 'I mean, thank you, that's a really good idea, but I think I'd better reveal him straight away and see what happens.'

'Ja, you're right. Legend and Kwanele both have a thing about honesty. Okay, so here we are.'

For the last fifteen minutes we'd been driving down an incline, so I'd seen that the main thatched lodge sat near the Crocodile River behind thick reeds and flat rocks before the sandy beaches that met the river. Yamihle was as exclusive as it got, with only three double chalets on either side of the main building, each with river frontage, separated from each other with dense bush and trees. We drew up to the main building, which nestled amidst lush green vegetation. A tall and intricately carved door stood open, flanked by lanterns and massive stone statues of elephant. As Marietjie drove past I caught a glimpse of a light and airy space and a blue flash of river beyond. About two hundred metres further on we arrived at the staff quarters in a large enclosed boma with six thatched bungalows.

'The big ones are for the male guides and staff,' explained Marietjie, 'and then the single ones are for all the females, and Kwanele as he's head guide.'

I felt relieved that I didn't have to share a room. Boarding school had definitely killed that cosy camaraderie for me. And besides that, I'm a noisy sleeper. I don't snore or anything, but apparently I talk and sometimes even laugh in my sleep, and that's actually really creepy.

My room was plain but nice. A single iron bed like the ones you get in national parks stood under a window, a small cupboard and a table, and a shower, basin and loo in an ensuite.

My guide's uniform, two pairs of khaki shorts and a couple of branded shirts, were laid out neatly on the bed.

Marietjie picked up one of the shirts and laughed.

'No ways these are going to fit,' she said. 'They've swapped the uniform, but I think you're gonna need an extra small. Don't bother to get changed then. Let's go to the main lodge so you can meet Legend and Kwanele. They should be there.'

Because I hadn't exactly taken care when I dressed that morning, I wished that I could have worn the uniform. I was wearing black jeans, a black T-shirt and a black hoodie, and probably looked a bit goth. I hadn't washed my hair for a couple of days and so my usually auburn hair also looked black with grease.

I went to the bathroom and looked in the mirror. My pupils were a bit dilated from lack of sleep and I could see grey smudges of exhaustion under my eyes. Plus, there were definite signs of a pimple forming on my nose. In fact, I looked terrible.

Marietjie and I decided to take Jackson with us for the introduction and not just tell Legend and Kwanele about him. We decided he looked so old and pathetic that only a very cold-hearted person would turn him away.

At first glance the decor inside the lodge was impressive, but I'm not an interior decorator's daughter for nothing, so I could see immediately that it was a bit tired. And also, my experience of game lodges was five-star on account of my parents. I mean, it was streets ahead of The Plains, but if you're paying over ten thousand rand a night, you have a right to expect something a bit more spectacular. 'It's all in the detail,' was Liesbet's favourite saying, and looking around I could see she was right. At some point an interior decorator had definitely had a go, because the furnishings were clearly expensive and top quality. But that would have been a while ago, because bits and pieces had been added that didn't quite fit in. The wood and furniture were all too dark, the fabrics slightly faded, and it was all just too heavy.

The actual space was amazing, though. It was completely open plan with a lounge, bar and dining area and massive floor-to-ceiling windows that cleverly captured the panoramic views from the front and sides.

We went to the lounge area, which led on to a deck overlooking the river, where a lone elephant bull stood silently, his trunk scooping water. The silent vista could not have been more perfect, with wide banks that sloped gently to the glistening water. Within the lounge, massive leather couches and wicker armchairs flanked a stone fireplace, not lit but still emanating a smoky smell. A large bar made from a single mahogany slab stood at the back of the room, the fans above circling steadily and lazily.

I recognised him immediately. Kwanele sat perched on a bar stool, his laptop in front of him. He was aware of us, but he took his time. Without any rush, he finished typing and then turned to face us. He looked me straight in the eye, consideringly, intensely, and then without any interest at all.

'Kwanele, this is Alex,' said Marietjie. 'And guess what? She's a girl!'

'So I see,' he said, standing up and coming towards us. He was taller than I thought, and much better looking than the images I'd googled, with strong, even features and dark-brown liquid eyes. He reached out and shook my hand. His felt cool and I was aware that mine must have felt hot and clammy.

'And a dog,' he said, looking at Jackson and then at me. It wasn't a question, just a statement that he expected me to answer.

'Yes, he's mine,' I said. 'But I can explain ...'

I stopped as Kwanele and Marietjie looked round.

Legend walked in, and I immediately knew it was him by the dreadlocks. As he came closer, I could see that his eyes were bloodshot, and it looked like he had fallen asleep in his clothes from the night before. Conspicuous, though mostly covered in stubble, was the sizeable scar running from just under his mouth to his chin, and it definitely looked as if his nose had been broken more than once. He was a bit taller than Kwanele and quite intimidating, to be honest.

'What the hell's that?' he said, pointing at Jackson.

'She brought a dog,' said Kwanele. 'This is the new guide, Alex.'

Legend didn't exactly look impressed, and so I immediately got a bit defensive.

'There wasn't anything in the contract that said I couldn't

bring a dog,' I said. 'But actually, I wasn't meaning to and then I found him on the side of the road on the way here and I couldn't leave him to die.'

Legend raised his eyebrows. 'Contracts mean fuck all. What I say goes because I own this fucking joint and it doesn't matter if it's on a damned piece of paper or not. What are you going to do if I tell you that you can't keep it here?'

I paused and wished I could send a message to The Mutual Protection Society.

'Well, I suppose I'd also have to leave,' I said. 'I rescued him so he's my responsibility now.'

He yawned and looked as if he was already bored with the conversation.

'Good answer. You can both stay but if he chases game and I mean even a goddamned bird he's target practice, understood?'

'Yes, totally, but I mean it wouldn't be his fault exactly because he's a dog and everything and he has instincts, but obviously you know that about animals and the limitations, but ... '

I trailed off because he was literally looking at me as if I was mad.

'Understood, Mister Legend ... um, Fletcher,' I said. 'And thank you for giving him the opportunity. I mean, he would definitely thank you if he could.'

Marietjie gave a smothered laugh and Legend eyed me suspiciously.

'Don't take the piss with me,' he said. 'Now get him out of my sight and meet me at the front in fifteen minutes. You're taking me and Kwanele on a game drive.'

He stalked out of the lounge and Kwanele went back to his laptop.

Marietjie took me by the arm and walked me back to my room.

'Shit, so he usually only gets a new guide to take him on a game drive after a week!' she said. 'Alex, you must gooi mielies and try to impress him. I don't want to worry you, but you mustn't get on the wrong side of Legend. I've never known him do this before and it's bladdy unfair if you ask me.'

I won't lie, it crossed my mind that what I should do right

then and there was ask Marietjie to take me back to Hoedspruit. Then I'd get in my car and go … somewhere. This wasn't how I'd wanted to start. It was meant to be my fresh start and it had all gone wrong within only an hour of arriving at Yamihle. Legend and Kwanele's first impression of me was supposed to be brilliant, but now they probably thought I was an annoying troublemaker to get rid of fast.

Marietjie left me to get ready. I took out my binoculars, and then realised that I'd left all my field guides in Cape Town. If I was a crying sort of person this was the point when I would have sobbed. But luckily I'm not. Not having my books with me was the last straw. It wasn't so much that I needed them, but it seemed then that it was just another thing that would hold me back. A huge wave of defeat washed over me, and I don't mind telling you that I felt defeated by everything at that point. I trudged off to the main entrance feeling as if I didn't care what impression I made on the game drive. And to be honest, that was quite a good feeling.

6

KWANELE AND LEGEND WERE ALREADY in the cruiser. Kwanele sat next to the driver's seat while Legend was sprawled out at the back holding a beer. He was wearing his sunglasses but from the set of his jaw I could see that he wasn't going to cut me any slack.

I got into the driver's seat and turned to him.

'Do you want me to take a rifle?'

'You tell me,' he replied.

'Yes, obviously. But I haven't been issued with one yet.'

'I've brought mine. It's on the back seat. Next to me.'

'Well, if I'm driving, then I need it up here with me.'

There was a long pause and then he turned and picked up the rifle and made as if to pass it over to me.

'No, don't do that,' I said getting out of the cruiser and taking it from him. 'If it's loaded, which I assume it is, then that's actually really dangerous.' I took the rifle out its case and checked if it was loaded (it was) and then put the safety catch back on. I placed it on the dashboard and adjusted my seat, wishing I'd brought a pillow from my bedroom because the seat was a bit indented from a bum much heavier than mine and way too low for me.

I started up the cruiser and of course I stalled it. Three times actually.

'Jesus,' said Legend. 'Are we ever going to get going?'

'Sorry, I'm having trouble with the clutch,' I replied. 'It's really stiff so you're going to have to check the cable at some point. And the discs. My guess is that the person who usually drives this has been riding on the accelerator.'

'It's my car, and there's stuff all wrong with the bloody clutch or my bloody driving,' replied Legend as the engine finally burst into life on my fourth attempt and we lurched forward. 'Okay, take a left here and then turn right where the acacias are. And try and get a bit of control because I nearly lost my fucking front teeth just now.'

I soon got the feel of the Land Cruiser as I'd driven models like it before. My feet barely touched the pedals, though, but I thought Legend would probably go insane if I stopped the car and adjusted my seat. Talk about a fiery character.

'We're clients,' said Legend. 'Do your stuff. Impress us.'

I suppose he said that to intimidate me, but the minute he uttered those words I relaxed. This is what I loved doing. Finding, explaining, discussing. And I knew I was good, really good. As long as there were no stupid people in my cruiser.

As a guide at The Plains, you knew exactly what you were going to see. Which was very boring. But here, right now, I felt the excitement of proper guiding as I drove down the unfamiliar dirt road. No one could predict what would happen or what we'd see. Living in the moment, ready for the unexpected.

The wet season brings migrant birds, and as we drove further and further into the bush, I could barely contain my excitement. It'd been a while since I visited Mpumalanga in the first months of the year, and I hailed each new discovery like an old friend. It seemed as if we stopped every five minutes for a sighting. I wasn't even aware of my correct identifications, and the enthusiasm bubbled out of me.

I was aware, though, that Kwanele was nodding as I spoke, and once, when I glanced across at him, he gave me a small smile. I found myself smiling back, which was unusual actually, and for the first time in a very long time I felt a little glimmer of happiness.

We traversed the Crocodile River over a low bridge and I stopped to point out a Saddle-billed Stork stabbing its heavy bill into the water. I scanned the surrounding marshes with my binoculars and saw a flash of white as a tiny bird lifted and landed behind thick reeds.

'Carry on,' said Legend.

'No, wait, I think … I can't be sure exactly, but I think I've seen a White-winged Flufftail.'

'Highly doubt it,' he said, but he lifted his binoculars. 'Where?' Kwanele had his out too.

'So, just beyond the rocks to your right, it's in the reeds.'

'I think she's right,' said Kwanele. 'Look, it's in the open now.'

'Holy shit!' exclaimed Legend. 'Well spotted! I've only seen one once before. Fucking rare and I haven't got my fucking camera.'

The flufftail rose again and disappeared, and we continued in a sort of camaraderie. Until I navigated a bend, with the overgrown bush making it tricky to see clearly ahead. Fairly close to us, a herd of elephant were browsing on the side of the road. I wasn't that experienced around elephant, to be fair, because the herd at The Plains were so used to people that they were kind of like pets. Oubaas had his moments, but he wasn't like a real elephant in the wild, if you know what I mean. But I was a trained guide, and I could read behaviour well enough. And this herd wasn't happy to see us.

I stopped a good distance away and shut down the engine.

'Go closer,' said Legend, and I swear it was like déjà vu with that maniac David.

'No, I don't think that's a good idea,' I replied after looking at them more closely. 'Look, there's a really tiny baby. They want to cross the road, so let's give them their space. And see that big bull that's just come out of the bush in the front? He's holding his tail at a right angle, and he's got his head raised high. He's getting annoyed.'

'Go closer,' he repeated.

I started the engine and then I turned it off again.

'No, I won't. It's about respect, firstly, and it's also about putting clients in danger. So if you're my client I'm not going closer so you can put a dumb video on YouTube about nearly being charged. And thirdly, as the owner of the fucking joint as you yourself put it, do you really want Yamihle to be the reason that a herd of elephant gets stressed out and becomes aggressive towards vehicles? And if the answer is yes then I'm totally not working for you, and you can shove your job right up your arse and give it to some pathetic and moronic person who doesn't mind being bullied because they're too thick to realise it.'

There've been many occasions in my life that I'd like to rewind, and this was definitely one of those. I knew immediately, without WhatsApping The Mutual Protection Society, that I could have chosen my words better.

'You passed the test,' said Legend, leaning forward. 'Good call. But you listen to me and listen hard. Don't you ever, and I mean ever, dare to speak like that to me again. You want to talk about respect? Who the fuck do you think you are? Consider this strike one. Strike two and you're out. Now take us back and don't say another fucking word.'

I didn't even dare apologise. I turned the cruiser around and somehow found my way back, although Kwanele did the occasional wave to show me where to turn. Out of the corner of my eye I could see that his face was expressionless. I could only imagine what he was thinking, and it wasn't good.

'Dinner in twenty minutes,' said Legend as we pulled into the entrance of the lodge. 'Don't be late.'

I still had to take the cruiser to the parking lot and feed Jackson. And I was desperate to take a shower and wash my hair, but there wouldn't be time for that. I messaged The Mutual Protection Society on my way back to my room.

First day a disaster.

A message came back.

Nooooo! What did you DO? Even worse than rocking up with the dog????

I felt a bit irritated that Saskia immediately assumed it was my fault, and also that she didn't even remember Jackson's name.

JACKSON (the dog) not a huge success but he can stay. I had to go on a game drive with the bosses and I said some stuff I shouldn't have. But I'll explain later.

I managed to at least brush my hair and then almost ran back to the lodge, stopping briefly when my phone pinged.

Alex. Pull yourself towards yourself. Just STOP it! DON'T ruin this. OMG.

Great, some support, I thought, and actually my eyes did prickle with tears just a bit.

There were no guests at Yamihle that night and so all the staff had gathered at the bar before dinner. Dressed in their khaki uniforms, they looked fresh and clean. And I looked manky. I'd spilled some Husky down my T-shirt while I was filling Jackson's bowl so I couldn't take off my hoodie, and I felt hot and sweaty, and my hair was by now sticking to my scalp.

Legend was sitting behind the bar counter, and he gave me this sort of piercing look, but he didn't say anything. Marietjie looked pretty, I noticed. She'd put on lip gloss and mascara and was chatting to a very good-looking guy with wavy dark hair. She looked up and waved to me.

'Hey, everyone! Here's Alex.'

They all turned and stared at me with varying degrees of interest. But not much interest in total, to be honest. I wasn't exactly a breath-taking sight.

The good-looking guy turned out to be Petrus of the snotklap fame. He seemed pretty harmless, but the way he looked me up and down made me feel a little uncomfortable. There were two other guides, Bandile and Mandla, both in their thirties and friendly. The manager, Dirk, was polite in a private school way, kind of more pleased with his manners than the effect.

Legend offered me a drink and I asked for a glass of water. It was all a bit awkward, as if my arrival had spoilt the atmosphere. Soon after that a waiter said dinner was ready and we went to the table. I ended up sitting next to Kwanele, and although I had really wanted to sit next to him, I now wished that I wasn't there, because I was feeling embarrassed about the game drive and everything. Plus, by this time I was convinced that I didn't smell very nice.

I tried to think of something to talk to him about but I couldn't think of anything, so I just kept quiet, happy enough to be invisible because I was also very tired and could hardly keep my eyes open. But then there was a pause in the general conversation, and Legend looked at me from the head of the table and said, 'Our new guide is a big fan of rugby. Who do you think will win the final on Saturday, Alex?'

They were all silent, waiting for my reply. In an interested way, almost respectful. But I had no idea who was playing, or even what final it was, like no idea at all because I knew nothing about rugby, and I'd only put that on my CV to sound like a guy. I felt like a cornered animal, and I actually wondered if this day could get any worse.

But I had to say something and so I dredged up random stuff I'd heard from my dad and the twins.

'Well, it depends,' I said slowly, playing for time. 'I mean, let's say that if it's a kicking game then it depends if the other team can, um, turn it into a running game, and I'm not sure if the pitch is conducive to that, and of course the scrums will be quite tricky on account of the fly halves and that, but I think it'll swing back and forth so who knows really?'

And certainly not me, I thought.

'What's your prediction?' I asked quickly as everyone was looking a bit confused, hoping that Legend would at least mention a side.

'The Boks are the strongest team,' said Legend.

'Definitely! I'm sure they'll win.'

'So it's a pity they're not in the final,' he continued.

And now you're taking the piss, I thought. You know I pretended to be a guy and you're gunning for me.

I looked him directly in the eye.

'I'm not talking about Saturday's match, obviously,' I said. 'That's a done deal. But going forward I think they're formidable.'

His lips curled and he was about to reply when Kwanele looked at him and said quietly, 'Ungabi nomoya omubi; mnikeni ithuba.'

I knew enough Zulu to know that he was saying, 'Don't be unkind, give her a chance.'

'Alex spotted a White-winged Flufftail this evening,' Kwanele continued. 'That was a good sighting on her first drive.'

I was the focus of attention again but this time I didn't mind because it was about the flufftail and not me.

The guides were excited and impressed, but a White-winged Flufftail is actually a very rare bird and possibly nearly extinct, and I would have been just as excited if another guide had spotted it. The conversation turned to birds, and suddenly it was easy to talk because they were all so knowledgeable and it was very interesting. I asked a lot of questions, probably too many, but no one seemed to mind. Legend said hardly anything, but at one point I was aware of him looking at me and his expression had changed. I mean, he didn't look exactly friendly, but he also wasn't looking contemptuous, which had previously been his resting face when he had his sights on me, to be honest.

While we'd been talking about the flufftail the chef had served us these massive helpings of mince lasagne. And that was all. No salad or veg or bread rolls or anything. Everyone was tucking in, but there was no way I could eat it, even though I was starving. I couldn't even bring myself to try and scrape the mince off the pasta. I pushed the lasagne around my plate, hoping no one would notice, but of course they did because it was pretty obvious.

'Don't you like lasagne, Alex?' said Marietjie. 'I'll finish it for you if you like.'

She didn't mean to draw attention to me, but it was in one of those moments when there was no general conversation.

'I'm vegetarian,' I said. 'But actually, it's totally fine. I'm not hungry and … '

Dirk tutted. 'It's not fine,' he said fussily. He clicked his fingers at one of the waiters. 'Tell Chef to come to the dining room.'

I looked at him in surprise and then at Legend. He didn't say anything. He just carried on eating. Everyone else looked uncomfortable and there was silence until the chef appeared and stood hesitantly near the table.

'Now, this is exactly what I was talking to you about last week, Dumisani,' said Dirk. 'Do you remember what we discussed about food allergies and preferences? Our new guide is vegetarian and now she has nothing to eat. What do you think would happen if she were a guest? Do you think this would make a good impression?'

I couldn't believe that he was using me to make an example of Dumisani and humiliate him in front of everyone. And I also couldn't understand why Legend was allowing him to do it. In fact, he'd now pulled out his phone and was staring at the screen, looking completely uninterested in what was going on.

I took one look at Dumisani's face, and it made me feel sick. It reminded me of school when someone would get picked on in front of the whole class by a teacher who was grandstanding just for the hell of it.

'The thing is, Dirk,' I said, 'I've literally only just arrived and to be honest there was nothing on your employee form that indicated dietary preferences, so I'm not sure how Dumisani could have found out that I'm vegetarian. I mean, he'd have to be kind of like a mind reader to do that. Plus, did he even know I was arriving today?'

I turned to Dumisani. 'Ubuwazi ukuthi ngifika lapha namuhla?'

I was conscious of Kwanele turning sharply to stare at me and also that Legend had lifted his face out of his phone.

'Cha bengingakwazi lokho,' Dumisani replied softly, shaking his head.

'He didn't know,' I said to Dirk. 'So, um, it's not really fair to blame him.'

There was an awkward pause. I hoped that Legend would break it, but he didn't. He was staring up at the ceiling, tight-lipped. I couldn't help but think he was a bit of a coward. He was supposed to be the boss, for God's sake.

'It's my fault,' I continued, trying to ignore the fact that Dirk looked as if he'd like to murder me. 'I should have told you I'm vegetarian and I'm *so* sorry about that – I know how annoying it is when people don't disclose their dietary needs upfront, especially when you're in the middle of the bush.'

Dirk gave me a thin smile, his eyes cold.

'You should have, indeed,' he said, waving at Dumisani to indicate that he was dismissed. 'Well, I'm afraid we can't offer you an alternative at this point, which I'm sure you'll understand.'

'Of course,' I said, 'I don't expect that at all.' I passed my plate over to Marietjie, who was staring at me as if I had two heads or something.

But it broke the awkwardness that everyone was feeling, because the other guides started teasing her and asking her to share.

'Where did you learn to speak Zulu?' asked Kwanele. 'You speak it well.'

'It was one of my subjects at high school,' I replied. 'And actually, I'm sort of addicted to *The Queen*. It's easier to learn if you really want to know what people are saying.'

He nodded but didn't say anything more. And I didn't mind that, since I'm not the world's greatest conversationalist. Plus, by that stage I was so tired and frankly so sick of being me that I was desperate to get back to my room.

Everyone started to get up from the table. The guides went to the bar to play darts, but I didn't join them. Actually, no one suggested that I should.

Instead, I walked up to Legend, who was still at the table looking at his phone.

'I'm sorry about the drive and everything,' I said. 'I mean, I was very rude to you and there's no excuse.'

He looked at me for a long moment, and I forced myself not to look away. Although I couldn't read his expression, I fully expected him to go off at me again, and this time maybe about what I had said to Dirk. I could feel my heart thudding in my chest.

But he just said, 'Apology accepted. You'll be training with Kwanele this week. Check with him what time he wants to start in the morning.'

I couldn't believe my luck. I thought I'd probably be going out with one of the senior guides, Bandile or Mandla. For the first time since I'd arrived at Yamihle, I smiled. I mean, a proper smile.

'And by the way,' he continued, 'you should smile more often.'

I wasn't sure what he meant by that, but I suppose he was trying to tell me not to always have a sulky expression or something. People tell me that a lot, but I don't mean to look sulky. It's just the way I look. I mean, you should see my baby pictures.

Kwanele had gone, but the waiter told me he'd said I should meet him at eight in the morning at the front of the lodge.

The soft breeze felt cool on my face as I walked back to the staff quarters, and I smiled when the almost deafening clicking of frogs stopped abruptly as I passed them, and then continued vigorously. Tiny flickers of lightning flashed far in the distance, too far away to hear the thunder. As I entered my room, Jackson struggled up from the pile of blankets I'd put on the floor for him, his stub of a tail quivering with pleasure. I let him outside, and as I watched him sniff around, I let it all soak in. The sweet smell of the bush, the quiet, the peace.

My new uniform was laid out on my bed, and there was a cheese sandwich and an apple on the table. I won't lie, I practically inhaled it as I checked my phone.

There was a message from The Mutual Protection Society.
Is everything OK?

I was still feeling a bit hurt, so my reply was brief.

Yes.

Then I felt bad, because that was actually being quite bratty. And also, of course Saskia was going to assume it had been my fault for obvious reasons.

I think it's going to be fine.

I nearly told Saskia about Dirk, but I thought that would throw her completely over the edge. Then I realised it had all been about me as usual, so I sent another message.

How are things with you?

👍 *I'm OK. My parents had marriage counselling today and then they had this huge fight. WTF?? My mom put their wedding picture in the wheelie bin. Ouma's just gone out in her nightie to get it.* 😂

Which was funny, but not really. I've only ever heard my parents have a proper fight a few times and it was always about me, which in a way is okay because it's not exactly fundamental.

There were two missed calls from Jess and one from my dad. I started thinking that I was a very selfish and self-absorbed person, and I that I should have sent a WhatsApp to our family group because if I were them, I would have wanted a message.

Hi. Got here. It's nice.

I called Jess back and I knew immediately that things weren't okay because she was speaking in this sort of high-pitched and deliberately cheerful voice. She told me Roger had gone to Mauritius on business and he'd only let her know on the morning he left, like it was funny or something. I said he was a narcissist and that was totally the wrong thing to say because she got all huffy and said I didn't even know what it meant, and that people always fall back on that label if they don't understand someone. I said I was sorry, and then we said goodnight in a bit of a stiff way.

I was so exhausted I had to force myself to take a shower. But once I started, it was difficult to get out. I stood staring ahead like a zombie and then I realised this position was a bit too familiar and not in a good way, and I made myself switch off the taps.

Before I went to sleep, I thought about who maybe liked me so far at Yamihle and who didn't. I was almost sure Marietjie liked me, so that was good. Legend didn't like me. Kwanele probably didn't either. Everyone else probably wasn't sure yet. But one thing was certain. I had definitely made an enemy on my first day, and that was Dirk.

7

I woke up to the sound of hippos grunting in the nearby river, and a few light thumps on the roof of my chalet signalling that the vervet monkeys had descended from the jackalberry trees in camp and were ready for action. Jackson was sitting up, his head cocked to one side, looking puzzled by the unfamiliar sounds.

'Today's going to be a good day,' I told him.

I scrutinised myself in the mirror after I'd got dressed. Because I'd gone to bed with wet hair it had gone all curly but at least it was back to its natural auburn colour. Miraculously, the pimple forming on my nose had decided to retreat. My uniform was a bit big, and the baggy shorts made my legs look skinny, especially as they ended in thick rolled down socks and clumpy hiking boots. But I definitely looked the part. A bona fide Yamihle guide.

I put Jackson on a leash and set out to explore the camp. I especially wanted to see the guest chalets, as every single review of Yamihle I'd seen on Tripadvisor mentioned how stunning they were. I followed a path that meandered towards the river and came across two of the housekeeping staff carrying fresh white towels and making their way to the chalets. They waved at me and then stopped, somewhat surprised to see Jackson with me, and introduced themselves as Grace and Ayanda.

We walked together to the chalets.

'The bedrooms have just been redecorated,' said Grace. 'They are very, very beautiful. I think you will like what you see.'

I expected to see standard safari style with muted, neutral colours, a touch of colonialism, and a good deal of dark wooden furniture, but the decor was far more exciting. It was eclectic and eccentric, from colourful beaded chandeliers and a delicately carved four-poster bed painted in sage green, draped in tie-dyed mosquito nets, and made up with Indian fabric covers and pillows, to a massive pink couch adorned with throws and cushions of so many hues that they should have clashed horribly but didn't. Not one piece of furniture or fabric was repeated. It was a glorious confusion of beautiful objects and colour, and it was exquisite.

Floor-to-ceiling bifold doors opened to a deck with similarly decorated day beds, a plunge pool and an outside shower. The deck was barely a metre away from the edge of the river, its smooth water still glistening in shades of pink from the early morning sun.

'Come look here,' said Ayanda, gesturing towards the bathroom. Almost as big as the bedroom, it was dominated by a sunken bath, a green velvet chaise lounge and a Moroccan rug. Three walls were entirely made of glass, and an elaborately woven grass chandelier threaded with ostrich shells hung from the ceiling. Oversized wrought-iron lanterns stood next to the bath, and a dresser alongside it was covered in candles and silver candelabras of every shape and size, amongst which stood somewhat inexplicably a large porcelain parrot. But it worked.

The style struck me as vaguely familiar, but I couldn't put my finger on it.

'I love it,' I said. 'It's like, totally over the top in a way, but you're right, it is beautiful. Who did the design?'

'This nice lady, Liz, who is famous,' said Grace. 'She's coming back soon to do the main lodge.'

I glanced at my watch and saw it was already past seven.

'I'd better go back,' I said. 'I'm going out with Kwanele just now.'

I hesitated. 'Grace, would you mind maybe just checking on Jackson if you've got time during the morning? I'm sorry to ask but I'm going to leave him in my room and ...'

'Leave the old man with us,' she said, taking Jackson's lead. 'He can have pap and gravy for his breakfast.'

I'd been so excited to go out with Kwanele and I'd been thinking about how amazing it was going to be and everything, but once I got into the cruiser and we'd driven out, I suddenly felt all shy and awkward. I thought about Liesbet saying I didn't know how to make small talk and I considered saying something about the weather. But Kwanele got in first.

'It looks like we're going to get a storm,' he said.

I smiled. 'Yes,' I said, feeling myself relax. 'Yes, I think you're right.'

'I want to check on the treehouse camp,' he said, turning the cruiser onto a narrow sandy road after we'd crossed the bridge. 'It's been closed for the rainy season, but we've got guests coming tomorrow and I have a feeling Legend might want to bring them here for an evening. We often just braai here when it's closed, and the road is okay to drive on.'

The road ended at a waterhole surrounded by muddy sand and thick bush just beyond. Raised high on wooden stilts and built around an old leadwood tree, the treehouse camp had six rooms connected by a walkway, and a huge deck that overlooked the water. A rudimentary shower room had been built below, screened by bamboo poles. It wasn't luxurious but it was certainly spectacular.

'Let us see if nature has overtaken it,' said Kwanele, getting out of the cruiser. 'We must check all the rooms, and then Grace and Ayanda can clean them tomorrow. The guests always want to explore even if they aren't sleeping over.'

Besides needing a good sweep, it all looked fine. Until I went into the last bedroom. I didn't spot it immediately, but I could sense I wasn't alone, and I was right. A couple of very large, very hairy legs were just visible under a pillow on one of the twin beds. I raised the pillow slowly, placed it back just as slowly and then went to call Kwanele.

'There's a spider on one of the beds in this room,' I said. 'Actually, it's a baboon spider and it's massive.'

I lifted the pillow again to show him and he swore softly.

'Shit, that's a big one.'

The spider raised its front legs threateningly and we both took a hurried step back. Then it decided to make its escape. It ran across the duvet cover and disappeared under the bed. We looked at each other and burst into nervous laughter.

'Haibo!' exclaimed Kwanele, now nearly out of the door. 'Man, I don't like those things.'

So, I won't lie, I don't like them either. Nothing personal, but a baboon spider is a flipping scary-looking thing. But I couldn't resist trying to impress Kwanele.

I took hold of a grass basket that was hanging on the wall.

'Can you get a piece of paper or something from the cruiser? I'll see if I can put this over it and then slide the paper under.'

He looked quite impressed. He came back a few minutes later with a map and a torch.

'Okay, I'm going in,' I said. I lay on my stomach and wriggled just under the bed. The hairs on my arms were standing up as I scanned around with the torch, and I prayed it wasn't sitting above my head. But then I saw it. It had squashed itself against the wall and a leg of the bed. It raised its legs again as I wriggled forward using the basket as a shield. Before it could run, I slammed the basket over it.

'Got it! Quick, hand me the map.'

Kwanele bent down and gave me the map, which I slowly inserted under the basket, praying that I'd sealed it. But then I was stuck. I was too scared to move backwards in case I lifted the basket.

'Um, Kwanele, can you pull me out by my legs?' I said. 'Like, really slowly so I can use both hands to keep the map under the basket?'

He took hold of my ankles and pulled me out from under the bed. Actually, he pulled me all the way out through the door onto the walkway. With one hand still on the basket, I stood up and Kwanele closed the door. I shuffled round to his side.

'You ready?' he said. I nodded.

I lifted the basket and we both ran. Luckily the spider ran in the opposite direction, and we saw it disappear down one of the wooden stilts.

But we carried on running until we reached the deck.

'You were the brave one,' he said, smiling at me. 'When it comes to spiders, I'm a coward. And I am beginning to think that you are fearless.'

Once we were back in the cruiser, I said a bit shyly, 'You know what, I've seen a YouTube video of you when you had a stand-off with this huge bull elephant, so I know you're brave. That's way braver than catching a spider. And actually, sometimes I'm afraid of quite a lot of stuff.'

'What are you most afraid of?' he said.

'Storms,' I replied. 'Like, very scared of them. I get terrified when thunder and lightning are really close, so if one approaches this week maybe you'll get to see that I'm not as fearless as you think.'

We didn't talk very much after that. The main purpose of going out with Kwanele that morning was for me to get my bearings on the roads in the concession. He showed me landmarks to look out for, the waterholes, and the boundaries I shouldn't cross over into the Kruger Park. But at the end of the drive, he asked me about where I'd worked before, and I told him about The Plains. Not about getting fired, obviously, but about the encampments and how it could possibly become a self-sustaining conservancy if there was more land. He was really interested, not just pretending, and so knowledgeable and informed about that sort of thing that I felt disappointed when we got back because I could have literally talked to him about it all day.

I went back to my bungalow and Jackson wasn't there. Grace had said she'd take care of him, but I had assumed she would take him back to my room, and I started to panic. I ran to the kitchen area and heaved a big sigh of relief when I saw him lying on the floor next to Dumisani, who was chopping vegetables. Although Jackson thumped his tail when he saw me, he didn't get up. Dumisani looked up at me and smiled.

'This inja is now the deputy of the kitchen,' he said. 'He has earned his promotion by cleaning the floor.' He pushed a piece of carrot off the table and Jackson snapped it up.

'Shall I take him back to my room?' I asked. 'I don't want him to bother you or anything.'

'No, he must stay here with us,' said Dumisani. 'He has not finished his work. I'll take him to your room later. And Marietjie was looking for you for a meeting. She's in her room.'

I went to find Marietjie. She was sitting on her bed crocheting a beanie and listening to Jeremy Loops.

'Crisis,' she said. 'Only two bladdy guests expected this week and now Legend's accepted a booking at short notice for a hele flippen group arriving tomorrow morning. Dirk is freaked out and he's called a meeting for now now, and all the guides and housekeeping have to attend.'

'And besides that,' she continued, 'Dirk's *already* properly the moer in. Petrus heard Legend skelling him out this morning for what he did to Dumisani at dinner last night. Serves him right. He's a bladdy bully. Petrus said Dirk tried to argue with Legend about it and then Legend yelled at him to fuck right off out of his sight.'

'Why d'you think he didn't say anything last night, though?'

Marietjie shook her head. 'Not his style. The thing with Legend is that if you do something stupid, he'll lose his temper and yell and carry on, verstaan? But no one really minds that much because he just goes a bit mal, but he won't shame you in front of everyone and make you feel like a poepol. Not like Dirk does. Hopefully he won't last much longer. He's just recently started throwing his weight around, and Legend's beginning to notice that.'

She put the beanie to one side. 'Come, we better go.'

We joined the others in the dining room. A few minutes later Dirk marched in holding a clipboard, followed by Bandile carrying a flipchart. Grinning, Bandile rolled his eyes at us and then took his seat.

Even though no one was actually talking, Dirk clapped his hands.

'I need your *full* attention, people,' he said importantly.

'Crack on then,' muttered Petrus, and Marietjie stifled a giggle.

'Now, you've probably heard that we got a last-minute booking today. As from tomorrow morning, we are fully occupied until Sunday morning. The group that's arriving unfortunately experienced a sudden change of plans and they're now coming to us for a *very* important occasion.'

He looked around expectantly, obviously hoping for a reaction, but everyone just stared at him.

'A *very* important occasion,' he repeated, 'and *very* important guests.'

Petrus gave a huge yawn and this time I also had to try not to laugh.

Somewhat deflated, Dirk soldiered on.

'A fiftieth birthday party,' he said. 'And we have to pull out all the stops. All hands on deck. Attention to *detail*, that's what this week is all about. No room for error. We have to impress the hell out of them. Are you up for it, people?'

As everyone mumbled that they were, I had this weird feeling he was going to make us stand up and do a haka or something.

'Right,' continued Dirk, passing around stapled documents. 'What you have in front of you are the room allocations, and a schedule of activities.'

For good measure he wrote it all down on the flipchart as well.

On Day One we all had to meet and greet the guests and sing some random welcome song. Depressing, because that's what we literally had to do every day at The Plains. Then brunch, game drive, cocktail party, dinner. The next day was a bush breakfast, a guided walk … it went on and on, until Day Four, which was the actual party, and that night there was going to be a marimba band, and dancing and whatever. Dirk banged on about the menu, impeccable behaviour, personal hygiene (what the actual?) and the importance of finding lions for the guests every single day.

He then swept out of the room like a headmistress at the end of assembly and everyone fell around laughing. Unfortunately, he swept back in again almost immediately, his mouth literally like a chicken's bum as he clocked the hilarity.

'Grace, I forgot to mention to you specifically that a complimentary fruit basket and bouquet of flowers goes in Room Seven on Friday morning. Kindly do not forget.'

He paused. 'I hope you are all taking this seriously, people. I can assure you that a written warning will be issued to anyone who performs poorly this week.'

There was silence, but then I felt that I had to say something, because it's really important to get the facts straight before you threaten anyone.

'Actually, Dirk,' I said, 'you can't give a written warning before you give a verbal warning. I mean, I'm sure you meant to say that, but legally you sort of have to give two verbal warnings before a written one.'

He glared at me and then tittered.

'Well, I'm sure you've had *plenty* of experience in that, Alex,' he said. 'I bow down to your very obvious knowledge of employee misconduct and stand corrected.'

After they'd made sure Dirk wasn't coming back, everyone started high-fiving me, and that wasn't good. I didn't want to be seen as a troublemaker. I tried to explain that I was just being honest, but they didn't really get it.

'Jeez, you're something else,' said Petrus, looking at me admiringly, and I totally didn't want that either, because Marietjie looked upset, and I realised that she liked Petrus. I mean, like as if she had a thing for him.

Kwanele hadn't been at the meeting with Dirk, but he came in a few moments later and briefed us on who we'd be guiding. Because I wasn't yet familiar with the roads, he told me I'd be going out with him and his group. I tried not to smile when he said that, but in fact, I felt like fist-pumping the air. Kwanele and Legend were the only pro guides so they'd be doing the guided walks, but he said we would go too on account of the groups being bigger than usual.

***

It was a bit tense later at dinner. Legend and Kwanele didn't join us, but Dirk did, and he wouldn't let anyone drink any alcohol because he said we needed clear heads in the morning. That didn't affect me, of course, but there was a lot of grumbling about it, especially since Mandla whispered to us that he'd seen Dirk chucking a huge tot of brandy into his coke.

I tried to avoid sitting next to Petrus, but he managed to manoeuvre it so that I sat between him and Marietjie, and then he got all stupid and flirty. Obviously Marietjie noticed and looked miserable, so I attempted to talk to her instead, but she kept shutting me down and eventually I gave up.

The three of us ended up walking back to our chalets together. I found myself thinking that I really wanted a friend at Yamihle, and so I decided to nip the whole Petrus thing in the bud.

'Goodnight,' I said. 'Big day tomorrow, I guess. I'm just going to give my boyfriend a quick call and go straight to sleep.'

I didn't look at either of their faces as I spoke, but I knew it would kind of sort things out.

8

THE GUESTS HAD CHARTERED A plane from Johannesburg and were landing at Hoedspruit Airport at the ungodly hour of six in the morning. Luckily only Bandile, Mandla and Petrus were driving out to meet them, but we were all up early as Dirk started banging on everyone's doors just after four o'clock.

Once the guides had left, he marched off with Grace and Ayanda to conduct probably about his fiftieth room inspection, and as there was nothing really for Marietjie and me to do, we went to help in the kitchen. Dumisani had just taken a tray of croissants out of the oven, and the sous chefs were mixing dough to make vetkoek. Platters of smoked salmon, sweet potato and feta frittatas, and cut meats had already been prepared, but Dumisani said he was far from finished.

'Where's my deputy, Jackson?' he asked as he placed a string of pork sausages into a massive frying pan sizzling with oil. 'He's late reporting for duty.' He made me go and fetch him when I said Jackson was in my room. 'From now on you can leave him with me during the day,' he said when Jackson bustled in and installed himself under the table. 'He'll keep the monkeys out of my kitchen.'

Just before ten we heard the cruisers arriving and Dirk herded everyone to the entrance. Legend was already there, leaning against the wall and smoking what appeared to be a joint. Actually, it definitely was because you can't mistake that smell.

'Now, as they get out, you start to sing,' said Dirk, pulling his face into a kind of grotesque welcoming smile.

'Fuck that,' said Legend, chucking his joint into the bushes strolling forward. 'Jesus, now I've heard it all.'

He shook hands with the guests as they got out of the cruisers, and I must say he was so charming that they were eating out of his hands in minutes. The women especially looked totally excited, and their husbands were sort of puffing themselves out trying to look as manly and rugged as Legend.

We all helped carry the luggage into the foyer, and once they'd been given their cold towels and orange juice, Dirk started his welcome speech, but no one really listened as they kept wandering off to go to the loo or look at the view from the lounge. It was a very glamorous bunch of people. Ranging from very blonde to very brunette to very braided, the women were sort of like sleek and well-kept racehorses. If you looked closely, you could see that they'd all had a bit of work, but it was really subtle and clearly very expensive. They were all dressed in couture safari wear and basically looked straight out of one of those old Peter Stuyvesant ads.

Shamilla and Gavin were the hosts, and it was going to be Shamilla's birthday. They'd brought four other couples with them, as well as their children, Julia, who was about fourteen, and Mikey, who was definitely ten, since he seemed to find it important to tell everyone how old he was the minute he arrived.

They all eventually listened to Dirk when he started allocating their rooms.

'Now, the birthday girl, the *young* lady to my right, and her husband,' he said with a coy smile, 'will be in our very special honeymoon suite, and no need to pull the blinds down because your privacy is *guaranteed* although there may be the odd naughty little monkey wanting to peep at you.'

He chuckled but everyone just stared at him.

'Fuck's sake,' I heard Legend mutter behind me.

Dirk continued giving out room numbers and then turned to Julia and Mikey.

'And these little people are in Room One because it's closest to the main lodge, so you can sound your panic horn if you get scared at night, and we'll be there in less than a minute.'

'I'm not little,' said Mikey. 'And I'm not afraid of anything. If a lion comes into my room, I'll kick it in the arse and twist its bloody head off.'

'Language, son,' said Gavin mildly.

'I don't want to share a room with Mikey,' said Julia, her face mutinous. 'He farts in his sleep and he's generally disgusting, *and* he makes a mess in the toilet. I want my own room.'

'Sweetie,' murmured Shamilla. 'Remember what we talked about on the plane? We're here for mummy's birthday celebration, so absolutely no fighting or doing anything that makes me sad.'

Julia opened her mouth to argue but just then Kwanele appeared, and she snapped it shut and blushed. I didn't blame her. Legend was sexy in a rugged and dishevelled way, but Kwanele was definitely *GQ* magazine cover material.

'Kwanele and I will help you take your luggage to your room,' I said to Julia. 'I bet you won't mind sharing with Mikey once you see it, because it's huge.'

'Brunch in one hour, ladies and gents, and don't forget to bring your appetites!' Dirk called out as everyone started going to their rooms. As we left, I heard Legend telling him to tone it the fuck down a notch or two.

They were all back on the deck before even an hour had passed. We guides hung around in the bar area, but Kwanele and Legend joined them on the deck, and it seemed like every five minutes Legend was popping open a bottle of champagne.

'They're going to be so vrot by the time we take them out,' said Marietjie. 'And making so much noise we're gonna see fokkol.' She looked disapprovingly at Petrus, Mandla and Bandile, who had surreptitiously taken beers from behind the bar and were pouring them into their water bottles.

'Better not let Dirk see you,' she said, and then giggled. 'Check, he's trying to chase the vervets away.'

The resident troop had taken up position in the trees, clearly poised for a raid. Dirk was ineffectually flapping his arms at them while filling glasses and snapping his fingers at the waiters to remove plates. We stopped laughing as he came back inside, and he looked at us suspiciously.

'Don't just sit around, people. Some of you help Dumisani bring out the coffee, and the rest of you can go and talk to the guests about the afternoon game drive.'

They all shot off to the kitchen and Dirk flapped his hands at me.

'Go on, get out there, and be *polite*, Alex.'

I had to admit that Dirk had got my measure by now. I went outside determined to practise small talk, but then I sighed when I saw that Julia was throwing pieces of apple to a vervet monkey who had decided the time was right for a strategic approach.

'Please don't do that,' I said. 'They can become a bit of a nuisance if they get fed.'

'It's so cute,' she replied, ignoring me, and tossing another piece of apple to the monkey.

'Very cute,' I agreed. 'Until she bites you in the face and then we'll have to shoot her. And that would be a pity, wouldn't it? Because she's probably got a baby and then it'll die too. A long and excruciatingly slow death of starvation.'

She gave me this really insolent look and then chucked a piece of toast at the vervet. I swear, I really didn't want to do it, but I picked up the catapult that's kept at the breakfast table of almost every lodge I've been to, loaded it with a small stone and fired it at the vervet. Not hard though. It hit her on the leg, and she squealed in fright and ran away.

Julia stared at me in shock and yelled, 'Mom, she killed the monkey!' and burst into noisy sobs.

The other guests looked around in consternation and I was glad that both Legend and Kwanele had gone inside at this stage.

'Oh, Julia darling,' said Shamilla, '*please* shut up and don't make a scene. It gives me *such* a headache.'

She smiled at me and rolled her eyes.

'She's simply stuffed full of hormones at the moment,' she said. 'It's the most frightful nuisance.'

'I promise you the monkey's not dead,' I said to Julia, now feeling sorry for her. 'Look, she's actually looking at us from the tree, already plotting her next move.'

Mikey had picked up the catapult and was aiming it at the vervet.

'Can I have a go?' he said. 'I bet I can knock it out of the tree.'

I snatched it away from him.

'No, you bloody well can't. And if you touch that catapult again, I'll shoot you in the bum.'

He found this incredibly funny and fell about laughing. 'Bum! Arse!' he yelled, 'Alex's going to shoot me in the banana cannon!'

I couldn't help laughing too because I'd forgotten what ten-year-old boys find funny. And he was quite a cute child with all his freckles and sticky-up hair.

Unfortunately, I hadn't noticed that Dirk had come back to the deck and had been lurking while all this was going on. He beckoned at me to go inside with him.

'The guests have just arrived, and already you've made trouble,' he said, his voice high-pitched. 'I am strongly tempted, Alex, *strongly* tempted, to give you your *first* verbal warning this very minute on only your third day with us.'

'A verbal warning for what?' said Legend, walking into the lounge.

'Alex upset that poor child Julia by shooting at a vervet with a catapult and then she threatened to shoot the boy in the bottom.'

'She was feeding the vervets and wouldn't stop,' I explained, 'and then Mikey wanted to have a go with the catapult.'

Legend laughed. 'Little shit,' he said. 'Show him how to hit cans with it.'

He turned to Dirk. 'Instead of giving Alex a verbal warning, you might want to check on the bar supplies. There's only one case of whisky in the store and I suspect this lot will go at it hard this week. And we've already been through a case of champagne. We can't run out for Chrissake.'

Dirk gave me a poisonous look, but he hurried away.

'I've been speaking to Kwanele,' continued Legend, 'and we think it's best that you take the kids out on their own, okay?'

'Just me?' I said, alarmed.

'No, you and him. I get the feeling they're going to cramp the adults' style on the drives if they get bored. So you might want to take them on shorter drives and do other stuff with them.'

I nodded. 'Okay, but I mean I don't know many kids, and to be honest I don't really like the ones I do know.'

'And to be honest, Alex,' he said mockingly but with a frown, 'I don't give a stuff whether you like kids or not. Guiding is not only identifying animals – it's about looking after your fucking clients, however old they are, and making sure they have a good time. Are you going to push back at every instruction? Because if so, you can piss off right now.'

'Sorry,' I said, my face going a bit red. 'Um, we could find animal poo and everything and get them to pick it up and sort of identify it and look for insects and stuff. And your catapult idea ... definitely brilliant. Totally.'

He stared at me. 'I've yet to figure out when you're taking the piss and when you aren't,' he said. 'But I think you'll find that you are good with kids. And Kwanele certainly is.'

After brunch, the adults all sloped off to sleep off the champagne. Kwanele and I took Julia and Mikey to an open area just near the staff quarters and we set up some cans and gave them catapults. Mikey loved it, but Julia was a bit disinterested and aloof and said it was childish – until she knocked over a can and then she got all excited. I suggested that we take on Mikey and Kwanele and then we got all noisy and silly and gave our teams funny names. The other guides joined us, and then it got even noisier and even more fun, and we lost track of time and were nearly late for the game drive.

Legend and Bandile were driving the adults and Petrus and Marietjie joined us. To be honest, it was one of the best game drives I'd ever had. Kwanele was brilliant with Julia and Mikey. We identified animal poo and tracked prints, and it turned out Marietjie had the same sense of humour as Mikey and rolled out toilet jokes until he nearly got sick he laughed so much.

We were just about to drive to the meeting place for sundowners when Legend radioed us.

'Lion kill,' he said. 'A pride has just taken a giraffe. About two kilometres east of uBhejane Pan.'

'Roger,' said Kwanele. He reversed and turned the cruiser, and we went at speed towards the pan. We soon spotted the other cruisers and Kwanele slowed down.

'Just keep very quiet,' he said, turning to Julia and Mikey. 'And don't stand up, okay?'

'Why?' said Mikey. 'Why can't I stand up? I want to see them properly.'

I leant back and whispered, 'Because if you stand up, they will jump into the cruiser and eat you.' He thought that was funny, but in retrospect it really wasn't the most intelligent thing I could have said.

Kwanele pulled up beside Legend's cruiser and cut the engine. A few metres away, in long grass, a pride of fourteen lions were crouched around a giraffe carcass. Judging from the noise they were making it was obvious that they hadn't eaten for a couple of days. The male growled ferociously as he pulled out chunks of meat from the rump, occasionally lashing out at the lionesses and cubs. Their faces reddened with blood and guts, the lions were still in their initial feeding frenzy, but it would take them several days to finish their meal.

We'd been watching them for about twenty minutes before Kwanele held up his hand. 'Did you hear that?' he whispered to me. I nodded. It was the unmistakeable sound of another male lion.

In the same moment, the pride paused, alert. The male stood up, his body stiff and eyes fixed on a clump of trees behind them.

Kwanele signalled to Legend, but he'd heard it too.

I turned to Mikey and Julia, putting my finger to my lips. 'There's another male approaching. Keep very still, it's going to be interesting.'

It was only then that I saw Julia's face. It was completely white. She was also shaking, hugging her knees. Petrus and Marietjie were behind her so they wouldn't have seen how terrified she was. Before I could say anything to reassure her, the second male appeared. He paused for only a couple of seconds, and then all hell broke loose. The lionesses and cubs scattered, and the two males went at each other, first standing at their full height, then rolling in battle on the ground, their roars deafening. We had drawn up close to the kill and so they were fighting frenziedly just a few metres away from us. It seemed like it could have been a fight to the death, but the second lion retreated and ran between the vehicles, pursued by the bigger male. For a moment I thought he might actually jump into our cruiser, but he turned and hurled himself back into the fight.

I leant back and grabbed Julia's hand. I don't think I've ever seen someone so frightened.

'Julia,' I whispered, 'listen to me, I absolutely promise you that they're not interested in us. It's a territorial fight. They're not even aware of the cruisers. I know it's scary, but it's just noise.'

She gripped my hand hard. '*Please*, can't we just go?'

'We can't now,' I said. 'Just put your head down and don't look, okay?'

Snarling, their jaws wide open, the males were now going at each other with a ferocity that was terrifying. They were so close it felt as if their roars were reverberating in my chest, literally in my gut. I kept hold of Julia's hand, feeling it shake in mine.

Within a few minutes it was over. The male retreated and the rest of the pride slowly and cautiously came back to carry on eating.

'It's okay,' I said softly to Julia. 'The other male has gone, and they're calm now.'

She shook her head, tears pouring down her cheeks.

'Alex, I weed in my pants because I thought one of them might attack me,' she said quietly in my ear. 'And now my shorts are all wet and everyone's going to *see*.'

I mean, that's basically the worst thing that can happen to a fourteen-year-old girl. I took off my jacket and passed it to her.

'Put that over your lap for now,' I said. 'We can't go back to the lodge but when we stop for sundowners, we'll sort it out, okay?'

It was almost sunset when Legend started his engine. He nodded to Kwanele and Bandile and we drove away.

A few minutes later we got to a waterhole and set up the drinks table. The guests got out, talking animatedly and the guides started pouring gins. I went to Shamilla.

'Julia was very frightened,' I said. 'So, maybe ...'

'Oh, for God's sake,' she said. 'I knew we shouldn't have brought the bloody kids.'

'Actually, she was so frightened she wet herself,' I said. I expected Shamilla would get all motherly and go to Julia, but she just stared at me, and I swear her left eye started twitching.

'But it's okay,' I said because I suspected she was going to go off the deep end. 'I'll make a plan.'

It was a bit tricky to sort out to be honest, so I just stayed in the Land Cruiser with Julia and gave her a blanket to put around her waist and hoped that they'd all drink up quickly.

But they were knocking back a second round of drinks and totally into the whole sunset thing, which was spectacular to be fair. A herd of buffalo had arrived at the waterhole, silhouetted by the warm golden glow that stretched over the plains behind them and intensified into rich and burning hues of orange flaming across the sky.

A couple of hippos rumbled in the water, their sound momentarily drowned by the long wail of a fish eagle as it glided across the water and landed on the top of a tree. I glanced over at the group.

They'd gone quiet now, soaking up the moment.

'It's beautiful,' said Kwanele coming up to the Land Cruiser. 'And never the same.'

'I read somewhere that a sunset is our reward for surviving another day,' I said. 'But I wasn't sure of that wording, though. It's more like a celebration of the day. You know, sort of a grand finale at an opera or something when the whole orchestra plays, and the singers reach a crescendo.'

He smiled. 'Do you like opera?'

'I like listening to it,' I said. 'But I don't like watching *and* listening. It's too much.'

'That makes sense,' he said, and was about to say more when Legend spoke.

'If you've finished your drinks,' he said, 'how about going back to the kill? I have a feeling that male is going to give it another go.'

Excited, the guests all agreed and started heading back to the cruisers.

'Cool,' said Legend. 'Empty your water bottles and we'll fill them with gin and tonic.'

He came up to my Land Cruiser and gave me a hard look. I supposed he was wondering why I wasn't socialising, but I couldn't exactly explain with Julia sitting right behind me.

'What do you think, Kwanele?' he said. 'We go back to the kill and then do a short night drive.'

'Dirk's wanting to serve dinner at half past eight,' said Kwanele, 'and he's planned a cocktail party before. It's just gone six now.'

'His cocktail party idea was bloody stupid,' said Legend. 'They're not staying at a fucking fancy hotel. Tell him to cancel it and push dinner back.'

Kwanele grinned at him. 'Radio him yourself. Your idea, your firing line.'

'Christ, you're meant to be my wingman,' grumbled Legend, walking back to the group.

I got out of the cruiser and took Kwanele aside.

'Look, Julia was really scared at the lion kill and she's not going to cope with it again. I think we should rather take her and Mikey back.'

He nodded. 'Yes, you're right,' he said, eyeing Mikey, who had climbed onto the top of an ant hill. He was preparing to slice it in half with a spade he'd nicked off the back of one of the cruisers. 'Petrus and Marietjie can go with Bandile.'

When we got back, Kwanele took Mikey to the main lodge, and I went with Julia to her room, where she started crying in earnest.

'I'm so embarrassed,' she sobbed, 'and I'm sure everyone *knew*, and I didn't want to come here anyway because I've never been to a game reserve and I'm scared of animals, and I want to go home. Promise you won't tell anyone?'

'Of course I promise, and Julia, no one knew,' I said. 'They were too busy getting stuck into their gins and I bet you every single one of those women have weed in their pants before. I mean, when you get to that age, you just have to sneeze to wet yourself.'

She started to laugh then, and I waited for her to shower and change and then we walked back to the lounge where Kwanele and Mikey were playing Uno.

'I'm so hungry,' said Mikey as we entered, 'I could eat a giraffe.' He fell about laughing. 'Did you get it, Alex? I could eat a giraffe!'

I grinned at him. 'I can always take you back to the kill,' I said.

He started jumping on the couch. 'I'll eat its tail,' he yelled. 'And then I'll eat its bum!'

Julia rolled her eyes at me. 'He's had too much Fanta. I think you'd better feed him.'

'Okay, let's go and chat to Dumi,' said Kwanele. Julia and Mikey insisted on coming with us to the kitchen, where we found Dirk chuntering about his scuppered cocktail party and harassing Dumisani about the timing of dinner.

'I'm a highly regarded professional,' he was saying, 'and I do *not* dance to anyone's tune, I assure you! Dumisani, I am *hoping* that you have a plan so kindly enlighten me what you intend ...'

He broke off as he saw us.

'No children in the kitchen. Health and safety rules.'

He clearly hadn't noticed Jackson, who was lying under the prep bench gnawing on something's knuckle.

'We are not children,' said Mikey, 'and I want a hamburger please. Can I also have chips?'

'Coming up,' said Dumisani with a grin. He turned to Dirk. 'Two types of curry tonight, just need to be warmed up.'

Kwanele looked at Dirk. 'Looks like it's well under control as usual. But if I were you, I'd check the bar. The red wine's running low.'

'I'm *well* aware of that, thank you,' said Dirk, but it was kind of obvious that he wasn't. 'Come on, children! Back to the lodge please.'

'I will eat my hamburger here,' said Mikey climbing onto a stool at the prep area. 'It's better than the dining room.'

'Sure you can,' said Kwanele, then raising his eyebrows at Dirk, who started to protest. So, it wasn't a big standoff or anything, but Dirk immediately shut up and left.

'All okay, Dumi?' said Kwanele. Dumi gave him a thumbs up as he handed Mikey and Julia a chunk of mince to make patties.

'Will you stay with Julia and Mikey and bring them back to the lodge when they've finished?' he said to me. 'I've got a couple of things to check on.'

I nodded, and he left. I felt disappointed because I'd wanted him to stay with us.

9

IT WAS HALF PAST NINE before the guests rolled in, and clearly their water bottles had been filled with gin a few times.

'Bloody spectacular!' said Gavin. 'A pack of hyena tried to move in, and then the second male tried his luck again, poor sod.'

He nodded at Dirk. 'Pour me a whisky, there's a good chap.'

'Perhaps a glass of wine?' said Dirk with a glassy smile. 'I think Chef is ready to serve dinner.'

'Balls,' said Legend walking to the bar. 'We'll have a drink first.'

'Bloody fine idea,' said Gavin. He raised his eyebrows at me. 'Kids?'

'They've had supper and went to their room just now,' I replied. 'All good.'

As a first night it couldn't have been a greater success. Fuelled by the excitement of the game drive and the alcohol that flowed, it was difficult to get everyone away from the bar, but they eventually sat down to dinner. At The Plains you only had to join the guests if you had guided them, but at Yamihle, Legend liked to have the guides eat with the guests every night. Luckily that excluded Dirk. The way he was starting to watch me like a hawk was getting on my nerves.

It was exactly the kind of group I liked. They were all friends, so I didn't have to make conversation and feel all awkward about that and think about what to say. Even though I'd eaten two cheese rolls while Julia and Mikey had their hamburgers, I was still starving so I could just concentrate on the food. And observe the guests.

Because it was Shamilla's birthday and it was obvious that they'd paid for all the guests to be there, Gavin and Shamilla were socially in charge and basically enjoying that. The three other couples were Clifford and Nicky, Simangele and Prem, and Tommy and Fredine. Besides noticing that Clifford and Nicky were a bit scratchy with each other, that Fredine appeared to be a functioning alcoholic (which was saying something with this group), and Shamilla was slightly self-obsessed, I could see they were pretty harmless but definitely geared up for a rave-up of a week.

Eventually they started murmuring about going to bed and Bandile and Kwanele went to get their rifles to escort them. I was about to leave the dining area when Legend stopped me.

'I don't know what you did with guests at your last job,' he said, 'but here I expect you to get out your damn cruiser and socialise when we stop for sundowners instead of staying in it and sulking for fuck knows what reason.'

'I wasn't sulking and obviously I would normally socialise,' I replied, 'but Julia had a problem, so I stayed with her.'

'What kind of problem?' he said, frowning.

'Actually, I'm not going to tell you,' I said. 'You don't need to know.'

'I'll bloody well decide what I need to know about my guests, okay?'

'Well, this time you're *not* going to know, *okay?*'

We glared at each other for a few seconds, and then Shamilla came up to us.

'Alex, thank you so much for helping Julia,' she said, oblivious to the tension between me and Legend. 'I'm sure you probably think I'm a complete and useless cow, but I swear I sometimes simply can't cope with all the bloody drama. What the hell, I can't believe she actually ...'

'It's fine,' I said, not looking at Legend. 'And Shamilla, maybe don't tell anyone about what happened because she was really humiliated and upset.'

'Quite funny though,' she said, 'but yes, you're right. Gosh, I'm sure I wasn't that uptight when I was her age. Anyway, good night!'

Legend continued glaring at me after she left, expecting me to explain.

'So, I'm still not going to tell you what happened,' I said, half-heartedly trying to sound conciliatory. 'Basically, it's not a big deal and I promised Julia I wouldn't say anything. I mean, you're just going to have to trust me on this one.'

He was about to say something when I saw Marietjie and Petrus heading out on their way to the guides' quarters and I quickly joined them, and to be honest I hoped that I was leaving Legend to stew.

Jackson was fast asleep on my bed when I got to my room, and that was good because basically that meant he was getting stronger. He definitely looked a bit fatter. His kitchen scrap diet was doing him good. I managed to squash myself into bed with him and opened a message from The Mutual Protection Society.

Hey girl! No news is good news? Are you behaving lol 😊 *Not sure if I should tell you this, but Jess and Roger were at the restaurant tonight and they were having a bit of an argument and Jess cried. I just thought you'd want to know. xx*

I did want to know. But then I couldn't sleep.

I tried to phone Jess in the morning, but her phone went straight to voice mail. I sent her a message asking her to call me and then I thought about phoning Charles to ask him to check up on Jess, but since he hates Roger as much as me, I thought he might actually phone Roger instead and then whatever was happening would get even worse.

94

So I WhatsApped The Mutual Protection Society instead.

Thank you for telling me, Sas. I haven't managed to get hold of Jess and I won't have a chance the whole day. Can you try call her, but I can't think of a reason so that she doesn't suspect anything?

It was going to be a busy day because new guests, Knut and Ursula from Norway, were arriving in the morning. Dirk tried to make me go and meet them at the airport, but luckily Kwanele overheard and said I was in training. When he spoke, he gave Dirk this kind of look to suggest that he was surprised he had even suggested it. It struck me that Kwanele was quietly in charge of a lot of stuff at Yamihle.

In the end Marietjie and Petrus went to collect them and Kwanele and I set off after breakfast with Julia and Mikey. It was an oppressively hot and humid day, grey and overcast. The air was stale and heavy with prickly heat, and the bush felt eerily quiet as no birds sang. Sometimes you get a sixth-sense feeling that you're not going to see much and today was one of those days. Julia and Mikey were getting bored and just starting to fight over a pair of binoculars when we came across a big troop of baboons hanging out under a jackalberry tree.

Most guests are happy to watch baboons for a while, but often after the first sighting they're not that interested in stopping to watch them. Which is a pity because there's always so much going on, sort of like a glimpse into the raucous life of a massive family where there's never a dull moment.

Julia and Mikey were enchanted, as with grunts, barks and squeals adolescents quarrelled and wrestled, harassed mothers rescued their babies jumping unsteadily through the branches of the tree, and the alpha male swatted any cheeky attempts to approach him.

Mikey gazed at two mating baboons with interest.

'My mom and dad mated twice,' he said. 'When I get married, I think I'll mate three times. Kwanele, are you going to marry Alex? And if you do, how many times …'

'Shut *up*, Mikey!' said Julia, giving him a push. Taken by surprise he hit his head on the side of the cruiser and then flung himself on her to retaliate.

'Hey! That's enough,' said Kwanele reaching over and pulling Mikey back onto his seat. 'Behave, both of you, or we'll leave you here, okay?'

There was a pause.

'Yes, Dad,' said Julia giggling. Mikey started giggling too.

'That's what our parents always say,' he said. 'But they never do it. If they die, and you and Alex get married, can we come and live with you?'

Kwanele turned to me, grinning. 'You go ahead and answer,' he said in an undertone.

'Your parents are not going to die, Mikey,' I said. 'Do you want Kwanele to get you a Fanta out of the cool box?'

'And there I was thinking you were fearless,' said Kwanele, raising his eyebrows at me as he got out of the cruiser.

I tilted my head and gave him a quizzical smile.

'Ditto,' I replied.

Mikey leant forward. 'And why do so many of them have such funny-looking bums?'

I waited until Kwanele came back with the cooldrinks. 'Mikey wants to know something about the baboons. I thought you'd better answer because I don't have a clue.'

As we drove back to the lodge, I was conscious of a feeling of something I couldn't quite figure out. All I knew was that I felt content and happy in that very moment and that I wouldn't mind if it carried on forever.

But it didn't, of course. When we got back, I went to the bar area where the Wi-Fi was better to check my phone. There was another worrying message from The Mutual Protection Society.

Jess's cell on voice mail so I phoned her at the spa. They said she wasn't in today.

I still didn't think it was a good idea to message Charles, so I sent one to my dad, since Liesbet was still in Kenya. I didn't say

I was worried or anything but asked him if maybe Jess' phone wasn't working.

'You must check this new oke, Knut,' said Marietjie, walking in. 'He's got so many tattoos it looks like someone sommer klapped him with a wet *Rapport*. Look, he's coming in now with his wife.'

Tall, blonde and massively well built, Knut looked like a Viking, but in terms of his personality he was more like a golden retriever because he was so friendly and enthusiastic. Tattoos of dragons, tigers, foxes and roses covered his body-builder arms like sleeves, culminating in a pretty spectacular rendition of a sleeping snake coiled a couple of times around his neck. Ursula was small and sturdy, with rosy cheeks and startlingly light blue eyes that twinkled with excitement. Both were dressed in brand-new safari gear, and it was obvious Yamihle wasn't the first lodge they'd visited on their trip because Knut's hat band was decorated with porcupine quills, guinea-fowl feathers and a dried seed pod.

By now the other guests had gathered outside on the deck for lunch and Knut caused a lot of excitement when he and Ursula joined them. I noticed Shamilla surreptitiously pushing up her boobs and Simangele leaning sideways off her chair towards her handbag, emerging with fresh lipstick on her lips.

It can be tricky when a new couple joins an established group, but Knut and Ursula slotted in immediately, and before lunch was even over, they were all swapping numbers and showing each other pictures of their children. Only Legend and Kwanele joined them for lunch, and before I left the bar area I observed them for a bit, thinking what a good team they made with guests because they really seemed to enjoy talking to people. I wondered if I was maybe getting a little better at it, and then decided it was too soon to tell.

We all set off again in the afternoon. It had hardly cooled down, so the bush was still quiet, but luckily the lions were still feeding, so Knut and Ursula could see them and take about a thousand photographs and videos, according to Marietjie. Kwanele and I decided to avoid the lions and concentrated on animal poo.

We all gathered at the waterhole for drinks, and by the evening, the sky was at its most dramatic as it displayed the dark purple clouds of the gathering storm. There was nothing to see. The waterhole sat still and abandoned as the animals had gone deep into the bush. The mosquitos were out in full force, though, and attacked us with a feeding frenzy that eventually became too uncomfortable, and we headed back early to the lodge.

Dinner was served inside as the wind had picked up by then, the slight breeze of the evening breaking into discordant and random squalls. The mood at the table was slightly subdued, with some of the guests looking nervously out of the bifold doors at the ominous but very beautiful sky lit up by both the full moon and jagged snaps of lightning, followed by rumbles of thunder that appeared to be steadily getting closer.

Knut and Ursula, on the other hand, were delighted. Knut kept on leaping up and going outside with his selfie stick and making videos.

'He makes the documentary for the YouTube,' explained Ursula. 'It is the same verever ve go.'

'I suggest you have nightcaps in your rooms tonight,' said Legend once everyone had finished dessert. 'We're going to get a ton of rain very shortly.'

We'd all been back in our quarters for about half an hour when Legend's prediction proved to be spot on. White sheets of rain hurtled relentlessly down from the skies, deafening and monotonous.

When I'd told Kwanele that I was scared of storms it was actually a massive understatement. They reduce me to a gibbering mess. The white flash that snaps and then you wait for the thunder. I couldn't even count to one before the thunder, which meant of course that the lightning was right on top of us.

And then my very worst fear came true. The lightning struck the roof of my chalet. For a moment I thought I had died. The glass in the windows shattered and the lights blew. Sobbing and sweating with fear, I grabbed Jackson and pulled him under my bed with me.

A few minutes later there was a loud thumping on my door and then it opened. It was Kwanele.

'Alex!' he shouted. 'Are you okay?'

'No. Yes.' It came out as a whimper.

'Where are you?' He flashed a torch around the room.

'Under the bed.'

'Come out. It's safe, I promise. I'll stay with you.'

'No, um, I think I'll stay here for a bit. You know, until it's over. And … and I think Jackson feels safer under the bed.'

Actually, he hadn't flinched once.

There was a brief silence, and then Kwanele crawled under the bed and lay down next to me, taking my hand. I hadn't held someone's hand for as long as I could remember and, in that moment, I briefly forgot about the storm because it struck me that I didn't instinctively snatch it away. Instead, my hand relaxed in his, and then I gripped it hard as lightning lit up the room followed by a violent roll of thunder.

'Do you think Julia and Mikey are okay?' I asked, feeling a bit ashamed I'd only thought of them now. 'Julia will be completely terrified.'

'I'm sure they're fine,' he said. 'Legend said they must stay in Gavin and Shamilla's room tonight. Mikey's probably loving the storm.'

I flinched at another explosion of thunder and turned my face into his shoulder.

'Blow, winds, and crack your cheeks!' said Kwanele in a deep and dramatic voice, and in spite of my fear I managed a shaky laugh.

'Your matric setwork?' I said.

'Yes,' he replied and then, as the thunder rumbled again, he shouted, 'You sulphurous and thought-executing fires, um, couriers to … something-cleaving thunderbolts!'

'Oak-cleaving!' I said. 'I also did it in matric. I loved it but I always thought everything was Cordelia's fault. Basically, if she had just made more of an effort to tell King Lear how much she loved him then everything would have been totally fine. I mean, how can you tell someone that you *really* love that you love them no more and no less than what you're expected to?'

'So, Act One. The end?' he said laughing.

'Exactly. Where did you go to school?'

'Nhlaralumi High in Komatipoort, which is where I met Legend. He got expelled from his private school in Joburg, his third expulsion I think, so his parents sent him to Nhlaralumi. He was the only white boy in the school. He had a fairly tough time at first, but being Legend, he made sure no one noticed the colour of his skin after a few weeks. We became good friends, and I spent every weekend on this concession with him and his parents. That's how I got to love the bush.'

'Listen, it's not raining so hard,' he continued. 'Do we still need to stay here? My legs are getting stiff.'

I realised I was still holding tightly onto his hand. Embarrassed, I let it go. And then I thought about how ridiculous my behaviour must have seemed.

'No, I'm so sorry … actually, you needn't have come to check on me. I would have been fine on my own.'

He didn't reply until we'd both come out from under the bed.

'I just wanted to make sure you were okay because you said storms scared you,' he said and then laughed. 'That's the first time I've ever experienced a storm under a bed.'

'Sorry,' I said again, but this time I knew it sounded a bit stiff. 'Hopefully it will be the last time. You probably think I'm really silly and I'm sorry for making you feel silly too.'

'That's not what I meant,' he replied. He scanned my room with his torch and then started picking up broken glass.

'I can do that!' I said quickly. 'Honestly, you *really* don't have to bother.'

He ignored me until he'd put all the glass into the bin and

hung a towel over the window. Then he smiled at me.

'Actually, I was doing it for him,' he said pointing at Jackson who was lying on the rug and snoring peacefully. 'Dogs get scared during thunderstorms.'

And then he left.

The storm dissolved into a slow patter of rain. For the second night I struggled to sleep. I lay fretting about Jess but mostly I tossed and turned worrying that Kwanele had left thinking I was rude and ungrateful. And that I hadn't wanted him there. Which I had. Very much.

10

I BECAME EVEN MORE PARANOID that I'd messed up things with Kwanele when the next morning Bandile said I'd be driving out with him and Knut and Ursula. I kept on hoping to get a chance to thank Kwanele for looking out for me, but with so many guests around it wasn't possible. It didn't seem like he was specifically ignoring me or anything, because he was distracted by all the arrangements for the drives and guided walks and stuff, but I couldn't help worrying about it. I was also worried because the storm had knocked out the Wi-Fi, and the network was down, so I couldn't get any messages or make any calls to see if Jess was alright.

There was a lot of indecisiveness at breakfast when Legend suggested a bush walk for anyone that was keen. At only eight in the morning, it was already over thirty degrees and not a lot of cloud cover, so most of them looked dubious.

In the end only Gavin and Shamilla and Knut and Ursula decided to go on the bush walk, while the rest went on a drive with Kwanele and Bandile.

'I'm going to take Alex with us, okay?' said Legend to Bandile. I felt my pulse quicken with excitement. Only professional guides can take guided walks and there certainly hadn't been any at The Plains. I'd gone on bush walks in my training, but I hadn't done one for ages.

Plus, Legend hadn't got his name for nothing. Guided walks were his speciality.

We drove about five kilometres away from the lodge and then set off walking in a line with Legend at the front and me at the back. After a while I realised that Legend was heading in the direction of the lion kill. He stopped about a hundred metres away from the clearing where they were.

'Okay, so we're going to approach the lions,' he said. 'They'll still be very full from eating that giraffe so they're not going to be interested in us. But just keep very quiet, stay behind me and Alex when we get there, and don't move unless I tell you to.'

Everyone nodded, but I noticed that Knut was busy unravelling his selfie stick from his backpack.

Legend gave him a sharp look.

'Put that away,' he said. 'We don't want to break our silhouette with that stick, okay?'

We carried on in our line, but when we were a few metres away I went and stood next to Legend. The lions were all lying under a tree about a metre away from the giraffe. Their bellies distended, they were panting from both the heat and gorging themselves. They must have been aware of us, but I guessed they were so stuffed they didn't really care.

But that didn't last long, because the next minute Knut broke the silence. He'd quietly moved away from behind us and was standing with his back to the pride, selfie stick held high in the air.

'Here ve are seeing ze lions in ze African bush,' he began loudly, but got no further as Legend reached out his arm and yanked him roughly back into the group.

'Goddammit, what did I tell you?' he hissed furiously.

But by now the lionesses had raised their heads and the male sat up, alert. After a few moments he stood up and took a couple of steps towards us.

'Oh shit!' whispered Shamilla. 'Now what?'

I was wondering that myself, to be fair, because his tail was stiff and jerking up and down, which is actually a sign that a lion is basically totally pissed off and about to charge.

'Just keep still,' said Legend, and cocked his rifle.

Which is when Knut leapt back and decided to climb a tree, with Ursula in hot pursuit, screaming her head off, and for a few seconds I thought everyone was going to scatter in all directions. It happened very fast after that. The lion sprang forward and charged us.

'Don't run!' yelled Legend, picking up a piece of elephant dung. He hurled it at the lion and hit him squarely between the eyes. 'Piss off, you fucker!'

Taken by surprise it stopped and then leapt back. But it didn't exactly back off entirely. It stood rigid and alert, its golden eyes fixed on us. We were now locked in a standoff. Sweat trickled down my legs and chest and I clenched every muscle I had to stop myself from shaking.

'See if you can get the radio out my back pocket,' said Legend quietly, now pointing his gun at the lion. 'Do it slowly, okay? Put the sound on low and radio Kwanele for backup and then switch it off immediately so the lion doesn't get startled by the sound.'

I shifted closer to Legend. Without taking my eyes off the lion I slowly pulled out the radio, my hand shaking. Then I took a deep breath and radioed Kwanele.

'Assist urgently,' I said, speaking so quietly that to be honest I didn't think he was going to hear me. 'Site of lion kill. Aggressive male.' I quickly switched the radio off.

Fifteen minutes of a standoff with a lion can seem like a lifetime. He didn't take his eyes off us once, and neither did the lionesses. I knew that if he charged again Legend would probably have to shoot him, and I desperately didn't want that to happen. Every now and again he took a step towards us, and then Legend yelled and moved forward. He moved back each time, but he was furiously angry, and every time he attempted to advance he seemed a little more confident.

I could have cried with relief when I heard the distant rumble of Kwanele's cruiser. He had Clifford and Nicky and Simangele and Prem with him, but luckily not Julia and Mikey. He approached slowly but then speeded up, and he'd obviously briefed them because they all started thumping on the sides of the doors and yelling. At the same time Legend ran forward, waving his arms and shouting. The lion shot off and the whole pride disappeared into the bushes.

Everyone hotfooted it over to Kwanele's cruiser and clambered in. Actually, they vaulted into the cruiser like Olympic gymnasts. Kwanele walked across to us.

'You okay?' said Legend to me.

I nodded.

'She was bloody brave,' he said to Kwanele. 'I better check on the guests and I'm gonna strangle that fucker, Knut.' He walked off.

I looked at Kwanele and burst into tears.

'Hey now,' he said and put his arm round me. 'You're fine. And it sounds like you did everything right. You should be proud of yourself.'

'Basically, I'm not, really, because I was so scared and I didn't want the lion to be shot and then I thought you probably couldn't hear me on the radio and I'm sorry if I seemed ungrateful last night,' I said, wiping my eyes and nose with the back of my hand. 'It's just that … I got all embarrassed because I was being so stupid and then I say stuff and …'

He squeezed my shoulders and then let go of me.

'I know that,' he said gently. 'Come on, let's go back to the lodge. And I want you to take the afternoon off. Your windows will have been repaired by now so you can have a good sleep.'

I nearly started crying again because I was actually exhausted by now. But I just did one or two more really disgusting sniffs and then we all managed to squash into Kwanele's cruiser and went back to the lodge.

All the guests' nerves were so shot that they also went for naps after lunch and slept for so long we didn't have to do an evening game drive. By dinner time, though, the adrenaline of the day's events was pumping and there was much hilarity as they discussed the standoff with the lion. By the end of the evening and after many glasses of wine, Knut was convinced he'd been incredibly brave and quick-thinking, and Shamilla was well on her way to irritating her girlfriends as she repeatedly told them that the incident hadn't scared her at all and that she doubted they'd have handled it as well as she had.

Knut and Ursula and Shamilla and Gavin had clearly developed a sort of trauma bond and they carried on drinking when everyone else went to bed. After midnight, when they called for a bottle of Jägermeister, Legend suggested that they gather at Shamilla and Gavin's chalet to drink it. Actually, that was quite unusual, because he was literally always the last man standing, but although he hadn't strangled Knut, he'd had enough of the stories and was trying not to show how pissed off he was.

'Bandile will take you all back to Shamilla and Gavin's room,' he said. 'And then keep an eye out for the night guard, okay? He'll take Knut and Ursula back to their chalet.'

The next morning was Shamilla's birthday. Although she and Gavin looked as hungover as rats, they were in fine spirits as the staff sang happy birthday, Legend presented her with a Yamihle shirt, and Dirk brought in a cake, which was a bit of a weird thing to do at breakfast to be honest, especially as Dumi had said it was for afternoon tea.

Knut and Ursula appeared a bit later, equally hungover, and said they'd only got back to their room just before five because they'd passed out in Gavin and Shamilla's lounge.

'Vot a vonderful surprise,' said Ursula, dumping a fruit basket and bouquet of flowers on the table. 'Delivered to our room this morning. Ve can all share it.'

Dirk gave a sharp intake of breath.

'Well!' he said. 'I'm afraid I must most sincerely apologise, Ursula, but that was intended for our birthday girl, Shamilla. All I can say it's simply unforgiveable that it was delivered to the wrong room!'

He hurried away and I knew he couldn't wait to find Grace and tell her off.

Knut guffawed. 'It vos not delivered to our room,' he said. 'Ursula, she picks it up from Shamilla and Gavin's door ven ve leave, and she brings it back to our chalet. I do not know vy.'

Ursula flushed with embarrassment. 'No doubt I bring it back to our room because my brain vos not vorking properly. It vos the fault of the Jägermeister.'

All the guests thought it was hilarious and then everyone was laughing. Basically, I knew that I should have left it up to Legend and Kwanele to sort out, but Dirk had a level of viciousness that made me worry about Grace. I slipped away to the kitchens, where I knew I'd find him.

I walked in, and true to form, he was going for Grace in front of all the staff.

'Grace, I am most disappointed.' Dirk was saying, 'You alone are responsible for *ruining* the client's birthday morning. Was it too much to ask that you remember which room to deliver the special gift? Do you take no pride in your work at all? I have no further words at this precise moment but rest assured, there shall be serious consequences and you may need to consider finding alternative employment in the very near future.'

Grace couldn't even say anything because she was crying so much. And because he was such a bully, everyone else stood there, frozen by her public humiliation.

I felt dizzy I was so angry.

'You're disgusting and cowardly,' I said to Dirk. 'You haven't even bothered to find out what really happened and you're already threatening poor Grace when you *know* she won't fight back. And nor will anyone else because you're the worst kind of bully. And basically, you're going to look like an even bigger arsehole than you already are when you find out the truth, and I hope ...'

'That's enough, Alex,' said Kwanele as he came into the kitchen followed by Legend.

'But he's telling Grace he's going to fire her!' I said.

'Bugger off, Alex,' said Legend. 'I'll deal with this.'

I left, but actually it ended up not being my finest moment because I decided to eavesdrop. If Dirk denied anything he'd said to Grace I was fully prepared to go back in there. So I didn't go back to the lodge. I leant against the wall next to the door.

'You're getting on my bloody nerves,' Legend said. 'Grace has worked here for over fifteen years and she's one of my most competent staff members. Where the hell do you get off threatening to fire her? And if anyone gets fired at this lodge, I'll fucking well do it. And let me tell you, you'd better be careful because your job isn't looking exactly safe at this point. Understand?'

I could just make out a mumble from Dirk.

'And now there's a highly embarrassed guest because you made such a big deal out of it,' continued Legend. 'The gift was delivered to the right room, but Ursula took it by mistake because she was probably still pissed from the night before. So get the hell out of here and smooth it over, okay?'

Dirk exited the kitchen at such speed that it was too late for me to get out of the way.

'You're going to regret this, you little bitch,' he hissed at me, his face alive with spite.

11

AFTER A PICNIC LUNCH AT the treehouse camp, where a massive herd of elephant obligingly visited the waterhole, and early sundowners on a plain teeming with buffalo, wildebeest and giraffe, the day culminated in Shamilla's fiftieth birthday party.

Dirk had been surly all day after he'd apologised to Ursula and Shamilla, but to be fair he pulled out all the stops for the party that night. He'd brought in a marimba band from Hoedspruit, and the lounge, bar and deck looked fantastic with fairy lights and lanterns twinkling from every rafter and tree. In the afternoon he'd spent ages laying the table and decorating it with summer impala lilies and wild dagga, interspersed with tiny candles.

As the guests gathered on the deck, there was an air of excitement and anticipation, because they had clearly got Legend's drift during the week and knew they were in for a massive party.

'Looks like he's gonna give it horns tonight,' said Marietjie as Legend handed out tequila shots. 'Bladdy unfair, he said none of us can drink tonight because we have to take the guests to their rooms, but he's already vrot. God knows when we're gonna get to bed.'

Dressed in a silver sequined vest and a leopard print mini, Shamilla was in tearing spirits and knocked back two shots in quick succession. By the time they all sat down for dinner she already had a bit of dronkverdriet, and Julia and Mikey looked furious as she kept on trying to hug them and slather them with kisses. Gavin made a really sweet speech, but then Clifford sort of ruined it as he followed up by describing their tumultuous courtship that ended up with them having to get married because Shamilla got pregnant with Julia.

I noticed that Kwanele was keeping an eye on Legend, who was drinking way more than anyone else. Marietjie was right. He was definitely raring to go. The marimba band had been playing quietly in the background during dinner, but after dessert Legend handed them each a couple of tequila shots and told them to step it up a notch. That basically put paid to any conversation and soon the guests were dancing.

Fortified by the alcohol, the marimba band soon reached a high point. Glistening with sweat, hands flying across the boards and occasionally tossing the sticks into the air, they launched seamlessly from one piece of music to another.

'What a scream,' yelled Shamilla, gyrating to the music, her left boob threatening to pop out of her vest. 'Happy birthday to meeee!'

I noticed that Mikey was working his way around the room, taking sips from glasses when no one was looking, and that Julia basically looked miserable and embarrassed as she watched the adults carousing. I went to Kwanele.

'I think Julia and Mikey should go to their chalet,' I said. Mikey was enraged when we took him back, but after ranting a bit, he soon fell asleep, and we left Julia engrossed in a movie she'd downloaded on her iPad.

A fine drizzle of rain fell as we went back to the lodge, and I stopped for a minute, breathing in the earthy and sweet smell of the dry soil soaking up the moisture.

'Look,' said Kwanele, shining his torch into a mopane tree. A barn owl peered at us, its white, heart-shaped face starkly foregrounded in the light.

'She's beautiful,' I said.

'He,' corrected Kwanele. 'Look, his throat is completely white.'

The owl made a strange throaty purring sound and then screeched as it flew silently over us.

'He's courting,' said Kwanele. 'He wants a partner. For life.'

'And when he finds her, it will be so uncomplicated,' I said. 'No arguments, no jealousy, no doubts. Just a simple instinctive decision. Imagine if humans were like that?'

He smiled. 'Some would say barn owls stick together for practicality only. But they show affection to each other even outside mating season. They've discovered the true secrets to a successful marriage.'

A piercing shriek followed by raucous laughter erupted from the lodge, and Kwanele raised his eyebrows. 'Let's get back to the complicated humans,' he said.

The party was well on its way to reaching a climax. I was surprised to see that Dirk was egging everyone on. I supposed he was trying to make amends for how he'd behaved that morning, but it seemed a bit over the top. He was refilling glasses in a kind of feverish way, and his health and safety concerns were clearly no longer an issue as he suggested that everyone dance on the tables and pose for pictures.

Kwanele beckoned to all the guides.

'You can all go back to your rooms,' he said. 'This isn't going to end anytime soon. I'll get everyone back to their chalets.'

'Truly, I don't mind staying,' I said to him as the rest of the guides left.

He smiled. 'I need all of you fresh for tomorrow. They leave for the airport at nine and that's going to be a challenge.'

I reluctantly went back to my room, feeling a little uneasy. I knew that it didn't take much for a party to get completely out of hand. I checked my phone but there was still no signal. With the marimba band thumping and shrieks and laughter in the night, I eventually fell into yet another fitful sleep.

I awoke to the sound of Marietjie thumping on my door at five in the morning.

'Shit show,' she said. 'Come see. Petrus got up early to check and it's a fokken calamity.'

I quickly got dressed and went with her to the lodge. Virtually every piece of furniture had been turned upside down or sideways. Bottles of wine, tequila and brandy lay scattered all over the wet and sticky floor. Lying in various forms of drunken slumber in the lounge, the members of the marimba band hadn't made it home.

'Kwanele found Legend asleep behind the bar and gave him a Vitamin B shot in his bum, but he only had a horse syringe, so Legend was the moer in and he took four painkillers and he passed out again,' said Marietjie. 'Now we got to get the bladdy guests up and make sure they get to the airport.'

Dirk was nowhere to be seen, but between the guides, Kwanele, Grace, Ayanda and Dumi, we managed to round up all the guests and put them on the cruisers. They were completely out of it, but Julia and Mikey clung to Kwanele and me as they said goodbye and I sort of got this lump in my throat because I was going to miss them.

Somehow Knut managed to take a final video as they left, but it wasn't entirely a success as he dropped his phone and then vomited out of the side of the cruiser.

'My liewe vader,' said Marietjie, waving them goodbye. 'If you thought this was bad, wait until Wednesday. The shareholders are arriving.'

'Shareholders?' I said, turning to her in surprise. 'I thought Legend owned Yamihle.'

'Ja, he does,' she replied, 'but his dad originally bought the land and started the lodge. And he made three of these friends of his shareholders so that they get two weeks each, every year, all on the house. Free booze and food and watookal. Legend can't stand them, and he's been trying to buy them out for years, but they won't budge. He can overrule them on everything, so it's not about making decisions, but they're fokken freeloaders if you ask me and bladdy difficult 'cos they always act as if they own the place.'

She sighed. 'I suppose we got to clean up the mess.'

It took the rest of the weekend to get Yamihle in order. Dirk was annoyingly sanctimonious as he supervised, taking care to express his dismay at the extent of the chaos whenever Legend was around. It was doubtful that Legend actually noticed, since his hangover was so severe that he only recovered towards the end of the weekend. By which time he had become aware that the shareholders were arriving within the next few days and descended into a black mood, snapping at everyone who crossed his path, except Kwanele.

A couple of guests arrived that week, and since they were incredibly meek compared to the last lot, the next few days were easy. I was still driving with Kwanele, but he said that I'd be guiding guests on my own within a week or so. Instead of feeling happy about that I actually thought I'd rather drive out with him all the time, and not only because he taught me so much. To be honest, my hero crush on him had gone up a couple of notches, and sometimes I thought he liked me. Not *like* like exactly, but he didn't *not* like me. Plus, he liked Jackson. I ended up telling him that I was worried about Jess, and since the Wi-Fi and network still hadn't been restored, he offered to drive with me to Hoedspruit to see if we could get a signal there. But before we could leave, Marietjie told us Hoedspruit was also still cut off, which was a pity. It would have been a nice drive.

It was just before lunch on Wednesday when the shareholders arrived. Mandla had gone to collect them from the airport and Dirk had been hovering for ages at the entrance of the lodge to make sure he was first to greet them. Kwanele had taken Bandile to check the roads for any fallen trees from the storm, and so Marietjie, Petrus and I positioned ourselves at the bar, pretending to work out schedules on our laptops but really to check out the shareholders. Legend hadn't been seen the whole morning.

Two men and a woman entered the lodge and I guessed they were in their seventies. The woman looked a bit anxious, as if she'd rather be at home knitting or something, but the two men

113

had a confident air about them, and the shorter one was dressed in a safari suit with a paisley cravat tucked into the collar of his shirt.

'The one that looks like a doos is Bertie Greenshaw,' whispered Marietjie. 'He always makes trouble, and I swear one of these days Legend is gonna klap him in sy moer in.'

Dirk started to fawn all over them. Bertie in particular looked as if he was loving it. Of the three he was clearly the ringleader and, as Marietjie had warned, definitely looked as if he owned the place. Arms folded, his feet apart, he looked complacently at Dirk.

'Welcome to Yamihle, Mr Greenshaw.' Dirk was saying. 'How wonderful to have you back in our midst and looking, dare I say it, a good few years younger! You simply must tell me your secret. And Mr and Mrs Lawson, so good to see you both.'

'Now, now,' Bertie replied, playfully shaking his finger at Dirk. 'Remember what I told you last time? We shall have no formalities. You must call me Bertie, and, as you well know, the Lawsons are Lawrence and Helen to you.'

'Well, I'm not sure I deserve that honour,' said Dirk coyly. 'But Bertie, Lawrence and Helen it shall be!'

Dirk escorted them to the deck, and when Legend eventually joined them, it was obvious that the atmosphere was distinctly less warm than it had been with Dirk. Petrus and Marietjie went back to their rooms, but I stayed, hoping that the Wi-Fi might reappear.

From my position at the bar, I could see out to the deck. Lunch was laid out on the table, which Bertie was eyeing greedily. After gins were served, there was the sound of voices, at first a murmur, but the volume increased – or rather, Legend's voice became louder.

After a few minutes he pushed his chair back and strode to the bar.

'Alex, get over here. I need you to take notes. These arseholes are up to something, and I need a record.'

He introduced me briefly to the shareholders and then turned to Bertie.

'Repeat what you just said.'

Bertie gave him a deprecatory look.

'Upon much consideration – and do believe me when I say that this is very painful to us all – we have decided to invoke section 162 of the Companies Act to declare you a delinquent director.'

'And what the fuck does that mean?' said Legend.

'It means that you have consistently acted in a manner that amounts to gross negligence. The way you run this lodge is reckless and, dare I say it, dishonest. As just one example, let us reflect on the monthly reconciliation of the beverages. I have no words except to say that it is a disgrace. The amount of alcohol that is unaccounted for leaves one quite confounded.'

'I gather that poisonous little turd, Dirk, has been reporting back to you,' said Legend, leaning back in his chair with a sardonic smile.

'An exemplary employee,' sighed Bertie. 'Sadly unappreciated and much maligned by yourself, if I may say so.'

'Could you tell us more about what you spent on the refurbishment of the chalets?' he continued, delicately picking an olive out of the salad.

'I could,' said Legend, 'but I'm not going to.' Suddenly furious, he shouted, 'Look it up yourself, you moron, you were sent all the documents. And get your fat, bourgeois fingers out of the salad. We've all got to eat it, for Christ's sake.'

'That is quite uncalled for,' said Bertie, with a meaningful look at Helen and Lawrence, 'but, I fear, true to form. I shall not take offence, dear boy. Regarding the figures for the so-called upgrade, suffice to say we are shocked at the expense. Not to mention the end result, which is most distressing upon the eye.'

'Anything else?' said Legend, his eyes glittering with fury.

Bertie looked smug. He'd saved his trump card for the end.

'Debauchery,' he said. 'Plain and simple debauchery.'

He paused, expecting a reaction, but Legend said nothing, his face expressionless.

Slightly disconcerted, Bertie took out his phone.

'It's all over the social media,' he said. 'Pictures indicating

115

the most shocking depravity. One imagines that you must have hosted an *orgy* this past weekend.'

He passed his phone to Legend, who held it so that I could also see the screen.

Yamihle's accounts had been tagged on Instagram and Facebook in photographs from Shamilla's fiftieth birthday party. What struck me immediately was that whoever had taken the pictures had deliberately – and, yes, spitefully – captured images designed to show the party at its absolute worst. There was no denying it had got a bit out of control, but the pictures weren't a fair reflection at all.

I also realised that the Wi-Fi was back on. My phone started to vibrate in my pocket as messages flooded in.

Legend stiffened as he scrolled through image after appalling image. Gavin licking cake out of Shamilla's belly button as she lay on a table shrieking with laughter, while Petrus poured tequila into her mouth. Prem about to launch himself off the bar counter. Tommy with someone's bra wrapped around his head. Fredine dancing with Clifford, except it looked more like they were having sex in public. And then, finally, the worst one. Naked from the waist up, dreadlocks flying, his eyes wild and a bit squinty from all the booze, Legend spraying champagne around the room.

Legend pushed the phone back across the table to Bertie. There was a long, uncomfortable silence as he contemplated each of the shareholders. Helen and Lawrence shifted uneasily in their chairs, but Bertie returned Legend's gaze with a superior expression that made me want to slap him.

'And what are your plans once you've made me a delinquent director?' said Legend at last, his face inscrutable.

'Run a tight ship for one,' replied Bertie. 'And I've been looking into timeshare. Jolly profitable, you know. Build more chalets for self-catering, communal braai areas, a couple of tennis courts perhaps, and those paddling ball courts that are all the rage. And naturally a share of profits. We haven't seen a cent as shareholders.'

'The agreement,' said Legend, 'does not entitle you to profits, as you well know. My father made you shareholders purely to give you right of access for a couple of weeks a year.'

'Yes, but that's precisely the point,' said Bertie. 'One feels that dear old Jack made a sad error there. I have always thought that he would have wanted us to benefit financially.'

'And what do *you* think?' said Legend turning to Lawrence and Helen. 'You haven't said very much.'

'Well,' twittered Helen looking nervously at Bertie, 'we ...'

'Completely agree with him,' said Lawrence. 'Yes, ah, completely agree.'

He blanched under Legend's scornful gaze.

'It's only fair that we get some money out of this place,' he finished feebly.

'I see,' said Legend. He looked around the table. 'Well, if you've all said what you want to say, you can leave now.' Lawrence and Helen scuttled out as quickly as they could without actually breaking into a run.

'I daresay you're right,' said Bertie. 'This is a most upsetting business, and I should like to take a siesta once we've had our lunch and commence the game drive. We can continue this discussion tomorrow.'

'We certainly will not carry on this discussion, and there is no sodding lunch or game drive,' said Legend. 'You can all get the hell out of my lodge and fuck off this very minute.'

Bertie puffed out his cheeks. 'We're here for the week!' he expostulated. 'You can't kick us out. We have a right to be here! I shudder to think what your father would say ...'

'Not only would he see you out, he'd pepper your arses with his pellet gun while he was doing it,' replied Legend. 'Don't tempt me, Bertie, I've had enough of your shit. If you want to carry on this discussion, you can do it through a goddamn lawyer. Now bugger off.'

By now Legend had stood up, his mouth set in an ugly line. Bertie spluttered out a few more half-finished sentences, but when

Legend took a threatening step towards him, he disappeared with the same alacrity as Lawrence and Helen.

I'd been looking through my messages by now, but there was nothing from Jess or my family. So I thought I'd see if Legend was on social media. He was. And so were the pictures.

'Um, Legend, you've also been tagged on your personal Insta and Facebook accounts.'

'That's not possible. I don't have any social media accounts,' he snapped.

'Actually, you do,' I said, handing him my phone.

Legend swore long and loudly and then looked bewildered.

'How the hell did that happen?'

I already had my suspicions, but I didn't want to send him off the deep end just yet.

'That doesn't matter for now,' I said. 'The important thing is to get the photos deleted. Look, I don't have social media accounts, but Marietjie does, and she's sort of obsessed with them, so maybe she knows how to delete pictures. Shall I go and get her?'

He nodded.

'Fok,' said Marietjie as she scrolled through the pictures. 'Skandelik. No man, sies, what was Knut doing with the cushion?'

Then she got all businesslike. 'Okay, so now I'm gonna call my cousin Schalk. He's in IT and he's bladdy dodgy, so I'm sure he'll help us. But we've also got to find who posted the pictures. D'you think it was one of the guests?'

I shook my head. 'No, I've checked their accounts and none of the pictures are on their profiles. It's just the Yamihle Facebook and Insta, and Legend's account.'

My phone pinged, and I felt a prickle of fear as I read a message from my dad that had just come in.

Alex, we're desperately worried about Jess. No one has heard from her. Contact me immediately if she's been in touch with you.

12

I TRIED TO CALL MY dad, but his phone was busy every single time, so I eventually left him a voice message asking him to call me. To distract myself from obsessively checking my phone every few seconds I went to the reception area, where Marietjie and Petrus had set up a sort of mini crisis command centre with their laptops. By now all the staff knew about the social media disaster and they gathered around giving advice – all except Mandla, who had to take the cowering trio of shareholders back to the airport. Dirk tried to get them to go back to work, but they ignored him. Actually, Dirk was looking very jittery, and I didn't think it was entirely to do with the fact that Yamihle's and Legend's reputations were at stake.

The advice from the staff wasn't needed, as Marietjie's cousin Schalk turned out to be every bit as dodgy as she claimed, but their enthusiasm was an excellent example of how loyal they all were to Legend. Although, to be fair, they also wanted to see the pictures. Marietjie put her phone on speaker, and we watched and listened fascinated as, armed with full access to the Yamihle social media pages and the website, Schalk remotely took control of the computers and dealt swiftly and efficiently with the pictures and comments. None of us really knew what he was talking about, but he said he gave each photograph a digital fingerprint and that helped him to spot the images across the internet and take them down. For good measure, he hacked into the social media accounts of all the guests of the past weekend.

'If it was any of them what posted the pictures, I've fucked up their accounts good and proper,' Schalk said. 'Most of them gonna be banned from Facebook and Insta for inappropriate content for about six months. Shame, really. They were bladdy clean except for this guy called Knut, but I saved his pictures. He had some lekker stuff. And there's a teenager, Julia, right? I didn't hack her. She's got mainly selfies, parties, kittens, unicorns, baby goats, shit like that. Unlikely she did it. Or do you want me to close her down too?'

'No!' I said before anyone could reply. 'That would be too embarrassing for her, and she's *very* sensitive.'

'Okey dokey,' said Schalk, and Kwanele smiled at me. 'Good call, Alex,' he said.

Deleting Legend's social media accounts was a bit more challenging for Schalk, though. There was a lot of really bad swearing, even though Marietjie kept on telling him to shut up because it was so skandelik and that she'd tell his mom. But eventually he managed to do it, and then ended the call abruptly because he said there was a politician in Gauteng who urgently needed his help.

Legend told Marietjie to courier Schalk a case of whisky, and then he said everyone should come to the bar for a couple of drinks. There was a general stampede in that direction, but I decided to try my dad again. And then, before I could call him, my phone rang, and it was Jess.

'Where are you? Jess, are you okay? Dad's so worried.'

Then a terrible thought occurred to me. 'Have you been kidnapped? Where are they holding you and is there a ransom because you know Dad will pay anything and I can literally get in my car right now and come and get you and ...'

'Alex, just calm down! I haven't been kidnapped and I'm okay.

And I've let everyone know that I'm safe. I'm in Elgin at this really lovely retreat and meditating and doing yoga.'

I exhaled with relief. 'But why did you just disappear and not tell anyone?'

'I needed to be on my own for a bit and I sort of hoped that no one would contact me because I didn't want to have to explain why I'd gone away. I wanted to think about everything … about Roger.'

'Well, doesn't that tell you something, Jess? If you had to disappear and make everyone worried just because you wanted to think about Roger, who literally everyone in this family hates because he's so mean to you, then obviously it's like a no-brainer.'

'I know, but Alex, there was a reason I married him, you know. I loved him. It's just that now everything's gone so wrong, and … and I think he's having an affair. Actually, I know he is, and I think he's going to leave me.'

'*Don't* let him leave you, Jess!'

There was a pause.

'Well, mom said I should first try and make it work and that we should go for marriage counselling, but I'm not sure about that because I haven't told her about the affair and also, it's not actually the first time and …'

'No! That's not what I meant. *You* must leave *him*! Surely it's far worse being with him than being without him? Why wait for him to leave you? I mean, even if he doesn't leave now, he's going to have an affair again. Jess, he's really just not a nice person. Maybe he sort of was in the beginning but he's not now.'

'Yes,' she said. 'I do know that. Alex, you're the only one I've told that Roger's cheating on me. Please don't say anything, okay? I just need time to sort out everything in my head. But I did want to tell you. And I'm sorry that it puts pressure on you, and I feel bad already because that's hard on you. But I just wanted to talk to my sister. And Alex, I just really wish …' She didn't continue.

'Wish what, Jess?'

'I wish I knew what has happened to you. I wish the old Alex was back. I know you can't bear it when I'm not happy, so can you imagine how I feel when every time I see you, you're more withdrawn and distant and you've got this prickly protective barrier around you, and no one can get through.'

She gave a choky laugh. 'Actually, you were always a bit prickly, and we all loved you for being so feisty. But now, I don't know, it's like you're on high alert all the time and so angry and it worries *all* of us.'

I couldn't say anything.

'Alex, look,' Jess said. 'Forget what I just said. Let's just keep in touch, okay? I'm going to be here for a couple more days, but I'd really like to talk to you some more.'

'Of course,' I said. 'And Jess, I really love you. And I hope you're going to divorce Roger because I literally hate his stupid guts and if I ever see him again, I'm going to punch him in his fat ugly face.'

She laughed softly. 'I love you too. You're my best thing ever.'

***

Later that evening it struck me that we hadn't checked Tripadvisor. I looked at recent reviews for Yamihle and it was all good, so no worries there. Shamilla and her friends had left five-star reviews and so had Knut. Actually, Knut's review was sprinkled with about a thousand exclamation marks and that's always a good sign.

On impulse I decided to take a look at reviews for The Plains. I stared in dismay as I trawled through the recent ones. They were really, really bad.

Avoid this place like the plague. We hated every minute and couldn't wait to go home.

Worst holiday ever. Would not recommend The Plains to my worst enemy.

Massive disappointment. Total waste of time and money.

No words, except to say don't go there!!!

We paid for two nights but left after one night. Enough said.

I couldn't understand it, because basically everyone who went to The Plains had a good time. And the odd bad reviews they'd previously had were specifically about the animals being in encampments and sometimes that the food was a bit weird. But other than that, there were never any Tripadvisor-type complaints about cleanliness or service. So it couldn't have been that. I mean, Antoinette was totally obsessive about hygiene, and she went out of her way to make the rooms nice even if the decor was a bit seventies. And all the guests loved Barend because he was so welcoming and enthusiastic about everything.

I went through the reviews again and I realised the complaints weren't exactly clear about what the problems were. And that was strange, too. People usually love going into the details if they're moaning about stuff.

The whole thing kind of unnerved me, so I sent a WhatsApp to Antoinette just as an exploratory mission, because I was even starting to wonder if she and Barend had sold The Plains or something. Like, maybe there was a new owner or management and that would explain the reviews.

Hi Antoinette, just to say thank you again for helping me get this job. It's going well. How are things at The Plains?

Almost immediately I could see that she'd read my message, but no typing followed and then she went offline.

My dad eventually got hold of me, and by this stage he was in a really bad mood on account of all the worry about Jess, but he was obviously relieved she was safe. He had a bit of a rant about Liesbet being stuck in a place in the middle of God knows where without signal and the same went for me, and he was seriously considering buying us all this new tracking device he'd read about that you wore on your wrist and that had its own satellite or something. I remarked that it sounded a bit scary and Nostradamus-y and he said wait until you have your own children.

Saskia and I sent each other a couple of messages through The Mutual Protection Society and then I lay on my bed listening to all the night sounds I loved in the bush. A few hyenas whooped in the distance, night birds chirped, and I heard the barn owl again. I hoped he'd find his lady owl soon. A feeling of contentment came over me as I realised that I didn't have anything pressing to worry about. I mean, I definitely could have thought of some big stuff like polar bears and bees. That feeling didn't last long, though, because then I remembered The Plains. I switched on the light and read the reviews again. Then I remembered Bertie. So I ended up fretting about quite a lot until I fell asleep.

13

'THE GOOD NEWS,' SAID MARIETJIE the next morning as we finished breakfast, 'is that after this week there are no guests for ten days. Next week we got to get all the furniture out of the main lodge and do the painting and then after that the interior designer comes to do the installation of all the new stuff. You're gonna love her, she's so much fun.'

'But the bad news is that bladdy Bianca is coming to stay the whole of next week,' she continued.

'Legend's girlfriend, right?' I asked.

'Ja, and moerse uptight and demanding. She thinks we're all her slaves or something.' Marietjie chuckled. 'She's not going to be happy when she checks you.'

'Why not?' I said,

'She's very jealous and she hates it if there are pretty women around,' she said. 'Like this one time, a whole lot of German models came to stay here for a photoshoot, so Bianca made sure she was here too. She didn't let Legend out of her sight the whole time, and then she made one of the models cry because she accused her of flirting with Legend and was sommer this close to giving the poor girl a klap. Verskriklike bladdy scene.'

She checked her watch. 'I'm supposed to be taking that American couple out but I'm gonna see if Petrus wants to swap. I'm tired of looking for bladdy birds.'

She wandered off to the guides' accommodation and then I saw Dumisane beckoning to me from reception.

'There's a man to see you,' he said. 'He says he wants to talk to you about his dog.'

My heart racing, I went outside and sure enough there was Johan leaning against the Jeep I'd traded in and picking his teeth with a stick. Even from a distance I could smell brandy fumes. He'd clearly had a long night because he was still definitely drunk.

'Nice car,' I said and then decided to cut to the chase. 'How did you find me?'

'Took a while,' he replied. 'But I got a few friends in high places. And the Nissan's got a tracker on it.'

'That's illegal, actually,' I said. 'You're not allowed to track a vehicle you don't own. Anyway, what do you want?'

'My dog went missing on the day I sold you the Nissan. Funny that, hey? Where is he?'

'I've got no idea what you're talking about. Why would I know?'

'You stole him,' he replied, now chewing on the stick, which was actually disgusting. 'That's also illegal.' He leered at me. 'A criminal offence. Worse than a tracker, which I'll say I forgot to remove.'

'So why have you waited for so long to contact me if you think I stole him? I mean, I don't have him, but it seems a bit weird if you ask me.'

'Had to think about it, see?' he replied, his words now slurring. 'Missing him. Man's best friend and watookal. I want him back and compensation for my pain and suffering else I need to get some of my friends to come here and you don't want that, believe me.'

The guests were due to gather at reception in literally twenty minutes and I wondered how on earth I was going to get rid of him. I definitely didn't want Kwanele seeing me have an altercation with Johan.

Marietjie came walking up with Petrus. 'What's going on?' she said.

'This guy sold me my car in White River and now he says I stole his dog, but of course I didn't because there's no dog here, right?' I replied hoping she'd catch on and of course she did because there are no flies on Marietjie, but Petrus was looking a bit puzzled.

'Dogs aren't allowed here,' Marietjie said, giving Petrus a nudge with her shoulder. 'If they come onto the conservancy we shoot them, verstaan? RIP, one shot.'

Johan gestured to me. 'She's a liar. And a thief.'

'Takes one to know one,' said Marietjie and then grinned. 'Listen Oom, you're barking up the wrong tree.'

'You think you're funny? Maybe I must now get the police and we do a search.'

'I was just making a joke, Oom,' said Marietjie, 'but by all means get the police if you want to look stupid.'

'Joke se moer,' said Johan. 'You better shut your bek, meisie.'

'Hey, you don't speak to my girlfriend like that,' said Petrus squaring up to him. 'You bladdy apologise or I'm gonna teach you a lesson.'

Marietjie blushed and looked delighted.

Johan spat out his makeshift toothpick and took a step towards Petrus, who put up his fists and started dancing around on his toes like a boxer.

The last thing I needed was a fight literally in front of guests. Plus, I didn't think Johan had gone to all this trouble to get Jackson. I knew he wanted money. So I stepped in front of Petrus.

'Okay, look,' I said to Johan. 'I did steal your dog. But I'm not giving him back to you and to be honest I think you know why. How much do you want for him?'

'Ten grand,' he said, looking business like. 'Valuable dog, that.'

'I'll give you a thousand,' I replied. 'And five hundred for your petrol money.'

'Make it two and a half grand and I'll leave now,' he said.

'Jislaaik,' said Marietjie, 'remind me never to buy a car from you. Bladdy extortion.'

Luckily I had lots of cash with me and I went to my room to fetch it. When I came back Johan was trying to sell Petrus my Jeep, while Marietjie looked on, her arms folded and lips pursed.

Johan licked his finger and flicked through the notes. Then without saying a word he got into the Jeep, revved the engine, and drove away while Marietjie held up her middle finger.

'Thank you,' I said to her and Petrus. 'Sorry you had to get involved and everything.'

'No worries,' said Marietjie, but she wasn't really paying attention to me.

'So it's official,' she said to Petrus. 'You and me?'

'Ja, may as well,' he replied.

She rolled her eyes. 'Bladdy romantic. Can't wait for the marriage proposal.'

She turned to me. 'Understatement of the year, but that doos can't be trusted. I just hope he doesn't try and get more money off of you.'

I hoped so too, and later that afternoon I even considered confiding in Kwanele and telling him that I'd stolen Jackson. I'd told him that Jess was safe, and I'd even told him about Roger. Actually, we'd had quite a long discussion about Roger and why he'd become a bully, but we concluded it was just because he was basically a creep. I ended up not telling him about Jackson because I was too scared to risk him thinking badly of me. Not for stealing Jackson, maybe, but for pretending I had just found him. Well, lying actually. And basically, the more I thought about it, there was quite a lot I hadn't been exactly truthful about.

Because I'd got myself into a worrying mood, I decided to worry some more about Antoinette and Barend. There was definitely a chance that she was so over me that she couldn't be bothered to reply. But there was also a chance that there was something wrong.

In the end I decided to phone Magnus.

'Hallo?' he said cautiously, and I couldn't really blame him because I think he was a bit scared of me at The Plains.

I didn't bother with any small talk.

'Magnus, I've been looking at the reviews on Tripadvisor, and they're terrible! What's going on there?'

There was a pause.

'Shew,' he said. 'It's not good, hey. We got a lotta guests in the last few months and we're doing everything the same and while they're here it's okay, but jislaaik they all complain on Tripadvisor and we don't know why.'

'And what do Antoinette and Barend think?' I asked.

'Barend cannot understand it,' he replied. 'And now he's depressed and he's started to drink brandy. So's Antoinette. Depressed, I mean, not drinking brandy.'

'Yes, but surely they can follow up with the guests to find out exactly what the problem was. I mean, they're not even replying to the reviews, and they should.'

'Ja, I suppose so,' he said. 'But what would they say?'

Trying desperately hard to suppress my irritation – I mean, that was so feeble – I said, 'For starters, like I just said, they could find out more details. Something like that.'

'Ja,' he said again and gave a sigh. 'You're right. But I don't know how they would do that.'

'Well,' I said, 'maybe they could email them or call them or just reply on Tripadvisor. Like, 'Dear whoever, please tell me more about your experience'. I don't know exactly! But they can't just accept it.'

'And they're worried about the developers,' he said.

'Yes?' I said, trying not to sound impatient. God, he was so slow. 'What developers? I don't know what you mean by that.'

'There's these people from a big company wanting to build a housing estate next to The Plains, like a village with roads and a supermarket and a bioscope,' he said. 'They're trying to buy the farms around us and Barend says they want The Plains as well.'

I paused for a bit. That didn't sound good.

'Okay, listen Magnus,' I said. 'I want you to find out who the developers are, okay?'

'Ja, but how?' he said, sounding alarmed.

I nearly screamed in frustration and took a deep breath.

'Here's the plan,' I said. 'When you get a chance, you go to Barend and you say, 'Barend, who exactly are these developers that want to build a housing estate?' Then you write down whatever he says and phone me or send me a WhatsApp.'

'That's a good idea,' he replied. 'Ask Barend. Let you know who they are.'

'Brilliant!' I said. 'I absolutely knew you were the right person to call. But Magnus, you must speak to Barend soon. Like tonight or first thing tomorrow morning.'

'Got it.' He sounded chuffed with himself. 'You can leave it up to me, Alex. Otherwise, how's it going there by you?'

'All good,' I said. 'I have to go now, but we'll chat soon, okay?'

He wished me a good day further and we ended the call. By now I was feeling like a private detective or something. Miss Alex Marple, Inspector Alex Clouseau or maybe George from the Famous Five. I had a lot to think about. And worry about, actually. Something wasn't right about Bertie's threat to make Legend a delinquent director, we still hadn't worked out who posted the social media pictures, and there was definitely something fishy going on at The Plains.

Legend had been in a foul mood since the shareholders' meeting, but he didn't take it out on anyone beyond going off at Dirk when he caught him demonstrating to Grace and Ayanda how to float flowers in the toilet bowls. 'We're on septic tanks, you moron,' he yelled, 'it's gonna take a huge fucking dump to get them down, and why would anyone want to piss on a bloody flower?'

But by Friday evening, when all the guests had left, he had calmed down a bit and briefed us over dinner about the activities for the next week.

'Painters arrive Monday, so we need to get all the furniture out of the lodge over the weekend and prime the walls. The renovation is costing a fucking fortune and we're closing for around a week, so you're the labour, okay? Painting starts on Monday but I'm on the board of examiners for professional guides, so I'll be in Nelspruit for the day. I'm relying on you all to make sure that there won't be a cock-up because the designer arrives on Wednesday for the installation.'

'You can take it a bit easy tomorrow,' he continued, 'but on Sunday the work starts. Everyone got it?'

Everyone nodded or murmured assent.

Dirk raised his hand. 'Might I enquire who is in charge whilst you're away?'

'Kwanele, obviously,' replied Legend ignoring Dirk's boot-faced look. 'No more questions, for fuck's sake. I've had a tough week. Marietjie, get a bottle of tequila and let's get plastered.'

***

'Legend and his bladdy tequila,' grumbled Marietjie as she put on her sunglasses the next morning while we sat inside at the bar. She took an experimental bite of toast and groaned. 'Fok.'

'Why didn't you stop me, Alex?' She put her head down on the counter. 'You're supposed to be my friend.'

'I tried, actually,' I replied. 'But you wouldn't listen. Plus, you said I was a bleeksiel. What does that even mean?'

She rolled her eyes towards me and grinned. 'Dork.'

I laughed. 'Thanks very much. And you're supposed to be *my* friend.'

This was friendly banter between friends, I decided. This is what friends did. Saskia and I never teased each other but I knew she had a more relaxed relationship with her other friends. Our bond was strong, but we both knew that the past we'd shared had created fragile boundaries that, once crossed, could shatter everything. I was to blame.

Marietjie looked at her phone and sighed. 'Bianca's nearly here.'

'How'd you know?' I asked.

'Insta,' she said, holding her phone out to me. 'She's an influencer so she documents every second of her bladdy life. Check, this was taken an hour ago at the White River Golf Club. She always stops there for a gin and tonic 'cos she likes to get the old ballies all worked up.'

It was difficult to see Bianca's face because she was wearing massive sunglasses and a straw safari hat that she'd tied to her head with a floaty animal print silk scarf. A tight-fitting low-cut khaki dress and vivid red lipstick that matched her nails completed the picture, which she'd captioned, *Heading off to the bush to see my hunky man and my attitude is as fierce as my outfit #socooltobeme #myfablife #nomakeup #firstworldproblems #skinnygirlproblems #successlooksgoodonme #mystomachisflat #hategolf.*

Within an hour Bianca pulled up at speed to the entrance in a white SUV. She hooted loudly and Dirk went tearing out, with Grace and Ayanda following rather more reluctantly in his wake. Dirk and Bianca double-kissed the air, and then Bianca turned to Grace and Ayanda, who were struggling to pull three enormous suitcases out of the boot.

'Can I ask you to not get them covered in sand,' she said. 'Last time they were absolutely filthy when I got to my room, and there was a scratch on one of them, and I can't deal with that. They're *very* expensive suitcases. No, *don't* drag them, carry them on your heads like normal African people.'

Now ignoring Dirk, she glanced around her and started punching a number into her phone.

'I've just got here. Where the hell are you? The least you could do is to be waiting for me when I arrive.'

Legend's reply was obviously brief, because she chucked her phone into her bag and stalked off in the direction of his chalet.

'You won't meet her until much later,' said Marietjie. 'When she arrives, they always go straight to bed. In the middle of the day, nogal. Skandelik.'

We debated whether to do some packing but decided against it and instead spent the afternoon on the deck in front of one of the guest rooms. After a couple of hours, we heard Dirk calling our names, and then one by one the rest of the guides joined us, including Kwanele.

'He wants to make lists,' said Bandile, settling himself into a lounger after helping himself to a beer from the minibar. 'So we got Dumi to tell him Kwanele was taking us to the shooting range. He won't look for us here.'

I'd brought my bird list with me, since I'd somehow become responsible for the official Yamihle bird list after I'd spotted the flufftail.

'Seen anything interesting?' Kwanele said as he sat down next to me on the cushions I'd propped against a tree at the edge of the deck.

'Nothing new,' I replied, looking at my list. 'Just a few plovers and a heron. I'm really looking out for a White-winged Tern because that's not on the official list, and although it's not that common, it actually should be on the list.' I rambled on a bit about birds that are commonly on lists at game reserves until I heard a slight snuffly noise. I looked at Kwanele. He was fast asleep. So I stopped talking and sat quietly, just absorbing the peace. And, to be honest, the proximity of Kwanele. It felt good, just as it had when we'd lain together under the bed.

In the evening we all gathered in the lounge before dinner to discuss plans for the next day, and after a while Legend and Bianca wandered in. They were holding hands, but actually Bianca was holding his hand, if you know what I mean.

Slim and slightly taller than me, with long and straight reddish hair which framed a pixie face with flawless skin, a full pouting mouth and huge green eyes, Bianca gave a first impression of feminine fragility, but the tenderness ended there. Every inch of her exuded confidence and a kick-ass attitude as she surveyed us with a slightly amused and superior expression.

Actually, it was sort of like she expected us to curtsy or something.

After bestowing cool greetings on everyone, Bianca gave me a long appraising look, her eyes slightly narrowed.

'So, you're the new guide who loves rugby and braai competitions,' she said. 'Legend told me all about your CV. Honestly, we had such a laugh. Are you braaing for us tonight?'

'Shut up, Bianca,' said Legend pouring himself a whisky, 'and stop being a bitch.'

Unperturbed, Bianca looked at Legend from under her eyelashes.

'Don't talk to me like that, baby,' she said. 'Get me a gin with lots of lemon.'

Legend began discussing the renovation with Kwanele, and Bianca turned her attention to me. She took a dainty sip of her gin and gave me a fake smile.

'Tell me all about yourself, Alex. Where did you go to school?'

So I knew her type. I knew she'd first ask me about school, then university, then about my parents. Etcetera. All the questions I didn't want to answer. All the answers I didn't want her to know. But basically, if Legend had told her stuff about my CV, she most likely already knew a lot about me already.

'Oakvale Primary in Cape Town, and then Fernwood Collegiate,' I said, praying she wouldn't recognise the high school, but I knew she probably would, and I was right.

'My *word*, a very fancy high school,' she said. 'Your parents must be loaded. So boarding school in Gauteng? How strange. Lots of my friends went to Fernwood, but they were from Joburg. How on earth did you end up there?'

I shrugged. 'Actually, there were quite a few of us from Cape Town. My parents were travelling a lot during the time and my mom was doing a lot of work in Gauteng, so it made sense.'

'Do you know Athena Williams?' she said suddenly. 'She must have been in your year. You're twenty-five, right? Athena's older sister is one of my best friends.'

The palms of my hands started to sweat, and I felt that I was literally going to throw up. Of course I knew Athena Williams. I instinctively turned towards Kwanele, and he looked up instantly. I don't know what my expression was. Pleading. Panic.

Terror. Something like that. I don't remember.

He didn't miss a beat.

'Sorry to interrupt, Bianca,' he said, 'but I need Alex to check on the generator in the kitchen.'

It worked, but it kind of didn't as well. I got up and escaped, but a quick glance at Bianca showed me that her antennae were up. On my way to the kitchen, I sent a message to The Mutual Protection Society.

Legend's girlfriend Bianca is here and she's best friends with Athena's sister. And B isn't a very nice person. And asking questions about me.

When I got back, Dirk and Bianca were sitting at the bar, and it was pretty obvious they were having a major gossip about me, as every now and again one of them glanced my way and gave a smirk.

Feeling slightly anxious, I checked my phone to see if there was a message from The Mutual Protection Society. Saskia's message mirrored the panic I had felt.

I can't believe what I just read. Just keep away from her as much as you can. I'm not sure what else to say. Try to make her lose interest in you by not saying anything. So sorry, this is awful.

At dinner I sat as far away from Bianca as I could, and I hoped she had actually lost interest in me because she didn't ask me any more questions. She was more interested in talking about herself and managed to make sure that we all listened and didn't have any secondary conversations. Towards the end of dinner Bianca leant in towards Legend and took a selfie. It couldn't have been a great picture because he looked pretty irritated. She started scrolling through her phone and frowned.

'That's so weird,' she said. 'Baby, where have your Insta and Facebook pages gone? It took me ages to set them up and now they've disappeared.'

Everyone went silent and stared at her.

'What?' she said irritably looking around at us.

'What do you mean *you* set them up?' said Legend eventually.

'I told you last week that someone had posted pictures onto accounts that I knew nothing about.'

'Yes, I know, I'm not *stupid,* and then you said someone took them down, but they didn't have to delete the actual pages for God's sake. Do you realise how much work it took to set them up and get you followers? Damn, now I've got to start all over again.'

'Bianca,' said Legend, his voice dangerously calm. 'Are you shitting me? Did you not think it was important to tell me at the time that it was you who set up the accounts?'

'I'm sure I did tell you at some stage, like a really long time ago. But as usual you probably weren't paying attention. You *did* know about it. You just forgot.'

'I did not fucking forget,' said Legend. 'Are you out of your mind, for Christ's sake? And don't even think about setting them up again. Jesus, sometimes I think you're a fucking hand grenade.'

Bianca glared at him.

'Here comes trouble,' muttered Marietjie to me under her breath.

'Do you even realise how ungrateful and selfish you sound right now?' Bianca said, her voice rising. 'I give you *so* much support and go to *so* much trouble promoting Yamihle, but you don't ever support my career! If you thought about this for one single second, you'd understand that celebrities can't have an invisible boyfriend, and you're just going to have to accept that being with me means media attention for you.'

He laughed incredulously. 'You're not a celebrity, for fuck's sake, Bianca. And when you talk like that, I'm strongly tempted to become permanently invisible.'

'Check, she's about to go mal,' whispered Marietjie.

The next minute Legend and Bianca were yelling at each other as if there was no one else at the table.

'Verskriklik. We should sell tickets,' said Marietjie, now not bothering to lower her voice. After a few minutes Bianca got up and stormed out of the lodge.

'Better go and escort her,' said Kwanele without looking up from his dinner. 'There were a couple of buffalo hanging around last night.'

'Fuck,' said Legend, grabbing his rifle and setting off after Bianca.

14

'Now, we need everything out of the dining area, bar and lounge, people,' said Dirk bossily. 'Sunday is not a day of rest for us this weekend! No rest for the wicked, as they say. Right, we must have a *system*. First the furniture and then …'

'Dirk, I forgot to mention, Legend wants you to take inventory of the storeroom this morning,' said Kwanele.

Dirk eyed him suspiciously. 'That's the first I've heard of it. And since I am not accustomed to taking second-hand orders, I believe I should check with Legend.'

Kwanele shrugged. 'Legend's spending the day in the bush with Bianca. Said he didn't want to be disturbed unless someone dies. Up to you, though. I'm just the messenger.'

'Did Legend really say that about the inventory?' I said to Kwanele once Dirk had stalked off muttering to himself.

'No,' he grinned. 'I just thought of it now.'

Marietjie brandished her speaker. 'Time for Jeremy Loops, ek sê.'

We paired up to sort and move the furnishings, and Kwanele and I ended up working together. Although, that sounds as if it was random. It wasn't. He allocated moving the heavy pieces to Bandile and Mandla, and shifting the pictures and curtains

138

to Petrus and Marietjie, while we sorted out the bar area. As we wrapped the glasses in newspaper, I thought how doing the simplest, most mundane thing can make you feel so happy if you're doing it with the person you like being with the most.

By lunchtime it was stiflingly hot, and we were all sweating with the effort of lugging boxes and furniture to the storerooms. But it was done.

'Everyone meet at reception in an hour,' said Kwanele. 'We're going swimming in the kloof.'

The kloof was on a citrus farm that belonged to a friend of Legend and Kwanele about half an hour from White River. It wasn't exactly a treacherous climb down, but it was steep and rocky, and we had to do a fair amount of bundu-bashing through scratchy bushes as well. Kwanele walked in front of me and, without saying anything, he took my hand at the tricky bits. I thought guiltily about how I'd snapped bitchily at Magnus' attempts to help me climb up some huge rocks when we'd been taking clients on a bush walk at The Plains. Needless to say, he hadn't tried again. I didn't say anything to Kwanele, though, and I didn't try and snatch my hand away. So we ended up walking hand in hand practically the whole way down, the only sound the crunch of stones underfoot in the heavy heat.

At the bottom of the kloof, basking in the sun, sat three cascading and translucent rock pools flowing from one to the other. Mandla and Petrus were already in the water, trying to persuade Marietjie, who was sitting on the edge with just her feet dangling tentatively, to plunge in.

I tried not to stare when Kwanele took off his shirt, but it was actually impossible not to. I caught Marietjie staring as well, and she gave me a wink before slipping into the water and popping up with a shriek.

Kwanele dived effortlessly into the pool, and I followed less elegantly, gasping at the shock of the icy water.

Soon there was a water fight, and I was getting the worst of it when, laughing, Kwanele drew me towards him and instinctively

I put my arms around his neck, our hips touching. Our faces were inches apart and he gave me this sort of slow smile.

'Your eyelashes are so long they're all tangled up,' he said as he brushed strands of wet hair from my cheek. And then the moment was broken as Bandile dive-bombed practically on top of us.

We lay on the smooth rocks, soaking up the warmth. I cast a sideways glance at Kwanele, who was lying next to me. He was looking at me too, and it seemed as if there was something new about his expression. The cry of an eagle soaring above us made us both look up.

'African Crowned Eagle,' we both said at once, and laughed.

'Good spotting,' murmured Marietjie, 'but I think we gotta go back. My skin's burning.'

The others went ahead as we climbed back up the kloof. Kwanele took my hand again, and it sort of felt that he was doing it because he wanted to, not just to help me. He turned and grabbed both my hands as I slipped on loose shale.

'I've got you,' he said as our eyes met.

We stood there facing each other and smiling until after a few moments we heard Marietjie calling to us.

Kwanele squeezed my hands and then let go. We continued to climb and then he turned to me again. 'It's been a good day,' he said.

'Yes,' I replied. 'It's actually been perfect.'

***

By late morning the next day, the painters had almost finished painting the bar area in a soft neutral colour, like pale mushroom. Kwanele was holding a guides' meeting on the deck, and we looked up as Dirk and Bianca approached from the front and walked past us to observe the lodge interior from the open doors.

Bianca glared at the walls. 'Oh my God, that colour's all wrong. I can tell you right now it's not going to work. It looks like poo.'

140

'Well, I am *so* with you on this,' said Dirk. 'It's simply hideous! And if you don't mind me saying so, I have often wondered why Legend didn't commission you to do the redecoration, Bianca. You have such an amazing sense of style.'

'I do,' she agreed. 'Everyone says that.'

She turned to the foreman. 'You'll have to stop painting immediately. I'm going to have to sort out this mess and choose another colour.'

Dirk looked a bit taken aback to be honest. 'Well, you're totally right of course, but I do wonder if we shouldn't first consult Legend and perhaps the designer,' he said. 'The paint has been paid for and we must consider the budget … '

'To hell with the designer, if she can actually even call herself that. Legend will go with whatever I say,' she replied. 'And anyway, he's only back this evening so I'm in charge now.'

Dirk looked a bit sour at this statement and gave Kwanele this sideways look as if he was hoping he'd say something.

'I wouldn't cancel the painting if I were you,' said Kwanele, looking up. 'Legend's approved the colour and the painters are on a daily rate. Not a cheap one either.'

'Legend is practically colour-blind,' snapped Bianca. 'And he's relying on me to keep an eye on things, which is exactly what I'm doing this very minute, so I'm afraid you're going to have to trust me and suck it up, Kwanele.'

Kwanele gave her an appraising look and then suddenly grinned.

'Well, if you're both sure about this, I'll leave it up to you to sort it out with Legend,' he said. 'He said he'd be back around five.'

'Talk about letting them dig their own graves,' muttered Marietjie.

'I know when he'll be back, thank you very much,' snapped Bianca. 'We can have a meeting later when he's here and I expect you all to attend so that we can troubleshoot how to get back on schedule.'

'No can do,' replied Kwanele. 'I'm taking my guides on a training walk.' He turned away and continued the meeting.

Marietjie caught my eye as we heard Dirk nervously trying to persuade Bianca to let the painters continue, and rolled her eyes. Far from annoyed at the interruption, the painters looked delighted and scooted off to settle themselves outside under a tree to take a siesta.

Later that afternoon, once it had cooled down, we drove for about fifteen minutes and then got out at a waterhole. Kwanele had told us we were going to focus on vegetation on our walk, but almost immediately he spotted a rhino track in the mud.

'Look,' he said, 'it's very wet, so definitely fresh, and I would say he's about five minutes away. Let's see if we can find the spoor.'

We followed the tracks and Kwanele stopped to examine one that was clearer than the rest. 'Okay, so it's a black rhino,' he said with a grin. 'Are you up for this?'

'Liewe vader,' said Marietjie as we all nodded. 'A bladdy black rhino on foot. Petrus, you better push me up a tree if it charges.'

As we walked, Kwanele pointed out the almost invisible signs that showed the rhino's direction. 'Always stop, look, and listen,' he said. Branches bitten off a bush at a forty-five-degree angle led us to move east, and the shrill warning cries of birds continued us in that direction.

And then we spotted it. A huge grey shape deep within a thicket. Using hand signals Kwanele quickly moved us downwind and to a safer distance.

The rhino browsed, completely unaware of us, until Bandile moved slightly to get a better look, and snapped a twig underfoot. It raised its head and looked in our direction, ears twitching. Kwanele put up his hand and quietly took a step forward so that he was in front of us. Although we didn't make a sound, I could feel the relief as we all exhaled when the rhino continued browsing after a couple of seconds and then slowly moved away. I would trust this man with my life, I thought. I remembered the words Kwanele had spoken the previous day. I've got you.

I stayed close to him as we walked back to the cruiser.

The sun was setting as we drove back to the lodge, and the first thing we heard as we pulled up at the entrance was Legend and Bianca yelling at each other.

'They're having another moerse fight,' said Marietjie happily. 'And I hope he's fired that twat, Dirk.'

Sadly he hadn't, because Dirk joined us for dinner, which we had on the deck. Legend had obviously had a go at him too, though, judging from his injured air as he picked at his food.

The tension at dinner would have been unbearable if I hadn't been thinking only about Kwanele and feeling cocooned in happiness. Both Legend and Bianca were still in a towering rage. His face set, Legend ate his meal in stony silence, occasionally glaring at Bianca as she threw spiteful barbs at anyone who caught her attention. I could see her frustration mounting as no one rose to the bait, and eventually she settled on Marietjie, who was tucking into her second bowl of ice-cream.

'You get bigger every time I see you, Marietjie, and now I see why,' she said in a phoney teasing way. 'You should try hypnosis to get your weight under control.'

Marietjie looked up in surprise at the attack, and her face went a dull red with embarrassment. She said nothing but she looked as if she wanted to cry.

The cocoon of happiness evaporated as I thought of how Roger always seemed to bully Jess the worst at mealtimes. And then before I realised it, I was speaking.

'Why are you picking on Marietjie?' I said.

Bianca looked at me as if she couldn't believe what she had just heard. She put down her wine glass and leant aggressively towards me.

'I *beg* your pardon? Who the hell do you think you are? And I am *not* picking on her ...'

'Well, it definitely feels like it,' I replied. 'I mean, don't you think it's basically very unkind to say mean things about Marietjie's weight in front of everyone? Especially when it's none of your business and there's actually nothing wrong with her weight in the first place.'

'Stem saam,' said Petrus, eyeing Bianca with dislike and then smiling at Marietjie. 'We all think Marietjie is perfect, and particularly because she's such a lekker person.'

'When you bite without thinking, you end up eating your own tail,' said Bandile, looking up at the ceiling and speaking to no one in particular. 'Which means think before you speak, especially when you are angry.'

'And I suppose that's directed at me?' snapped Bianca. 'Well, I don't have to sit here listening to all your sanctimonious shit when I was actually trying to help Marietjie *and* I was only trying to be constructive today about the decorating and got stuff all thanks for it, and I don't mind telling you that I feel *very* misunderstood and unappreciated.'

She stood up and stalked off towards the lounge, tripped over a rolled-up rug and planted her face on the floor.

'Fuck's sake,' said Legend getting up and going over to her. 'Are you okay, baby?'

'No, I'm not,' she sobbed, curling into a foetal position. 'I've broken my wrist and I did *nothing* wrong, and now everyone hates me and it's all Alex's fault.'

He bent down and scooped her up in his arms.

'No one hates you,' he said, turning round and glaring at us. 'Isn't that right?'

We all sort of mumbled that we didn't hate Bianca and then he walked away, her head nestled against his neck.

'Who's for more ice-cream?' said Bandile once they were out of earshot.

'I suppose you're feeling satisfied with yourself, Alex,' said Dirk, giving me a nasty look. 'Always on the moral high ground, aren't you? Personally, I think you're a stirrer and a troublemaker. You need to learn to keep your mouth shut.'

'That's debatable,' said Kwanele. 'But I'll tell you one thing, Dirk. Alex reports to me and Legend. So you leave her alone from now on. Not one more word to her, and that also goes for the rest of my guides. No more instructions, no more comments, no more criticism. Just keep out of it and stop interfering.'

We all literally gaped at him. I mean, he said it so calmly and reasonably, without a trace of anger, but with quiet authority. Dirk tried to rally.

'Don't you speak to me like that, Kwanele,' he blustered. 'I'm going to have to tell Legend and …'

'That's enough,' said Kwanele. 'Do as you wish, but for now, I suggest we call it a night.'

Dirk walked off, trying to look dignified, and the rest sort of melted away to their rooms, but I held back.

'I'm sorry,' I said to Kwanele. 'Dirk's probably right that I'm a troublemaker, but I sort of had to say something because it wasn't fair to bully Marietjie, and I suppose I shouldn't have and rather let Legend say something to Bianca, but it kind of came out before I thought about it.'

'Fight or flight,' said Kwanele. 'It's an instinct. Your instinct made you fight, so don't second-guess yourself. I'm glad you fought back for Marietjie. You went in like a lioness, quick and decisive, before anyone else could react. There's no point in wondering what would have happened if you hadn't been the one to say something.'

We walked slowly back to our chalets. 'Everything unfolds as it should,' said Kwanele as we reached my door. He briefly put his hand against my cheek before he walked away. 'Trust your instincts and don't worry so much, Alex.'

I decided not to tell Saskia what I'd done. Even if The Mutual Protection Society had hundreds of members no one could protect me if Bianca decided to retaliate in a way that I dreaded.

Bianca insisted on Legend taking her for an X-ray at the White River hospital first thing in the morning and returned looking smug, wearing a sling and a bandage on her wrist.

Dirk rushed up to her. 'Oh my God, you poor little thing! I suppose it's broken?'

'I'm totally convinced it is,' she replied, 'but the nurse was so mean and said it was just bruised and I had to practically *beg* her to bandage it and give me a sling, and she wouldn't even let me have an X-ray or see a doctor. I told her I could see a lawsuit coming her way, but she just laughed. Dirk, take some pictures for my Insta.'

She stood cradling her wrist and looking pathetic. 'Make sure you can see the sling.'

'Jesus wept,' muttered Legend and then smiled as he looked around the lodge. 'Bloody well done, you lot.'

Kwanele had got all the staff to help the painters and we'd nearly finished the first coat. Actually, it was fun, except that Kwanele hadn't managed to get rid of Dirk, who had worked himself into a state with so many people to harass, but couldn't on account of Kwanele's warning the night before. So he had to settle on the foreman, who very quickly put in his AirPods and occasionally gave Dirk a thumbs up when he saw him talking.

He took the AirPods out when he saw Legend. 'First coat will be dry by late afternoon. If we paint tonight, we'll finish it, but I'll need everyone to help.'

'Well, *I* can't, obviously,' said Bianca before anyone could say anything. 'And nor can Legend. I'm not going to sit in my room on my own in absolute agony.'

'Get Dirk to watch a movie with you or something,' said Legend. 'Or take some bloody pills to knock you out. We've got to get this done and I'm sure as fuck not going to sit around while my staff are working, okay?'

We waited for the explosion but unexpectedly Bianca smiled. 'Fine. Actually, Dirk and I have got quite a bit to talk about.'

By three in the morning, we'd finally finished and, arms aching, we put down our rollers.

'What time does Liz get here?' asked Dumi, stifling a yawn. 'Breakfast?'

'No, she's driving in with the trucks with the new furniture, so not until after lunch,' replied Legend. 'Everyone can sleep in tomorrow morning, but she's only here until Sunday morning, so we'll have to get cracking as soon as she arrives. Okay, let's all get some sleep.'

As I got ready for bed, I wondered briefly about what Bianca had meant when she'd said she had a lot to discuss with Dirk. Perhaps it was about the delinquent directorship, or who had uploaded the pictures. Or just a gossip. In which case I hoped it wasn't about me, because she had looked at me in a weird sort of way when she said it. Maybe I was being paranoid. Maybe it was innocuous. Although deep down I knew almost for sure it wasn't.

15

WELL INTO A ROUTINE, JACKSON woke me four hours later by persistently scratching on the door so that he could head off to the kitchen to greet Dumi and take up his position under the table. I went with him in search of coffee. Dumi wasn't there but Kwanele was, filling the kettle and taking eggs out of the fridge.

'Did you know Dumi makes Jackson an omelette every morning?' he said. 'And a slice of toast.'

I smiled, wishing that I'd brushed my hair and wasn't wearing ancient leggings and a T-shirt that had a picture of Donald Duck on it.

'I didn't know that, but it sounds good. Are we raiding the fridge?'

'We are and I hope you don't mind, but Jackson and I are having bacon. Lots of it.'

'How did you learn to be a tracker?' I asked once we were eating.

'At first from my grandfather,' he replied. 'He died when I was eleven, but my brothers and I sometimes stayed with our grandparents on their farm during school holidays and my grandfather showed us how to track the cattle and bring them home. Guiding courses also cover tracking, as you know, but both Legend and I learnt the most from a master tracker, Jonas, who worked here for years, but he retired recently. He said it was like reading a book where every track is part of the story. They show you what's happened and what's about to happen. You have to read slowly because everything you see is a clue.'

'Stop, listen, and look, like what you said the other day when you found the rhino.'

'Exactly. Listen carefully. Look carefully. Take your time. Pause and then move. And always be on high alert. Just like you are. You'd make a good tracker.'

'Is that what you think? That I'm always on high alert?'

'It's not a criticism,' he smiled. 'I think you're responsive and intuitive. What I said the other night. We can do some tracking this week. The other guides need some practice too.'

I smiled back at him. 'I'd like that. And maybe it'll help me refine my intuition, because sometimes I think it doesn't work very well.'

Kwanele took our plates and started stacking the dishwasher. 'Intuition almost always works. See how Jackson found his way to the dishwasher to help us rinse.'

Later I spent a couple of hours on the deck putting my bird list into a spreadsheet. Actually, I also googled the meaning of Kwanele's name. *It is enough.* And he really was, I thought. I was heading towards reception, just about to go back to my room, when I froze. Legend was greeting the interior designer, and when I heard her reply there was no mistaking that voice.

The interior designer was my *mother.*

I literally felt like a trapped animal. Beyond climbing out of a window there was no escape, and so I just sort of stood there until Liesbet and Legend walked into the lounge.

'Alex, darling,' said Liesbet, looking delighted and giving me this huge smile. 'Whatever in the world are you doing *here*? I thought …'

'Hi, Liesbet,' I said as casually as I could. 'Gosh, it's been such a long time. How have you been? And how's the family?'

149

She gave me a puzzled look and I could see she was just about to explain to Legend that I was her daughter when I quickly intervened.

'I've met Liesbet before,' I said, managing to frown at her and look innocently at Legend at the same time. '*Years* ago. What an amazing coincidence to see you here and you look so well!'

She stared at me for a bit.

'Yes,' she said eventually, 'well, it's ... quite extraordinary, isn't it?'

So she took my cue but it was terrible, to be honest. I mean, she looked so hurt. And she had every right to be. I had literally just disowned her in front of my employer.

No flies on Legend. He gave us both a sharp look but then luckily Marietjie appeared, and she gave Liesbet a huge hug. And then all the staff came running to greet her and she was enveloped in affection, which was another weird sort of situation, because it made me realise that I didn't really know how others saw her. And I felt proud and sad and guilty and panicked all at the same time. Because basically all the plans I had laid were now turning into this massive mess.

I hadn't taken any notice when Dumi and Grace had spoken about Liz. But now I realised they'd abbreviated her name. Liz. Liesbet. Of course. There was no question now about my going back to my room or anywhere. Legend and Liesbet got stuck straight into discussions about the design, and Legend told us to stay so that we could get a feel for what needed to be done after the next couple of days. We followed Liesbet as she walked through the lodge outlining every detail.

'She's bladdy amazing, hey?' whispered Marietjie, and then gave me a nudge. 'Check, here comes the royalty. This should be interesting.'

Bianca and Dirk hadn't met Liesbet before, and so our progression paused as Legend introduced them. Bianca gave Liesbet her signature languid up-and-down inspection, and I swear I almost wanted to warn her that messing with Liesbet was not going to end well.

'Lovely to meet you, Liesbet,' she said. 'And thank you for helping us out a bit with this reno. Legend and I appreciate it *so* much. Now please don't take offence, but I'm afraid the colour you chose for the lodge interior is not on trend and it's actually a bit of a disaster.'

'Bianca,' said Legend warningly, 'Liesbet is taking us through the design, so hold your thoughts for another time, okay?'

Marietjie gave me another nudge, and even Dirk looked alarmed.

Ignoring Legend, Bianca continued. 'Gosh, it's so awkward, but someone had to say it and I hope you're not feeling disappointed, Liesbet. I think you've made a huge mistake, but don't take it to heart because it can happen to *anyone*. You may not know this but I'm a well-known influencer and I've got about two thousand followers. I'm *very* clued up on colour ways and I've got some suggestions that I think you should look at and then rethink your design. I usually charge for my advice, but I'm happy to do this pro bono, since your reputation is at stake, and of course Legend and I need this reno to *really* showcase our lodge.'

'Did I miss it and they got married or something? What's with the "our lodge"?' muttered Petrus. Marietjie snorted and quickly turned it into a cough.

Liesbet gave Bianca The Look, which I'd seen her give Charles and Richard very often when they were teenagers. Basically, raised eyebrows and a 'I know you didn't really mean to say that, so I'll let it go, but get back in your box or else there'll be trouble' sort of look. It always worked for Charles and Richard, except for this once when they were fourteen and polished off a bottle of Amarula when they were meant to be studying for exams and got really drunk. It worked immediately for Bianca, though. To be fair, she tried her very best to maintain eye contact, but it's incredibly hard to stare down Liesbet.

After giving Bianca The Look, Liesbet carried on talking to Legend as if she didn't exist.

'As I was saying, the mirrors on the north-facing walls will reflect the changing light of the backdrop of the river, since we have morning and evening light from the front of the lodge. Now, let's move to the bar itself, which I'm going to clad so that we can get rid of all that dark wood in the front of it, and I'd like to show you two options.'

She moved off, with Legend following, and I must say it was the first time I'd seen him looking so tame, and he didn't even give Bianca a backward glance.

'What a cow,' said Bianca staring after them. 'Who does she think she is?'

But she said it under her breath, which was a really good call.

After she'd supervised the unpacking of the trucks, it was late in the afternoon when Grace and Ayanda took Liesbet to her chalet. I volunteered to escort her to dinner, and I went to the chalet early so that I could at least attempt to explain what was going on. I still couldn't believe that she'd turned out to be the interior designer and, to be honest, when the trucks rolled away, I was strongly tempted to chuck Jackson in and go with them.

I tapped on the door of her chalet and went in.

Liesbet was sitting in front of her dressing table applying lipstick and glanced at me through the mirror. She looked at herself critically, put on another layer and then reached for her mascara. She didn't say anything, and it was a bit unnerving to be honest.

'Why don't you want them to know that I'm your mother?' she said eventually, turning round to face me.

'Um, it's quite complicated,' I replied.

She rolled her eyes. 'You're going to have to do better than that, Alex. If I'm going to play along with this charade I need to know why. And it had better be for a good reason.'

I sat down on the bed. 'Well, it's just that this job was my absolute ultimate dream, and if you really want to know I was actually fired from The Plains because … you're right, I don't have people skills and I was rude and everything to guests although I totally didn't mean to be, but it just happened. And then also everyone knew who I was and that my family was

152

wealthy, and I had this big brand-new Jeep and everyone else had really old cars and they didn't like me even before I arrived at The Plains.

'And so I thought I'd just try a fresh start and be ordinary. But somehow it's not exactly working because I keep on doing weird stuff, but now if everyone knows you're my mother it'll look like I was lying, which I actually did do this afternoon, but I didn't mean to hurt you. I mean, I'm actually very proud of you because the lodge looks amazing, and I can see that they all really like you a lot.'

I considered telling her about how I had stolen Jackson but then thought it was a step too far. Liesbet definitely wouldn't understand because she wasn't mad about domestic animals and only barely tolerated Clive and Tulip, who left fur and stuff on her furniture.

Without replying, Liesbet turned back to the mirror and then spent ages choosing earrings.

'You are who you are,' she said at last. 'You realise there's no escaping that?'

'I know. I was trying to see if I could get a filter, but it hasn't really worked.'

Liesbet turned back to me. 'No, I meant you can't pretend that your life is different from what it is. Your background is a done deal. If someone doesn't like you because of that, there's nothing you can do about it. And if that's the reason they don't like you then you wouldn't want to be friends with them anyway.'

She fiddled with her rings a bit and then said, 'Of all my children, I think I've failed you the most.'

'But why?' I asked, taken aback and feeling a bit hurt. 'I mean, I'm not doing drugs or anything. Plus, I don't drink.'

She smiled. 'No, I don't mean that sort of thing, and it's *we* that failed you, not the other way round. Dad and I feel that we didn't give you enough attention and then we sent you away to school, and now neither of us feels that we can get through to you or get close to you. Even the twins feel that you're shut

153

down, and God knows they only think about themselves. And so of course, we worry about you. We just want you to be happy, Alex.'

It was all getting a bit deep and meaningful for me, and so I changed the subject.

'Don't worry, you didn't fail me. So anyway, I spoke to Jess the other day.'

Liesbet sighed and got up. 'We were so worried when she took off like that. I sent her the name of a really good marriage counsellor.'

'So, Liesbet, I'm going to tell you something, but you must promise not to tell Jess that I told you. Roger's having an affair and he's had one before. Maybe even lots more. I swore I wouldn't tell anyone, but I think you need to know so that you can help Jess get a divorce like really fast.'

Actually, I'm very good at keeping secrets so I sort of surprised myself when I let this one out. For the second time that day Liesbet looked hurt.

'But why wouldn't she tell me and Dad?' she asked. 'Jess is usually so open.'

'I don't know,' I replied. 'Maybe she wanted to protect you or something. She said she needed to think about what to do. But that didn't make sense to me because obviously the only thing she can really do now is get rid of him.'

'Yes, but there are emotions involved,' said Liesbet. 'It's not always so black and white, Alex. It's no simple thing to end a marriage.'

I was about to reply that in certain circumstances it was, but I knew if we carried on talking, we'd get all tetchy with each other, so I said we should join everyone on the deck to watch the sunset. We walked there without saying anything more, but I was aware of a heavy feeling of misunderstanding between us.

Liesbet didn't blow my cover. Without actually ignoring me, she ignored me, but not in an unkind way if you know what I mean. Not like how she ignored Bianca. Actually, that wasn't unkind either. She just didn't pay any attention to her. Without any posturing or grandstanding, Liesbet casually stepped into the position of alpha female. Uncertain how to react, Bianca made a couple of attempts to assert herself and then finally descended into sulks. The brilliant thing about someone getting the sulks, of course, is that they don't say anything.

Bandile escorted Liesbet back to her room as, just before we ended dinner, Magnus called, and I left the table to speak to him. I walked towards reception, away from all the chatter because I could hardly hear what he was saying.

'Where are you?' I asked. 'Do you really have to whisper?'

'Near the front gate,' he said hoarsely, 'on account of imparting confidential information.'

'Magnus, you're literally like half a kilometre away from your room. No one's going to hear you.'

'You never know,' he said nervously, but speaking louder. 'And listen, you didn't hear this from me, okay? I don't want to get into trouble.'

Head Boy syndrome. I mean, it can actually last for your entire life.

'Understood,' I said. 'Totally. What did you find out?'

'The developers have made an offer for Oom Marius' farm on our northern boundary. And they've also made offers on Oom Piet's farm on the eastern side and Tannie Santie's farm on the west.'

'That's a huge amount of land,' I exclaimed. 'It must around forty hectares in total!'

'Ja, just about,' he agreed.

'But then why do they want The Plains?'

'The Brak River,' he said. 'None of those farms got a natural water source. It's all borehole. They don't want to rely only on dams and groundwater. And apparently a river is a big selling point.'

'So who are the developers?'

'Horizon Heights,' he said. 'They're a start-up and Barend

says they're very aggressive. He says Oom Piet and Oom Marius are not certain what to do because it's a lot of money they're offering and Oom Marius is now thinking of a nice retirement house in Mossel Bay where he and Tannie Bets can fish, you understand. But Tannie Santie said if they ever come back to her farm, she'll let Duiwel loose on them.'

'Duiwel?'

'Her rottweiler,' he clarified. 'Very unstable. A bit mal actually. Duiwel killed a ram when she was only five months old. Barend said Tannie Santie said she got it by the horns first, see, and then …'

'No, it's okay, I don't need to know,' I said hastily. 'Listen, Magnus, you've been a huge help, honestly. I'm going to see what I can do from my side to find out more, but you must let me know if you discover anything more. You're like, totally amazing.'

It wasn't usually my style to praise people, mainly because I'm always too angry to notice good stuff. Plus, I realised I hadn't been sarcastic one single time while I spoke to Magnus, and that was rather nice, I must admit. And it was also nice to say goodbye in a friendly way.

I googled Horizon Heights when I got back to my room, but the results didn't tell me very much, other than that their main pitch was luxurious exclusivity. They had a very fancy website, and it didn't seem like they'd done many developments. There was one in progress in Plett that looked quite nice, but the tightly packed houses were eye-wateringly expensive. They were definitely into the exclusive village vibe with clubhouses, golf courses and tons of amenities so that you wouldn't actually have to ever leave the estate until you died or something. I totally wouldn't have been surprised if they had turned out to be bespoke developers for weird cults.

I definitely needed to find out more, because the situation seemed urgent if Horizon Heights were waving tons of money at Oom Piet and Oom Marius. I liked the sound of Tantie Santie. At least there was someone who was straightforward and difficult.

16

I WAS ON HIGH ALERT the next day in case Liesbet called me darling or something, but I needn't have worried. She was in full-on work mode, and as this was a side of her that I hadn't seen before, I almost forgot that she was my mother. The painters were replaced with electricians and tilers and a grumpy handyman called Percy, who nearly caused chaos when it was discovered that he had forgotten to bring his drill to hang pictures. Kwanele and I had to drive out to the hardware store in Hoedspruit a few times, and each day I found myself hoping that Percy would discover something new he needed but hadn't brought.

Bianca and Dirk lurked in the background as the rest of us were given orders by Liesbet and Percy, occasionally passing snide comments but always when Legend and Liesbet were well out of earshot.

'Verskriklik. Talk about sour pussies,' commented Marietjie as she sat on the floor trying to untangle strings of solar lights destined for the deck. 'And that Dirk mustn't be thinking that Legend's not noticing that he's parking off and not helping, because he is. Legend's got eyes in the back of his bladdy head.'

She gave me a speculative look before glancing around to see if anyone was in earshot. 'I also got some eyes in the back of my head, verstaan? What's going on with you and Kwanele?'

'What do you mean? We're just friends,' I said a bit lamely, taken by surprise.

She shook her head. 'Ja, and I'm Prince Harry. Luister, I can see he likes you a lot. And you like him. But what about this boyfriend of yours?'

'Um, about that …' I said, going a bit red.

'I thought not.' Marietjie grinned. 'And I know why you pretended you had one. Bladdy Petrus. But anyway, I think you must just go for it. You won't get a better man than Kwanele. The only thing that could be a problem is his ma.'

'Why?' I asked. 'Have you met her?'

'Ja, we all have. She's nice, hey. But very traditional and proud of her family lineage. I don't think she's planning for Kwanele to marry a white girl. Liewe vader, she'd probably have a bladdy thrombosis.'

'That's looking a bit far ahead,' I said, smiling. 'I mean, we really are just good friends right now … but I do like him a lot.'

'Just saying it could be a problem,' she replied. 'But problems are there to be solved.'

It made me think, though. On top of all the problems I'd created there could well be another looming in my future. But if being with Kwanele resulted in that problem then I'd rather have the problem than not be with Kwanele. I put it out of my mind, but then I wondered what Liesbet would think.

***

A few days later, we all stood in the lodge admiring the renovation. Liesbet had literally transformed the reception, lounge, dining area, bar and deck. The decor was slightly muted in comparison with the rooms, but it was eclectic, unexpected and breathtakingly beautiful. An entire wall in the lounge area had been wallpapered with cheetah print, forming a backdrop to the myriad framed black and white wildlife photographs, all of which had been taken and signed by the guides. Woven grass lampshades hung in clusters to mimic chandeliers, and tiny downlights lit up any dark corners, turning the huge space into something quite magical.

True to her signature style, vintage floral fabric mixed effort-lessly with animal print, colourful patterned fabric and dark, bold colours in sheshwe print. All the furniture was antique, restored, polished and elegant, and complemented by pot plants, baskets of all shapes and sizes and colours, candle holders, piles of vintage safari books, quirky old ornaments, vases of dried grasses, wooden sculptures – it all formed a tableau that you could stare at for hours and still find something new.

'Do you like it?' Liesbet said to me almost shyly.

I nodded. 'Actually, I love it,' I said. 'It sort of draws you in and it's so different to other lodges.'

She looked pleased, and then we turned as Legend popped open a bottle of champagne.

'One drink to toast the renovation,' he said. 'And then we're all having a braai in the bush this evening to celebrate.'

He then made this really nice speech, thanking Liesbet, and also saying he was proud of how we had all rallied to help. Only Bianca and Dirk looked sour.

Liesbet and I sat on the back set of seats as we drove to the treehouse. 'I've been thinking,' she said, 'and I'm not going to tell Dad or anyone where you are. I feel that this place is good for you so I'm not going to interfere.'

I told her about my and Saskia's plan to reveal where I was after my three-month probation and explained we hadn't exactly thought about the details. Liesbet said that was probably a very good time to tell the truth and that she was sure everyone would be very happy for me. We didn't say much after that. Just sat in contented silence.

We arrived at the treehouse camp just before sunset. Grace, Ayanda and Dumisani were already there and had set up a long table in front of the waterhole. The fire had been lit and a herd of buffalo had arrived, wading deep into the water from the opposite side, grunting with pleasure as they quenched their thirst.

Legend had supervised the packing of the drinks and ordered Petrus to mix springbokkie shooters. Personally, even if I drank alcohol, I don't think I'd be able to imagine a more disgusting combination than Amarula and crème de menthe. But everyone got very excited, including Liesbet, and very soon Petrus was mixing a second round. I noticed that Kwanele didn't have another one and opted for a beer.

'Why aren't you drinking, Alex?' said Bianca as I took a bottle of water from the cooler box. 'Are you an alcoholic or something?'

I'd begun to notice that she always waited for a gap in the conversation to take me on.

'Jesus,' said Legend frowning at her. 'Try for a little tact, okay?'

'I was just *asking*,' she said, giving him a wide-eyed look. 'I didn't know it was a secret or a sensitive topic but it I suppose it is and now you're blaming me. Again.'

Actually, it was a sensitive topic, but I managed to smile at her and say, 'Of course not. There's no reason. I've just never really taken to alcohol.'

'Well, then, if there's no reason, have a drink now. Maybe you'll like it. Petrus, give her some wine.'

'Alex, can you give me a hand with lighting the lanterns?' asked Kwanele, and at the same time Legend asked Liesbet if she'd like to look at the treehouse accommodation.

As we walked away, I could hear Bianca muttering, 'It's just a glass of wine, for God's sake. *She's* the one that makes a big deal of everything.'

Liesbet and Legend came back while I was placing the lanterns on the table.

'That treehouse has so much potential,' Liesbet was saying. 'Honestly, Legend, I'd love to decorate the rooms, and I'm buzzing with ideas. Shall I put it in my diary for May? That will give you plenty of time to work on the structure.'

Bianca tried to push her way into their conversation, but again she wasn't a match for Liesbet, who, with her usual flair, managed to ignore her, much as she would an irritating and spoilt child. Disgruntled, Bianca wandered off towards Marietjie and Petrus. Marietjie looked so horrified it was almost comical, and after a few seconds she stood up and came over to me.

'Hierdie perd gaan nie flippen geselsies maak met haar nie!' she said. 'Let's go help Dumi with the braai.'

Like ghostly shadows, a couple of elephants silently appeared at the waterhole while we ate. Apart from the quiet rumbles and soft splashes, you'd hardly know they were there. I slipped away and walked to the water's edge. Kwanele joined me and we stood side by side watching the elephants.

'What would scare you most? If one of these guys charged us right now or if a baboon spider ran up your leg?' he said quietly.

I smiled and considered. 'So, definitely if a baboon spider ran up my leg. And the reason is, if an elephant charged us, you'd be totally unphased and know what to do, *but* if the baboon spider was on my leg you'd literally scream and run away and leave me to deal with it.'

He laughed softly. 'If it was anyone else, I'd do that,' he said. 'But for you there's a chance, a very small chance, that I'd flick it off your leg.'

'That's the most romantic thing anyone has ever said to me,' I quipped and then blushed furiously. 'I mean ...'

'It was meant to be romantic,' he said, turning to face me and smiling. 'So, tell me, if I was in the middle of the bush in the middle of the night in the middle of a storm and my cruiser had broken down, what would you do?'

'Um, I'd tell one of the guides to fetch you immediately,' I said. 'And I'd send an umbrella and a raincoat with them?'

'No go,' he said. 'They're all somewhere else.'

'Well then, I'd come and fetch you. But then you'd have to drive back.'

'I forgot to mention my right leg is broken, and so is my left arm.'

'No, you can't add to it! But, okay, then I would drive us back even though I'd be doubly traumatised and then I'd make you drink a whole bottle of brandy and then I'd set your arm and leg except I'd do them both the wrong way round and then for the rest of your days you'd have to drive backwards.'

'Then I've changed my mind because that's incredibly brave of you and I wouldn't mind about my limbs,' he said. 'Without even thinking about it, I'd remove the baboon spider off your leg with my own hands and then ...'

'Then what?' I demanded.

'Then you'd be so grateful that you'd kiss me,' he said. 'And feel free. I've been virtually very brave.'

'Are you flirting with me in front of the whole staff?' I said with mock severity.

'I am,' he agreed, smiling at me again. 'Do you like it?'

By now I was smiling back at him like a loon and was about to say that yes, I did, very much, when everyone joined us and then we all stood quietly watching the elephants until they melted quietly into the darkness. As we went back to the table, I noticed that Bianca and Petrus hadn't come to look at the elephants. Petrus was leaning away from Bianca, his arms folded and looking a bit scared.

We went back to the lodge in two cruisers, and this time I sat in the passenger seat next to Kwanele. We didn't say much but I loved the quietness between us. Occasionally he glanced at me and smiled, and each time I met his eyes and smiled back at him. Although I was relaxed, I was aware of his every move as he drove, his body so close to mine, the conversations taking place behind us muted. Even if this sounds stupidly romantic, it really seemed as if there were only the two of us.

'Kwanele seems nice,' Liesbet said casually as I escorted her to her room for the last time. Actually, she was trying to sound casual, but it totally didn't work. Nothing escapes Liesbet. But at least she didn't have a problem with it.

'Yes,' I said, glad that it was so dark that she couldn't see me smile. 'He's very nice, but I mean he's sort of my boss and everything in case you're thinking that I *like* like him, and anyway, even if I did, I'd probably mess it up and it would definitely be a disaster, especially when he really got to know me and …'

Liesbet stopped and put her hand on my arm.

'Alex, don't be afraid to live your life,' she said. And then she carried on walking.

'One other thing,' she said when we got back to her room. 'Stay as far away as you can from that Bianca. She's pure poison and I can't understand what Legend sees in her. She reminds me of that dreadful girl at your school. What was her name?'

'Um, Athena?'

Even saying her name made my stomach twist into a knot.

'That's right. Her mother was a piece of work too. Actually, a complete bitch, and I'll never forget how she forced darling Sally Thompson to resign as head of the parents' committee. She was completely devastated, poor woman.'

I said goodnight quickly, because it looked like Liesbet wouldn't mind settling in for a bit of a gossip. As I made my way back to the lodge, I could see Kwanele and the other guides at the bar. But the mention of Athena had made me feel insecure and self-despising and I knew I wouldn't be able to claw back to my happy mood. So I bypassed the lodge and went to bed.

Liesbet left early the next morning, and I was both sorry and relieved to see her go. Sorry because it was comforting having her at the lodge. I'd felt protected somehow. But also relieved because it was a bit of a strain pretending that she wasn't my mother. Everyone gathered at reception to wave her goodbye, and I felt proud that they liked her so much. And proud of what she had done. I knew I was going to miss her, and it was a bit of a weird feeling, to be honest.

We'd all been hoping that Bianca would leave and go back to Johannesburg, but she announced at breakfast that she was staying to give Legend support. The renovation had distracted

Legend for a few days, but as soon as Liesbet left he descended again into a black and foul mood as he no doubt ruminated about the shareholders' meeting. Now given full access to the website, social media and emails so that she could monitor any negative feedback, Marietjie told me that Bertie had followed up his meeting with Legend with a pompous and threatening email where he demanded another meeting, but this time at his home in Johannesburg. 'Legend is moerse bad at tackling problems,' she'd said. 'Most of the time it's Kwanele that sorts everything out, but heaven knows what he can do about this. It's a whole different story now and it's not going anywhere.'

'My wrist is in agony,' said Bianca after dropping her bombshell and managing to look pitiful and triumphant at the same time, 'and I definitely need to see a specialist and will probably need an operation, but my man needs me. I'm going to work remotely, and can I kindly ask you all to use the Wi-Fi as little as possible because I'm going to need a lot of bandwidth.'

It was obvious that she hadn't consulted Legend, because he looked almost as horrified as we did. It was a bit awkward, to be honest, because no one said anything, and we all just carried on eating. The silver lining was that from the afternoon, the lodge was full. We'd be so busy that Bianca would be unplugged. Like, literally, if the guests used all the Wi-Fi.

I had been puzzling over how to find out more about New Horizons. The obvious person was my dad, but Liesbet must have told him how I'd blocked her at Yamihle and he'd probably have a few things to say about that. I decided to practise avoiding avoidance behaviour and called him.

Luckily, he was in a meeting when I phoned him, so that put paid to any lawyery type questions about me, plus I'd get the information really quickly, because when his children called he would never say he'd phone back, but always got brisk and to the point if he was busy. I ignored the slight impatience in his tone and set about questioning him.

I started off by asking him about delinquent directors and

rights of shareholders and contracts. I could tell he was puzzled and asked for more details, so I ended up telling him what was happening to Legend. Although I didn't use his real name because my dad would have recognised even the nickname, to be honest. He had a lot of interesting things to say about it and I scribbled a few notes. Then I moved on to Horizon Heights. His comments were much more decisive. Actually, he snorted when I mentioned the name.

'Fly-by-nights and cowboys,' he scoffed. 'I shouldn't be surprised if they're on *Carte Blanche* sometime soon, not to mention in an exposé in the *Daily Maverick*. It appears the main issues are the dubious ways they finance their projects and questionable due diligence before they begin development.' He suddenly sounded suspicious.

'Alex, you're not getting into some hare-brained scheme to invest with them, are you? Because if you are, all I will say is that I can guarantee it's going to be a disaster and your mother and I will certainly not …'

'No, of course not, don't worry,' I said. 'And I don't have any money to invest anyway. So, it's all good.'

'Well, yes,' he replied, sounding incredibly relieved and a bit evasive at the same time. 'Yes, there is that, thank God. I thought for a minute … never mind, but tell me why you want to know about Horizon Heights.'

'Just for a friend,' I said. 'But now we know. Or at least, they will know shortly. And thanks for that.'

That was a bit weird, I thought, as I said goodbye. He knew I didn't have the sort of money you'd need to invest in property. I mean, I'd literally have to have millions handy to do that. The thought passed as I read over my notes about what he'd said about Legend's predicament. I was excited to tell him what I'd learnt, but from the time the guests arrived there literally wasn't a chance. Plus, Legend was also in a strange mood, distant and guarded, which we'd all put down to Bertie and the pictures and delinquent director scandal. I could see that as each group of guests arrived he was digging deep to greet them with his usual enthusiasm and charm.

Kwanele had told me I was ready to take guests out on my own, which I had mixed feelings about because I wouldn't have actually minded carrying on driving with him for the rest of my career. Or the rest of my life, actually, because at that stage I was pretty much in love with Kwanele and torturing myself wondering if he felt the same way. But allowing me to take guests out on my own showed that he trusted me, and that was good.

My group were elderly, and that was good too, since the elderly are much tamer and so less likely to cause trouble for any reason, such as drinking, room swapping and unreasonable requests. They were all friends (also good), spoke excellent English because they were from the UK (perfect) and, best of all, had never been on a safari, which meant that they would be extremely easy to please (ideal). I decided that apart from going out of my way to show them everything, I would also be the perfect hostessy guide. I'd be interested in all their boring stories and ask them about their grandchildren, and not get irritated when they asked stupid questions. Plus, I would be more outgoing at dinner and not just shovel my food down and keep quiet. Basically, I'd make great conversation with the whole table as if I was a master of ceremonies or something. I even briefly wondered if I could do a quick toastmaster's course online.

I googled 'How to make great conversation with guests' and made a list. It seemed quite simple actually.

'What hobbies do you have?'

'I really like your earrings. Where did you get them?'

'I love your accent. Where are you from?'

'What do you do on your day off?'

'Would you like to hear a joke?'

Once the guests were settled in, we took our groups on an afternoon game drive, which would end with my and Kwanele's guests meeting at uBhejane Pan for evening drinks. So I set off with Ian, Dawn, Martin and Angela, and it was clear from the beginning that they were taking their safari really seriously. They asked lots of intelligent questions and the conversation flowed all through the drive and during drinks with Kwanele's group. I picked up that they were a bit nervous around big game when we came across a herd of elephant on the way back. They all agreed they didn't want to get too close, which was a pity as it was a very relaxed herd.

Kwanele's and my groups had been placed together at dinner, and I was planning to be in the middle of everyone because the conversation was easy, plus, I wanted to sit near Kwanele. But before we sat down Marietjie drew me aside and asked me to help with her group, who were a bit tricky and sitting further down the table.

'I got the lemons,' she said. 'They're up their own bums and they think they know everything. Verskriklik. And the rest aren't any better. Check, Legend's got the teetotallers and Petrus got some Rotary mense from Canada, and Bandile's and Mandla's groups speak almost fokkol English.'

'But I'm terrible at making conversation,' I said. 'I mean, really terrible.'

'Ja, I know that,' she sighed. 'But at least we'll be sitting opposite each other.'

I gave in because it was a good opportunity to practise conversational skills. It didn't seem that much conversation would be forthcoming from Legend, as I noticed that he was in a foul mood and that Bianca was retaliating by deliberately trying to wind things up.

'How awful for you to be Russian,' she was saying to the couple opposite her as I took my seat. 'I'm surprised that you're even travelling, actually. I suppose you feel incredibly judged wherever you go.'

Luckily they didn't understand what she'd said, but it was totally awkward because literally the whole table went silent with shock, so I leant towards the Canadians and blurted out, 'Do you have any hobbies?'

And then it was amazing because they said they were truffle hunters for the restaurant industry. I asked if they used tracker dogs to find them and they actually did instead of pigs. The teetotallers got all excited and told us that they bred bloodhounds, and then they all started asking Legend about tracking dogs for anti-poaching, and we spoke about that until coffee was served. Bianca tried to tell an anecdote about her grandmother's yorkie, but Legend kept on interrupting her, and she descended into sulks and glowered at me as I contributed more and more to the conversation.

Kwanele had joined our side of the table and he sat close to me, our shoulders touching. 'You're quite something, you know,' he said to me softly at some point and put his hand on my knee. I covered it with mine and said, 'So are you.' It was a private moment, just a perfect moment, when we both knew there was more than a spark, and that something special was going to happen. But after smiling at Kwanele and then looking up, I saw that Bianca had noticed our perfect moment. Her face hard, lips tight, she stared at me and then, looking scornful, turned away.

To make matters worse, Legend said right in front of Bianca as we prepared to escort the guests to their rooms that he was impressed with my knowledge about using tracker dogs. He said he'd like to discuss it with me and Kwanele sometime soon because they'd been thinking of establishing their own anti-poaching squad at Yamihle. I said that would be great because I also had something to talk to him about.

'Sure thing,' he said, and went off with the Canadians.

'Well, aren't you the little suction that everyone thinks is so amazing?' said Bianca as I was about to go to my group. 'But no one really knows you, do they?'

I hesitated, about to ask her what she meant, but I remembered Liesbet's warning. And what Saskia had said: Stay far away from Bianca. Although it was too late for that. I shrugged and walked away.

17

BIANCA'S WORDS LINGERED, THOUGH, AND the more I thought about what she had said, the more threatening it seemed. But a few hours into the day I managed to put it to one side. A full lodge doesn't give you too much time to think about much else than making sure everything flows smoothly. A braai had been planned at the treehouse for that night, and as the guides weren't all needed, only Bandile and Mandla went with the guests. I'd hoped for a chance at some point in the afternoon to talk to Legend, but he'd taken his car to Hoedspruit to get the clutch sorted out.

Marietjie had told me that another email had arrived from Bertie, who, it appeared, was not giving up easily. She said that Legend had replied to his request, or rather demand, for a meeting in Johannesburg with only a subject line: Fuck off. Bertie had retaliated by sending Legend a lawyer's letter and had attached the lawyer's invoice. So Legend sat down to dinner with us in another bleak mood and we ate mostly in silence.

Dirk joined us, and occasionally he looked at Bianca expectantly as if he was waiting for her to say something. She certainly had a smug expression, as if biding her time before she made some kind of announcement or something. I was right, but I wasn't entirely prepared for what was coming.

'I was looking at Liesbet's Facebook page this morning,' she said as Dumi removed the plates. 'I suppose since you know her, you're a friend of hers on Facebook, Alex?'

'I'm not on social media, so no, I'm not,' I said. But I knew where this was going.

'Well, you are in a way,' replied Bianca, 'because you're in most of her family pictures.'

Everyone looked up at this and stared at me. I said nothing, forcing myself to thank Dumi as he put a bowl of fruit salad in front of me.

'Liesbet has four children,' said Bianca, looking at Legend while counting on her fingers. 'There's Jessica, Richard, Charles ... and Alexandra. And that's you, isn't it, *Alex*?'

I didn't say anything.

'And Alex's dad is none other than Edward Carnell-Ellis, one of South Africa's richest men,' she continued. 'How hectic is that? Lucky you, growing up with a silver spoon in your mouth. And so I'm quite curious to know what you're doing here. Your dad could afford to buy you your very own game reserve with his small change. But maybe he's planning to buy you Yamihle once Legend's been made a delinquent director and loses everything? I wouldn't be surprised if you're a mole or something, you know. No one here put those pictures all over social media, and seeing as you're so deceitful, it seems to me that it could have been you.'

'It was *not* me!' I said. 'I would never do something like that and ...'

'But you're not denying that you lied about being Liesbet's daughter?' cut in Legend, his eyes cold.

'No, but I can explain that,' I replied, 'I mean, what does it even matter? I had reasons and I can explain, I promise you ...'

'I don't like being lied to,' said Legend. 'That's what matters. And I couldn't give a flying fuck about the reason.'

Bianca leant back in her chair, enjoying the moment.

'Liesbet lied to you too,' she pointed out to Legend. 'She also pretended that Alex wasn't her daughter. So I suppose it was all part of the plan. How coincidental that just after a week Alex arrives all those pictures go up.'

'Liesbet did not lie! And there was no plan,' I said. 'She didn't even know I was here, and I didn't know that she was the interior designer for Yamihle. But I explained everything to her, and she understood and it's really not a big deal. It makes no difference to *anything*.'

'Well, I still think the whole situation is really weird,' said Bianca, taking a slug of her wine before she moved in for the kill. 'And I would imagine the reason that you're not on social media is because everyone at your school hated you so much. My goodness, imagine being tagged in pictures of parties that you weren't invited to. No wonder you deleted your social media accounts. And that clip when your partner for the Grade 11 dance told you he'd only been messing with you and was going with someone else. That was quite a set-up, and they had planned all along to actually *video* it! It makes me wonder what you did to be so unpopular. And now I totally understand why you don't drink, after seeing all those pictures of you completely out of it. *So* embarrassing.'

I stared at her aghast. 'Where did you see all of that? And I wasn't ... they spiked my drink and ...'

'Stop it right now, Bianca,' said Kwanele. 'You're being spiteful. Nobody needs to know things like that.'

She stared at him derisively. 'You think? I'd expect you to defend her, though, seeing as you've obviously got a crush on her for some reason. What a joke. You're making a fool of yourself, Kwanele, and I bet she thinks so too, because your precious Alex already has a boyfriend. I'm sure she's neglected to tell you that little detail.'

'I don't have a boyfriend,' I said desperately, looking at Kwanele, who turned away, his face rigid.

'Then why did you say you did?' said Bianca, leaning forward.

'Come on, tell us! Or are you just some sort of psycho liar and manipulator?'

'For Christ's sake, shut the fuck up, Bianca,' said Legend. 'What's got into you?'

'Nothing's got into *me*,' she hissed at Legend. 'She's your little pet too, isn't she? And speaking of which, ask her about that dog of hers. You stole it, didn't you, *Alexandra*?'

I glanced involuntarily at Marietjie and Petrus. They were the only ones who knew I'd stolen Jackson.

'Wasn't me. I didn't tell her *anything*,' said Marietjie. She glared at Petrus. 'Did you say anything about Jackson? And did *you* tell her about Alex's supposed boyfriend?'

He looked shamefaced. 'It was that night we had the braai and the springbokkies,' he mumbled, 'and she was asking me stuff about Alex.'

'You and your big bladdy bek,' said Marietjie. 'One or two springbokkies and you must start to skinder just like an old tannie at the church fete and ...'

'Did you steal Jackson?' interrupted Legend, his eyes fixed on me.

'Yes, I did, okay?' I said. 'But it's not what you think! I had to steal him because ...'

'Fucking hell,' said Legend. 'Jesus, I've had enough for one night, but you've got a shitload of explaining to do, Alex.'

I'd also had enough. I stood up.

'I've been trying to explain this whole entire time,' I said, my voice trembling, 'but you just won't let me.'

And then I took off. I went to my room and climbed into bed and turned off the lights. Marietjie knocked on my door a while later and so did Kwanele. But I didn't answer and lay awake for what seemed the whole night, staring into the darkness and thinking that this was what it felt like when your worst nightmares come true.

I'm still not sure how I did it, but the next day I managed to avoid everyone. I woke up early, before anyone could come to

172

my room, took my guests on a game drive, and brought them back for lunch. And then I disappeared until it was time for their afternoon drive. I met them minutes before it was time to leave, and I avoided looking at any of the other guides. I knew that after the game drive and dinner Legend or Kwanele or probably both would want to speak to me, but I put that out of my mind. What I didn't know as I headed off with my guests was that I was about to commit one of the worst mistakes or crimes, whichever way you look at it, that any guide could make. And that the nightmare I thought I was in was nothing compared to what was to follow.

Before it happened, it was a successful drive. I was on autopilot, but we had a lot of good sightings and I know that my group were excited and happy. And relaxed. I was still mindful that they preferred to watch big game from a distance. I was about to start driving in the direction of the pan where we were due to join the other groups for sundowners when we stopped to look at the resident troop of baboons. I remember thinking that my guests enjoyed watching them, just as Julia and Mikey had. My eyes were focused on a young female with a tiny baby clinging to her stomach, which couldn't have been more than three days old.

It was a peaceful scene, but within seconds that changed as alarm calls sounded around us. Francolins squawking, the distinct cadence of squirrels on high alert, and warning barks from the male baboons. The troop scattered, most disappearing rapidly up surrounding trees. And then a leopard flashed before us, taking the female I'd been watching in a scuffle of dust, followed by a high-pitched cry, and the baby flung from the safety of the mother's stomach before her predator carried her away. It happened so quickly that it took us a while to register what had just taken place. The rest of the baboons vanished in seconds, but the baby was left alone, terrified and bewildered, and then it made its way unsteadily into the bush.

They all started talking at once, but I gestured to them to keep quiet, and we sat in silence. I waited. I really did. Hardly breathing, and hoping that one of the baboons would come back for the baby, and I never took my eyes off the spot from where it had disappeared. After half an hour I knew I should drive away. My guests were restless, dusk was closing in, and we should already have joined the other groups for sundowners. Perhaps the troop would still come back for the baby. Perhaps they wouldn't. I should have left well alone, let nature take its course. But I didn't.

First mistake. I got out of the cruiser.

'Stay here,' I said. 'I'm going to see where the baby baboon went, and check if the troop are nearby. I won't be long.'

Second mistake. They were uneasy, fearful at the thought of being left on their own. Of course they would be. They asked me, they begged me not to leave them, they demanded that I stay, but I didn't take any notice and I walked away. After about fifteen minutes I found the baby crouching under a bush, terrified and helpless. There was no sign of the troop. I sat next to it for a while, and by then I wasn't wondering what to do. I knew what was going to happen next. I picked it up. It struggled, uselessly baring its toothless mouth, and then it clutched at me. I covered it with my jacket. By now it was past sunset and raining.

They were still sitting in the Land Cruiser. Huddled under the dripping canopy, blankets around their shoulders. They looked as if they were in shock, and I wasn't surprised. It was the worst thing that could have happened to them, to be left alone in the bush like that. Kwanele's cruiser was pulled up beside them and he was sitting in the driving seat of my cruiser, holding the radio. His first expression when he saw me was relief. Followed quickly by anger. He got out of the cruiser and walked towards me.

'Do you realise,' he said, his voice cold and measured, 'what you've done? I have no idea how they managed it, but your group got on to the radio. I got to them quickly, but you've caused a big problem, Alex. They were scared and now they're very angry and want to leave Yamihle tonight. You call yourself a guide? I think you're irresponsible and a liar and the sooner you leave Yamihle the better. You're not who I thought you were, and what you did today shows me you're definitely not cut out for this job.'

'Kwanele,' I said, '*please* just listen to me. I promise there's a good reason why I left them.'

'There is never a good reason to abandon guests,' he almost shouted, 'and they've already told us what you did. How could you even think of trying to find that baboon and leaving them on their own? What was the point? You could lose your guiding licence over this!'

I didn't reply and clutched the baby baboon closer. He hadn't noticed it.

'I'm driving them back to the lodge,' he continued. 'Follow us in my cruiser. Legend knows about this. They all know by now, even the other guests. He's going to have his work cut out to smooth this over.'

I still said nothing. I turned and went to his cruiser and put the baboon on the floor in front of the passenger seat. I covered it again with my jacket and prayed it wouldn't try and leap out. But it did try, and I had to stop briefly as I followed Kwanele and put it on my lap, holding onto it tightly with one hand.

We pulled up at the lodge entrance. Legend was waiting for us. Besides giving me an angry and contemptuous glance, he ignored me and ushered the guests inside.

Kwanele and I then drove the cruisers to the parking bay next to the guides' accommodation. I got out, the baboon in my arms, still covered in my jacket. Restless and frightened, it cried.

Kwanele stared at me. 'Don't tell me you've got the baboon,' he said. 'Alex. Are you completely out of your mind?'

'Probably,' I replied, my voice shaky. 'But I had to go after it and see if it was okay. And it wasn't. If I hadn't brought it back with me, it would have died.'

He shook his head. 'It will probably die now anyway. Do you realise that? Did it even cross your mind when you took it what you were going to feed it tonight? It will probably die of starvation or dehydration overnight. If you'd left it, it may have had a chance. Now you've given it a death sentence.'

We stood silently facing each other in the rain and I braced myself, thinking that he was going to tell me to drive back to where I had found it and leave it in the bush. And I knew I wouldn't be able to do that. But I also knew Kwanele was right. Beyond taking it, I hadn't thought of how to make sure it survived.

'Don't come to the lodge,' he said finally. 'It's going to take a while for Legend to sort this out. Alex, I can't believe you've got us into this mess, and I can't even begin to tell you how angry Legend's going to be when I tell him you've also taken the baboon.'

'I'll take it to my room then,' I said, 'and I'll try to think of what to do. Maybe … is there a sanctuary or something nearby?'

He shook his head. 'No. There's nothing we can do to help it now.' He strode off to the lodge without looking at me again.

18

WHILE I WAS DESPERATELY GOOGLING what to feed a newly born baboon, a WhatsApp flashed onto my screen from an unknown number.

I want another two grand for my dog. I'm coming to get the money tomorrow.

Johan. Marietjie was right. He wasn't going to stop. I thought about everything that was going to happen the next day. Johan arriving, because I had no doubt that he would. Legend's fury. And all the shouting and accusations because of the huge mess that I was in and that I had no idea how to solve. I shivered, getting this weird buzzing noise in my ears as panic set in. I needed help and I couldn't think of who to turn to. I wasn't going to find it at Yamihle. And so I started to pack. I threw everything I'd brought with me randomly into my bags and took the baboon and Jackson with me to where we parked the cruisers at night. The keys were always left in the ignitions, and I got us all into the first one and drove away. I was halfway to Hoedspruit when I realised that I was driving Legend's cruiser. So basically, it couldn't have got any worse.

It was raining hard by now, and I drove slowly, with one hand on my backpack where I'd made a nest for the baboon. Tiny rumbles of thunder and flashes of lightning made me break into a sweat, and I could have cried with relief when I eventually saw the sign to Hoedspruit Airport. The Nissan was where I'd left it and I parked Legend's cruiser nearby. I wasn't sure what to do with his keys, so I buried them in a pot plant next to the entrance to departures.

By now it was nearly midnight, and as I drove into the town, I didn't hold out much hope that anything would be open, and definitely not a shop that stocked formula for babies. The streets were completely quiet, as I expected, but then I spotted a strip mall and sighed when I saw a huge lit-up green cross.

There was a neon sign on the door that said 'Open,' but it was locked. It took a bit of knocking and then banging to get anyone's attention. Eventually a sleepy looking woman in her fifties emerged and let me in.

'I suppose you want a condom?' she said, looking a bit disapproving but resigned.

'Um no, actually I'm looking for formula for, like, a really tiny baby.'

'Too late, then,' she said, yawning. 'How old?'

'About three or four days,' I replied. 'To be honest, I'm not entirely sure.'

She raised her eyebrows and eyed my boobs. 'With a baby that small you should really persevere, you know. Have you tried supporting your breast while feeding?'

'It's not actually for me,' I said hastily. 'And basically, the mother has tried everything, and plus, this is sort of an emergency.'

Fifteen minutes later we'd gone too far into the shopping to explain that the baby was actually a baboon, and so I left with a massive bag of different types of formula for a newborn, a breast pump, three bottles with various nipple sizes, two receiving blankets, nappies, a mobile, a pair of booties, and some cabbage leaves which she said she always kept in the fridge at the back just in case. Also, at the last minute I added a syringe because I had a feeling that this wasn't going to be easy.

I pulled over a few kilometres out of Hoedspruit and mixed the formula. And I was right, it wasn't easy. The baboon was desperately hungry, but it couldn't latch on to the nipple of the bottle. I managed to squirt some formula into its mouth, but it wasn't enough, and it kept spewing it out.

I googled the route from Hoedspruit to The Plains. Because by now I knew where I was going. Barend and Antoinette were the only people I could think of who would properly help me. Antoinette would have a lot of sharp words, but I was okay with that because she'd know what to do. And Barend was so kind and trustworthy. I needed solid people. Google said it would take me fifteen hours and six minutes. It was now two in the morning and so that meant I'd get to The Plains at five in the evening. And I'd have to stop and try to feed the baby with the syringe every hour.

I closed my eyes and I think I actually whimpered. I considered driving back to Yamihle for help, but then I thought of Kwanele's cold anger, Legend's fury, and the scornful reception that I'd get from everyone. I turned on the engine, put my foot down flat on the accelerator and sped into the night.

When adrenaline is coursing through your bloodstream it keeps you awake whatever the cost. Fight or flight? I was doing both. I ignored the speedometer, only concentrating on the mileage, as I knew that I had to make up time while it was still dark. Adrenaline doesn't last for more than a few hours, though, and by the time the sun had properly risen my eyes were pricking with exhaustion. When I reached the outskirts of Pretoria, I considered that I was a safe distance from Yamihle, and I pulled over to send a message to Kwanele.

By now you know I've left and it was the best thing to do. I've got the baboon, but I'll look after it. It's still alive. I'm sorry about everything but I'm not actually a liar, it's just complicated. I don't have a boyfriend. I only said that because Petrus was flirting with me this one time and I didn't know what to do because I knew Marietjie liked him, and I wanted her to be my friend. I took Legend's cruiser. It's at Hoedspruit Airport. The keys are buried in the big orange flowerpot outside the doors that go to departures. I'm really sorry, I know I've messed up everything.

I switched off my phone and carried on. The bad times were when I stopped and tried to feed the baby. It choked and cried as I squirted formula into its mouth. I imagined it was getting a little in, but I also knew it was getting weaker by the hour, as each time we stopped its tiny body seemed limper and weaker. Jackson kept on pushing his huge head through to the passenger seat where it lay, and after a few hours I pulled over and put it in the back seat with him. In the rearview mirror, I could see it holding on to him as he licked it and curled his stomach around it to keep it warm. Or to comfort it. I didn't know.

The worst time was when I had four hours to go, and I was in the middle of endless flat plains and the long straight highway that seemed as if it would never lead to anywhere. I'd driven for eleven hours, and I felt as if I couldn't carry on. It was too much. I pulled over to the side of the road and laid my head on the steering wheel. It would have been easy to go to sleep, I wanted to go to sleep. But then I had this sort of hallucination, or image, or whatever, that when I woke up everything would be a hundred times worse. Four hours is only eight times thirty minutes, chanted my brain, and only sixteen times fifteen minutes. I decided to break it up into the fifteen-minute equation. After that, it wasn't so bad.

I was driving through the gates of The Plains when it occurred to me that I didn't exactly have a very well thought-out plan about how to explain my presence. Although, I thought hazily, I did have information about the developers, and surely that would evolve into a plan. But first there needed to be a plan about the baby baboon, and then a plan about that plan in case any of the plans didn't work. I realised I was getting into a sleep-deprived delirium again, so I parked the Nissan, let Jackson out, cradled the baby against my shoulder and sort of sideways sleepwalked into Antoinette's office.

She looked up from her computer and stared at me as if she couldn't believe her eyes.

'With a dog and a fokken baboon,' she said eventually.

'You may as well know right now that I stole the baboon and also this dog,' I said, gesturing to Jackson.

She held up her hand. 'I don't want to know. Fok.'

I think she was about to ask me why I was there when she looked properly at the baboon and her eyes softened. 'Come to Ma,' she said, getting up and taking it from my arms. It put its skinny little arms around her neck and chattered a bit, and then made a runny poo all down her immaculate white shirt.

'Shame, man, it needs a nappy.'

'So, I bought some on the way here,' I said, 'but I couldn't work out how to put them on. And I'm sorry about the poo and everything, but it wouldn't take the bottle so I used a syringe, and it was probably the wrong formula, and I'm scared it's going to die because it's very hungry and it's literally taken in nothing, and I've driven fifteen hours and six minutes to get to you and please will you help me?'

I sat down on a chair in front of her desk and started to cry in a sort of weak and feeble way. Antoinette picked up her walkie-talkie. Actually, it was a radio, but she always called it that. 'Barend, Barend, kom in, Barend,' she said. 'Verskriklike krisis. Office.'

She reminded me of Marietjie then, and I giggled in a bit of a crazy weird way, tears still pouring down my cheeks.

Barend appeared in like seconds, looking around wildly as if he expected to see robbers or something. Then he stared at Antoinette in amazement, and you couldn't blame him, really. I mean, she was holding a baby baboon and covered in poo. Then he turned to me, his face full of concern.

Antoinette nodded towards me. 'She's overwrought. Get her some sugar water and put a bit of brandy in it. And a headache powder.'

They are so nice, was my last thought before I lost consciousness after drinking the concoction that Barend handed me.

When I opened my eyes the next morning, the first thing I saw was Jackson's head on the frilly white pillow beside me and his body stretched out on top of a pink satin quilt. He was still fast asleep, a damp patch of drool under his mouth. After a while I realised that I must be in Antoinette and Barend's house in their spare room. A tiny shaft of sunlight streamed through a gap in the vivid floral curtains, and I could hear Jeremy Loops faintly from somewhere, probably from the kitchen. Antoinette and Marietjie would like each other, I thought, and then closed my eyes and drifted into another deep sleep.

I woke up for a second time, my heart pounding, and leapt out of bed. This time Jackson wasn't in the room, and I began to panic about the baby, imagining that it hadn't survived the night and all I had done was sleep.

I walked down the passage towards where I thought the kitchen must be and I heard Antoinette talking. 'Jislaaik, but you're an ugly baby,' she was saying. 'But Ma loves you, okay? Now, we going to give you another bottle so you can get lekker vet.'

I stood in the doorway transfixed. Antoinette was sitting at the kitchen table. She had put a bib around the baboon's neck and held it cradled in her arms, its tiny face peeping out of a pink blanket. It was sucking on the bottle as if its life depended on it, which it did actually. Jackson lay under the table, his front paws just peeking out from beneath the tablecloth.

I was so relieved the baboon was alive that I started crying again, but this time it was that seriously sort of ugly crying with snot running out my nose and huge shuddering sobs.

'Ai siestog, Alex,' said Antoinette, getting up and handing me a roll of paper towel and guiding me to a chair at the table. She made me a cup of tea and set down a plate of rusks. 'Tell me everything.'

So I did. Every single detail right back from when I was at school. It wasn't chronological, though, and I was still crying most of the time, so it was a bit of a jumbled mess, and it took three cups of tea for me and two nappy changes for the baboon by the time I finally finished. Antoinette didn't say anything, but every now and again she shook her head and her lips tightened.

When I got to the bit about Johan and Jackson at the end, her lips got so thin they disappeared into her face. She held up her hand to make me stop talking.

'We deal with that one first,' she said. 'Dial his number and then give me your phone.'

Johan answered after one ring, and I handed the phone to Antoinette.

'Luister,' she snapped, 'you're speaking to Antoinette Snyman and not the girl you've been bullying. She's paid for the bladdy dog and if you know what's good for you, you delete this number otherwise you're going to be bladdy sorry.'

There was a pause, and I could hear Johan's voice, loud and indignant.

'Yes,' Antoinette said, 'I am threatening you, that's right, and I'm glad you understand, you bladdy troll. Alex is under my protection now and so you deal with me and my husband. And the police, and the SPCA, and every other organisation I can think of. Verstaan?'

There was just a mumble then from the phone, and Antoinette looked triumphant. 'Have a good day further,' she said and ended the call. 'The rest we deal with later. For now, you need to learn how to put on a nappy.'

As I took back my phone, I could see that I had tons of WhatsApps and missed calls. I didn't want to see who they were from, let alone read them, so I switched it off again.

It took a while to put on the nappy because the baby was so wriggly and sort of slippery, but I was managing to get it right almost expertly when Barend appeared, and for the first time since I'd been back at The Plains, he gave a proper smile.

'It's a little girlie,' he said. 'She needs a name.'

'Brunelda,' said Antoinette, taking its tiny paw and looking besotted.

Overcome with emotion, Barend brushed his hand over his eyes.

'My mother was Brunelda,' he explained to me. 'It's a beautiful gesture from Antoinette, hey?'

Antoinette gave him a sharp look and handed him a list. 'No time to be sentimental. I need you to go into town and shop for the baby.'

'Brunelda was a wonderful God-fearing woman,' she said once he'd left. 'This baby's got a lot to live up to.'

'Now you must call that Legend character,' she continued. 'He needs to know everything you found out.'

'Antoinette, I *can't*,' I replied. 'He's going to be so angry and say terrible things ... Maybe I can send him an email or something and not look at his reply?'

'You are many things, Alex,' she said. 'But you are not a coward. You know it's the right thing to do.' She permitted herself a grim smile. 'Unless you want me to call him?'

'No!' I said hastily. 'I'll do it right now so it's over and done with.'

I went to my room and sat on the bed and stared at my phone for a few minutes until I switched it on and then, my hand shaking, I tapped on Legend's number.

I spoke quickly before he could say anything.

'Legend, please listen to me because I've got something really important to tell you.'

'Go ahead,' he said, his voice cold.

'So I was speaking to my ... friend who is a lawyer about the shareholders trying to make you a delinquent director. And the first thing he wanted to know is, is Yamihle actually a registered company?'

'No,' said Legend. 'It's a private property. I own it.'

'Well then, if it's not a company then you can't be made a delinquent director. And secondly, is there a written agreement that Bertie and the others are shareholders or that they have any kind of right of access to Yamihle?'

'No,' he said again.

'Are you totally sure? I mean, that's what my friend said is really crucial. Did your dad maybe mention it in his will?'

'No. It was verbal. They were his friends and fuck knows why.

184

He gave them the two weeks a year as a gift.'

'Okay, so then basically the situation is that you're the sole owner of Yamihle and there are no directors, and also, the agreement with Bertie and the others was between them and your dad. My friend says that if that's the case then you don't have to honour the agreement unless you really want to.'

'You're saying there are no issues, and I can tell Bertie to piss off.'

'Yes. Plus … I'm not sure if I should even say this, but I think Dirk posted the pictures. I don't have any proof, it's just a hunch.'

'I think you're right, but we'll never know for sure because I fired him. Look, Alex, thank you, but where the fuck are you? We need to talk. You can't just fucking disappear like that.' His voice was rising in anger, and I paused before speaking, waves of nausea rising in my stomach.

'It doesn't matter where I am. I know that you're probably worried about the baboon, but she's totally fine and safe, so you really don't need to be concerned about her, I promise. Plus, there's nothing really to talk about because I know you don't want me back and I understand that. I'm very sorry about all the lies and everything.'

I ended the call. He rang back immediately, and I quickly switched off my phone.

I went back to Antoinette. 'I did it,' I said.

'That's two problems out of the way but there's still a lot to sort out,' she replied. 'Now you must have a shower and wash your hair and then you can have something to eat. Then you can sleep some more and then we talk.'

It was really nice having someone to tell me what to do, I thought as I went off obediently. And in small manageable chunks. I wondered briefly if I was having a nervous breakdown or something, but then I decided it was just lack of sleep.

Antoinette woke me up just before seven that evening. I followed her to the kitchen where Barend was sitting in a big armchair with Brunelda. She was fast asleep, her paw holding on to the collar of his shirt. Although he looked up and smiled at me as I came in, I could see the strain in his face and eyes. He looked desperately unhappy.

I sat down at the table. 'I know about the developers and everything. And I saw all the reviews on Tripadvisor.'

'Ja, Magnus told me so,' he said. 'I think it's all over for me and Antoinette.'

Antoinette banged a frying pan onto the stove with unnecessary force, but she didn't say anything.

'So, I hope you don't mind and think that I'm interfering, but I found out some stuff. I phoned my dad. He's a property developer and a lawyer and he knows who these developers are. He didn't have anything good to say about them. Actually, he said they were really dodgy.'

'Ja,' he said again. 'But there's nothing we can do to stop them.'

'But could you not buy the surrounding farms yourself? Then you could make The Plains a proper reserve with free-roaming animals.'

For a brief moment his eyes lit up, but he shook his head. 'We don't have the money. It would cost millions. And now someone has reported us to the National Consumer Commission for false advertising and for non-compliance with the rules of the Department of Tourism. There's going to be an investigation.'

'But Barend, don't you think that's a bit suspicious? I mean, you know the developers want your land, and now suddenly there's bad reviews and people reporting you. And how are you going to reply to those claims? There are obviously no grounds.'

He shrugged. 'There's no point. People like us don't stand a chance against the big players.'

'You mean bullies,' I said. 'Because that's what they are. And bullies rely on the fact that their victims won't do anything. They … they choose them carefully and pick on people who they think won't stand up to them for whatever reason. But it's a whole new thing for them if a victim won't back down.'

He shook his head again. 'It would cost too much. Lawyers

and all that. No, if we sell The Plains, Antoinette and I can start again. We can buy a guesthouse maybe in Durbanville and do wine tours and suchlike.'

'I don't want a guesthouse in Durbanville and I'm not having you drinking wine all bladdy day,' snapped Antoinette. 'And how the hell are we going to keep Brunelda in the Cape?'

'Look, Barend, I know you don't have the money,' I said, 'but surely there's no harm in doing an investigation just to see if your neighbours would be willing to sell their farms to you instead of the developers? You'd be making no promises, just putting out feelers. And then you take it from there. I mean, you never know, maybe you could find investors or something. Don't give up. The Plains is so important to you. It's always been your dream.'

'She's right, Barend,' said Antoinette. 'You and me need to grow a pair of fokken balls.'

Barend looked mutinous, and then he stood up and handed Brunelda to Antoinette. 'You forget that at month end we got to let another three staff members go. There's no money, liefie, and I'm not a businessman. I don't know how to find investors, I'm sorry.'

His shoulders slumped, he walked out of the kitchen.

'This crisis has klapped him right in the centre of his manhood,' remarked Antoinette, watching him go. 'At the end of the day, every one of the male species thinks he's a bladdy caveman. If he can't provide, he falls apart.'

Barend did look well and truly defeated, and in the state he was in, it was going to take a huge amount of time and effort to coax him into some kind of action. I didn't mind the effort, but basically we didn't have the time.

'Antoinette, I don't want to interfere or go behind Barend's back or anything, but do you think maybe I should speak to Oom Piet and Oom Marius and Tannie Santie just to sound them out? And I think it's a good idea to let them know the troubles you're facing, on account of you being neighbours and that.'

187

She didn't reply for a few moments because Brunelda was now wide awake and had climbed onto her head.

'Maybe a few direct questions would be a good idea,' she agreed, patting her perm back into shape once she'd extricated Brunelda, and giving me a slight smile. 'And I can't think of anyone better to do that.'

19

I DIDN'T GO ON MY discovery mission immediately because I spent the next day poring over maps of The Plains and the adjacent farms. I got increasingly excited because it appeared that integrating the land would be pretty seamless. A bit of internet research showed that portions of the land on two of the farms were listed as succulent Karoo hotspots, which made me wonder how Horizon Heights had got planning permission. Remembering that my dad had called them cowboys, it crossed my mind that they may not even have got that far. When I showed Antoinette the maps and explained how I thought the integration could work she gave a slight smile. 'It brings to my mind your employee feedback form.'

I set off first thing the next day, and Magnus came with me because I didn't know how to get to the farms. Barend and Antoinette hadn't yet told any of the staff that I'd arrived back at The Plains, so it was a bit of a shock for Magnus when Antoinette summoned him to the office, and he found me there waiting for him. As we set off, he said that the guides were all very surprised when Brunelda appeared, but now that he knew I had returned it made complete sense. So that didn't make sense to me, but I didn't really want to hear the explanation.

As we drove to the northern border of The Plains, I found myself seeing it through fresh eyes. The landscape was iconic semi-desert Karoo with low-lying shrubs, grasses and succulents dotted with sedimentary rocks and sandstone formations glowing red and golden yellow in the sun. It was perfectly preserved, and a growing sense of enthusiasm grew in me as I imagined what it could become if quadrupled in size.

'This is Oom Piet's farm,' said Magnus, leaping out of the Nissan to open a wonky old iron gate. Basically, the gate set the tone for Oom Piet's farm, which showed significant signs of neglect. Rusty windmills no longer working, abandoned tractors and the sad shabbiness of his farmhouse indicated that Oom Piet had lost interest and hope.

Being widowed for a few years, Oom Piet told us that he was bliksem lonely. His daughters didn't want the farm since they had both moved to Florida in America and they wanted him to join them there. He said he was greatly encouraged by the number of single ladies in Florida on the online dating sites and that it was time for a new chapter in his life. Admitting that he hadn't taken to the Horizon Heights representatives, who he described as donners high-handed, he said he would far rather sell to Barend if there was the opportunity. Oom Piet was shocked by the news that Barend and Antoinette may be forced to sell The Plains, and when we left him it seemed that he was a bit more energised.

Oom Marius and his wife Tannie Bets were next. Dazzled by the sum Horizon Heights had hinted at, they'd been googling properties in Mossel Bay and had found a nice house on the beach with a swimming pool and a jacuzzi. Tannie Bets explained that their predicament was that the farm had been in their family for three generations, and it would be hard to never see it again if they sold. We talked about that for a while and then Magnus had this genius idea that they keep the farmhouse and a couple of hectares and have it as a holiday home. They were literally ready to sell the rest of the land then and there, but I had to explain that Barend and Antoinette would need time to find a way of buying it.

The Horizon Heights people hadn't made a good impression on them either, but they seemed less flexible than Oom Piet in terms of timing. Basically, they were keener on the fishing and the jacuzzi in Mossel Bay than being sentimental about the farm.

They also mentioned something that was a bit worrying. Horizon Heights was ready to pay a deposit as soon as they signed a contract of sale. Oom Marius was sympathetic about Antoinette and Barend's plight, but he explained that the deposit would pay for the new house and a really nice fishing boat and maybe even a sauna.

We'd left Tannie Santie for last because, one, her farm was at the northern end of the potential land Barend could buy, and, two, she was likely to be the toughest nut to crack. Also, Magnus was worried about Duiwel and said if he were going to be mauled it would be best if it happened after we'd spoken to Oom Piet and Oom Marius.

As we drove onto Tannie Santie's farm, I could see immediately that her land was the best of the lot. For the most part it had fallen fallow. There were no discernible crops and only a few sheep were dotted around the landscape, which looked promisingly populated with indigenous scrub. Basically, the land had been neglected for years from a farming point of view, which was perfect in terms of rehabilitation. From what I could tell from the short drive to the farmhouse, her land also looked to be the most beautiful, with picturesque and dramatic koppies soaring from the scrubland.

At the sound of my car pulling up, Tannie Santie came out of the farmhouse. Short and wiry, with a wizened face and small dark eyes, she looked a bit like Brunelda. Standing beside her was the biggest rottweiler I'd ever seen in my life, who I guessed was Duiwel. Duiwel must have weighed about sixty kilograms of pure muscle, and as soon as I'd switched off the engine she leapt forward and started biting the tyres of my car.

'Leave it!' screeched Tannie Santie in a voice surprisingly powerful for someone so tiny. Duiwel backed off and eyed us shiftily as we followed Tannie Santie into her house.

Walking into the farmhouse was like going a hundred years back in time. A cool and dark hall tiled in slate led to a vast kitchen and sitting room at the back of the house, cosily furnished with numerous doily-bedecked armchairs. Framed cross-stitch samplers on the walls admonished us to mend our ways while an ancient tape deck rather incongruously belted out Bob Marley.

Sniffing appreciatively at the sweet smell of baking, Magnus attempted to charm Tannie Santie. 'Tannie's looking well, and how are things going with Tannie today? I hope this is a convenient time to visit Tannie?'

She threw him a contemptuous look and pointed a finger at me.

'Who's this girl?' she said. 'She better not be from the police, because they're not welcome on my farm.'

I assured her that I wasn't from the police, but she continued to stare at me suspiciously. 'And you better not tell me you're employed by those developers, because then you must leave before I get out my rifle.'

While she was talking, I absent-mindedly put out my hand to pat Duiwel, who snapped at me tetchily, her tail wagging and her bum wiggling with pleasure. Definitely not a full box of chocolates.

'Didn't your ma tell you never to pat a strange dog?' said Tannie Santie, handing Duiwel a piece of biltong and giving her a pat of approval.

'Sorry,' I said, smiling at her. I explained why we'd come to see her, and her reply was quick and decisive.

'I'm starting a new business on my farm,' she said, which was a bit unexpected, to be honest. I mean, she was way over eighty. 'Me and my grandson, Gert. We're entrepreneurs, if you follow me. So we cannot move, but we don't need all the land. I don't want a village built around my ears and people spying on me, but in principle I would consider selling to Barend because Gert says we need adventurous capital for our long-term growth potential.'

'How much land would you need to keep?' I asked.

'Let us ask Gert,' she replied. 'But first I will give you tea and rusks.'

I declined the rusks because they had a bit of a funny smell, but Magnus dipped about three into his tea, which pleased Tannie Santie a lot. Actually, she seemed to find it funny and even put some in a Jiffy bag for him to take home.

After tea Tannie Santie took us through the back door to a big tunnel greenhouse that stood some three hundred metres away from the house. A bearded man of about thirty with long wavy hair and wearing a tie-dyed shirt and khaki shorts came out and walked towards us. He clasped his hands in front of him and bowed.

'Namaste,' he said.

'Um, namaste,' I said, bowing back.

'Num num,' giggled Magnus, bending over double in the deepest possible low bow. 'Num num stay.'

I glanced at him in surprise, but Tannie Santie gave a cackle of laughter. 'This is Gert,' she said. 'He'll show you around.'

Once inside, I gazed around the tunnel at row upon row of lush green and incredibly healthy-looking plants. Tannie Santie and Gert were growing cannabis, but definitely not as a hobby. The set-up was professional, with LED lights, fans, temperature gauges, distillers and humidifiers. They were serious players. It also dawned on me that Magnus had eaten at least three rusks stuffed liberally with the harvest. His eyes rolling, he was looking upwards, entranced, as if he were taking part in the rapture.

Gert gave him a gentle smile. 'Leave the brother,' he said. 'He just had some good shit and he's rejoicing.'

Tannie Santie briefly explained why we'd come, and I asked Gert how much land they'd need to keep for their new business.

'Not less than six hectares,' he replied, tenderly redirecting Magnus, who was trying to switch off a humidifier. 'We're getting a lot of attention from the overseas market, including some big pharmaceuticals, and I'm planning on building a couple of yurts and becoming a spiritual guardian to lamas for facilitated human therapy.'

Gert admitted that he liked the idea of living adjacent to a reserve since it would be a good business offering to the therapy guests and also because he suspected he had a deep mystical connection with animals, which he was keen to explore. He shook his head gravely when I told him Horizon Heights were trying to push Antoinette and Barend off their land, but he had no practical suggestions about that except to say that they should smudge their house with sage as a matter of urgency.

Gert and Tannie Santie walked us to my car and Gert presented me with a packet of cannabis. 'Um, no, that's really not necessary,' I said, backing away slightly and feeling that my life was complicated enough as it was without my becoming the custodian of a sizeable stash of weed.

'Take it anyway,' he said, pressing the packet into my hand. 'Your root chakra is blocked. I can sense you're out of control and fearful. Maybe this will help.'

Not a chance, I thought, as Magnus peered myopically at Tannie Santie and said, 'Bye-bye. You're a funny little monkey and I don't think I like you. But maybe I do. I dunno.'

It was quite an annoying drive back, because Magnus became convinced that aliens were after us and kept on trying to get out my car to fight them. But then luckily he spotted some giraffe, and he spent the rest of the time laughing so much about their long necks that tears ran down his cheeks.

I drove Magnus straight up to the guides' accommodation and managed to put him to bed. I remembered to confiscate his rusks, which was a bit tricky, as he was clutching the Jiffy bag like a vice. I stashed the weed in the glove box of my car and then set off to debrief Antoinette.

She was in her office, staring at her screen, which basically wasn't a good sign, because whenever I'd been in there when I was working at The Plains, she was always typing really fast with all ten fingers. 'Only two bookings for the Easter weekend,' she said. 'Usually by this time we're full and I'm turning people away.'

'Where's Brunelda?' I asked.

'Barend got depressed when we went through the booking sheet, so he took her for a walk,' she replied.

I filled her in on my meetings, but I didn't mention that Tannie Santie was growing cannabis since it didn't seem to me that Antoinette would approve of that sort of thing. We were talking about what everyone had said and how to go about finding investors when Antoinette looked out the window at the sound of an approaching car, and then looked a bit awkward and maybe even embarrassed, which was a totally strange expression for her.

'What?' I said. 'Is it guests or something? I thought ...'

But then I also looked out the window and there was no mistaking the massive black Range Rover coming slowly down the road. It was my dad and Liesbet, and Jess and Saskia were in the back seat.

I leapt out of my chair in a wild panic. 'Antoinette, it's my parents and ... I have no idea how they know I'm here! I can't face them yet. I promise I'll send them messages and everything, but can you pretend I'm not actually here? I mean, you can say I *was* actually here, but I've left and I'm totally safe, but I *can't* see them.'

Then I looked properly at her expression. 'Please don't tell me you phoned them.'

'Alex, don't be bladdy stupid. Of course I bladdy phoned them. And Barend agreed. You need your family's support because you're in the middle of a fokken crisis.'

As they all got out of the car and began to walk towards the office, I felt like it was an intervention or something, and I had visions of being handcuffed and stuffed into a white jacket and taken to the loony bin. But, being my parents, they were quite practical.

'Another daughter on the run,' said my dad with an austere smile. 'Now all I'm waiting for is Charles and Richard to phone me from Dubai to say they've got a couple of hitmen after them.'

'God, Edward, don't *say* that,' said Liesbet, 'I honestly wouldn't be surprised. Alex darling, I do wish you had called us and I'm sorry to say that I'm going to have to put my foot down and insist that we talk about this.'

'Mom, just chill for a bit,' said Jess. 'Maybe she doesn't want to talk! Alex, are you surprised to see Sas? I thought it would nice if she came too.'

Saskia hugged me. 'When I didn't hear from you, I got all worried, so I phoned Jess and here I am!' She paused. 'Alex, is that man over there carrying a *baboon*?'

Barend was thrilled to meet my family and he busied himself allocating rooms and sorting out luggage. It appeared that he'd said everyone could stay for as long as they wanted. They all started to drift off towards the lodge (in quite a holiday mood to be honest), and I was about to follow when Antoinette held me back.

'Now listen, okay?' she said. 'Just because your family is here doesn't mean you got to go back with them. Me and Barend want you to know that you can stay here for as long as you like. I'm not going to employ you again, so we get that straight, but you leave when you're ready.'

'Thank you,' I said, feeling relieved. I didn't want to go back to Cape Town. And also, I didn't know where I wanted to go yet. But The Plains was a good place to think about all that.

I found Liesbet and my dad in their room. It was one of the nicest because it had a beautiful view and a huge bathroom.

'Oh dear,' said Liesbet gazing around her. My hackles went up a little because I felt quite protective of The Plains. It was one thing for me to criticise but quite another when someone else did it.

'Actually, it's not so bad considering the rate,' I said. 'And it's very clean. And Antoinette tries *very* hard with all the little details.'

'Yes,' she agreed hastily, eyeing the inexpertly decoupaged tissue box and vase of dyed grasses on the dresser. She turned towards the bed and spotted the stuffed toy lion propped up against the cushions holding a no smoking sign and a Bible. She said nothing but then our eyes met, and we both smiled.

So right then and there they did have an attempt at an intervention. Actually, to define it correctly, it was more like just a conversation with Liesbet and my dad where they wanted to go into deep stuff, and I didn't. I explained that I'd left Yamihle because I'd stolen the baboon and I panicked, and I also told them about Jackson and Johan. I decided it wasn't necessary to tell them about Bianca and that terrible night, and it seemed Legend hadn't told Liesbet about it either, because, one, she didn't say he had, and, two, if he had told her she would have definitely brought it up.

But they kept on probing and asked if I was unhappy or depressed or confused and suggested that I see a psychologist. Almost gritting my teeth with the effort of batting them off any soul-searching conversation starters, I eventually, in complete desperation, asked them if they'd been to any nice restaurants lately.

They both gave me quite a strange look.

'Alex, Mom and I also want you to know that you've got options,' said my dad, ignoring the question. 'We bought the spa for Jess when she was twenty-one and of course we bought a business for Richard and Charles, but only when they were much older.'

'But I thought Richard and Charles had made all their money modelling, and they used it to build the padel courts,' I said, surprised.

My father rolled his eyes. 'Hardly. They drank it, ate it, snorted it and travelled with it until they were broke, and had to come home. No, I funded the padel courts. Bloody good investment, though.'

'We'll obviously do the same for you,' he continued. 'As long as it's a sensible investment and something you're passionate about.'

'But why are you only telling me now?' I asked, interested. 'I mean, it's not as if I'm irresponsible with money or anything.'

'You most certainly are irresponsible with money, Alex,' said my dad. 'Don't think we don't know you gave all your twenty-first birthday money to the SPCA. You could have bought a flat for cash with it, for God's sake. Not to mention trading in your Jeep for that beat-up Nissan.'

'It's only done 135 000 kilometres and it's a 2014 model. And it has a full service history.' He looked quite impressed, to be honest.

'Anyway, that's not the point,' he continued. 'What I'm saying is, perhaps you might like to have your own business. It might give you some focus and confidence. Something of your own.'

'No thank you,' I said hastily. 'I mean, it's really kind and generous of you and everything, but I'm not good with people, and if you have a business you have to make lots of conversation and stuff, and basically people don't really take to me as a general rule.'

'Alex,' said Liesbet looking upset, 'the way you've just said that, in such a matter-of-fact way, is very concerning. *Of course* people like you! It's just ... it's just your approach, darling, that you might need to work on a bit.'

'I don't have any friends,' I said simply. 'Except for Saskia. I sort of had friends at Yamihle but not any more.'

They both stared at me with such troubled expressions that I wished I'd said I'd love a business like maybe a laundry or something and then dealt with getting out of it later. 'Please don't look like that. I promise you I'm fine and you mustn't worry about me. Maybe I'll stay at The Plains for a bit and think about stuff.'

'Perhaps even a gap year somewhere overseas?' said Liesbet perking up. 'You could go to the Australian outback maybe, on a sheep farm, or ... Texas on a cattle ranch. Where you could be with animals. You love animals!'

'Livestock farming is incredibly cruel and bad for the planet,' I said, frowning. 'And I'm a vegetarian, remember?'

Liesbet sighed and looked defeated. 'Yes,' she said, 'of course you are. What was I even thinking?'

20

WE ALL HAD DINNER IN the lodge dining room, which was basically empty because there were no guests. Even though Magnus and the few other guides that were left at The Plains joined us, the cavernous space seemed even more awful and inhospitable than it had before. I noticed Liesbet looking around her speculatively, and if I'd been seated next to her, I would have definitely asked her about her ideas.

'OMG, Alex,' whispered Saskia to me, 'you were totally right about the food. It's like so vintage that it could almost be trendy, you know what I mean? And also, you never said a single thing about you getting to work with so many *men*. That one over there, I think his name is Magnus, is he single? Not that it matters, it just seems that he's really nice.'

'He's absolutely single,' I said, even though I wasn't entirely sure. 'And he is nice. Uncomplicated and everything. I *think* he was head boy of his school.'

'So perfect,' she murmured, taking out her phone to photograph the aspic salad.

Later I joined Jess and Saskia in the room they were sharing, and we sat on the beds. This was the second intervention, but I didn't really mind.

'Now Alex,' Saskia said, 'this is only my opinion, but I think maybe you should phone Legend and talk about everything.'

'Like, so that he can tell me how terrible I am and then formally fire me?' I didn't say it in a snippy way, though.

'Well, I suppose he'll be angry, but perhaps you aren't fired? There's a chance that he might want you to come back. I mean, why is he keeping on trying to call you? If he's going to fire you, he would have done it on email or WhatsApp by now, surely?'

'Saskia's right, you know,' said Jess. 'And Mom said this one guide – Kwanele I think? – has phoned her about a hundred times.'

'He's definitely really angry with me,' I said, flopping onto my back and staring at the ceiling. 'That's probably why.'

'Angry?' Jess looked puzzled. 'If he were angry, why would he phone Mom? No, I don't think so, Alex. Mom said he sounded really worried. And Legend has phoned Mom too. She didn't say what he said, though. Actually, he sent her a few WhatsApps while we were driving today.'

'He's probably just worried about what's happened to Brunelda. What I did was illegal and he's definitely very angry with me. Do you think Liesbet told him where I was?'

Jess said she wasn't sure, and I fretted about it for a bit. But then I relaxed. Legend and Kwanele and Yamihle were a whole world away.

We were silent for a bit and then I said, 'What's happening with your parents, Saskia?'

'It's all worked out really well and they're getting a divorce,' replied Saskia.

I sat up straight at that.

'Oh no, I'm sorry. That's awful.'

'Not really,' she said. 'Actually, they're both much happier and they even took Ouma out for dinner to celebrate. She was so furious and insisted on wearing a black armband. The only thing they're sad about is that they didn't do it sooner.'

I raised an eyebrow at Jess, and she smiled. 'The wheels are turning. Roger moved in with the woman he was having an affair with, and then after two days he came back. He said she had all these cats and old sheets and he realised that I was his soul mate. But I just gave him a lawyer's letter and told him to go away. And it was weird, because when Mom came back from Yamihle, she did this about-turn on couples therapy and made me see a lawyer immediately.'

'Um, well, that's good,' I said. And I relaxed even more about Legend knowing where I was. Liesbet could definitely keep a secret.

Barend insisted that I take my dad and Liesbet and Jess and Saskia on a game drive the next morning. I asked Magnus to join us because I was beginning to think that he wasn't the fool I had always thought he was. Plus, Saskia asked me if I would invite him.

I hadn't had the chance to take Liesbet on a game drive at Yamihle, and so this was the first time my family had seen me in action. At first, I didn't bother to talk about the game we were viewing since they'd all been on game reserve holidays so often that I assumed it wasn't necessary. But then Saskia started asking me a few questions and I slipped easily into guide mode.

As we moved from one encampment to the next, I realised how much I had learnt from Kwanele, and I felt a sharp pang of longing, wishing he were sitting next to me. Up until that point I'd been feeling absorbed, maybe even happy, but suddenly missing him diminished all that and I struggled not to retreat into feeling sad. But by this time, we were in the elephant encampment, and luckily Oubaas distracted me. He really was a gentle giant, but I could see immediately that he was bored and in the mood to cause a little trouble. Not for the first time I thought how he needed more space to be a proper, free-roaming elephant.

He did a couple of mock charges, so I slapped the side of the cruiser and yelled at him. He retreated and wandered off a few metres, but changed his mind and came towards us from the side.

Judging by his approach, which I'd seen a few times before, I just knew he was going to do his favourite thing ever, which was to have a good scratch against the cruiser. Everyone had been silent up to this point, but as I turned around to explain what he was about to get up to, I saw that they were all looking completely terrified. Oubaas was on Saskia's side of the cruiser, and she was leaning so far away from him that she had practically climbed into Magnus' lap. Jess had also shifted over to Liesbet's side and was half standing up. 'Christ!' said my dad. 'Is he going to push us over?'

'No,' I said, 'definitely not. Everyone keep very quiet and stay still. He's just going to have a bit of a scratch and then he'll move away.'

In fact he had a fairly thorough rub against the cruiser, but luckily not a very long one. I waited for him to wander off again and started the engine.

'Let me tell you people something,' said Magnus when we were on our way. 'Of all the guides, Alex was the only one that kept calm around Oubaas. I nearly shat in my pants when he did that to me. He doesn't mean anything by it, but, sjoe, Alex got nerves of steel and she could always predict what he was going to do. Like now.'

'Well, thank God for that,' said Liesbet. 'Wasn't she wonderful, Edward?'

'She was indeed,' replied my dad. He turned to me. 'You're very good at all this.' He sounded a bit surprised, to be honest.

'Ja,' said Magnus, 'and a crack shot. You should see her at the shooting range.'

'Really?' My dad looked impressed. 'Well, that's quite something. And rather unexpected.' He glanced at my rifle on the dashboard of the cruiser. 'Funny, I've never thought about you having to handle a gun.'

'She escorted me to my room every night at Yamihle with her rifle,' said Liesbet. 'I didn't say anything, darling, but I did feel very proud that you were protecting your mother from heaven knows what. There are no fences at Yamihle, Edward, so you never know.'

The admiration was getting a bit much for me because I wasn't exactly used to it, so I pointed out a random bird and talked about it for a while. Plus, I didn't feel it was very deserved, considering the massive failure I'd turned out to be at Yamihle. And then I couldn't help thinking about that for the rest of the drive. So when we got back to the lodge it was almost as if I had conjured up a physical image of all the guilt and shame I'd been feeling. Because, parked next to Antoinette's office stood a Land Cruiser. And it was branded: Yamihle Private Game Reserve.

21

WEARING DARK SUNGLASSES AND LOOKING like something from the pages of a magazine, Legend and Kwanele stood towering over Antoinette, who had her arms folded and was looking at them with no small degree of hostility.

'My goodness,' said Liesbet a little too brightly. 'It's Legend and that lovely guide who is so handsome.'

I swung round furiously. 'You *knew* they were coming, didn't you? And why wouldn't you have warned me? Don't you think one ambush is enough?' I immediately felt bad and apologised because I was honestly getting much fonder of Liesbet.

'It will be fine, darling,' she said, squeezing my hand. 'Poor Legend was so worried, and I'm afraid I was a tiny bit harsh on him when he told me you were missing. So it'll be very good *therapy* for you both. To be honest, I actually didn't know Legend was coming, but I'm really very pleased.'

She gave a slightly mischievous smile. 'And besides, I think you need to have a talk with Kwanele.' She gave Legend an airy wave and then announced that she was going to leave us all to it since she was dying for a cup of tea, and disappeared into Antoinette and Barend's house.

The rest of us walked up to Legend and Kwanele since there was nothing else we could do, really. I looked at Kwanele, but he didn't smile at me or anything, and since he was wearing sunglasses, I couldn't see his eyes. They usually told me what he was thinking. In fact, I didn't smile at him either. I could still hardly believe what I was seeing.

Legend had clearly already rubbed up Antoinette the wrong way because, as we got nearer, she turned and said, 'Don't you even begin to think I invited this bladdy onbeskof Rastafarian and his sidekick. My liewe fok, I'm not surprised you ran away.'

Barend then came out of the office carrying Brunelda on his stomach in a bright pink baby sling. He always carried her facing outwards on account of stimulation or whatever, and she chattered excitedly when she saw us.

'Jesus Christ,' said Legend. 'Now I've seen it all.'

'Here we do not take the Lord's name in vain,' said Antoinette, pointing a long red fingernail at him. 'You mind your fokken language on my property.'

I expected him to say something rude, but he looked at her appreciatively and gave a slight smile.

'May I ask what you intend to do with that baboon?' he said, turning his attention to Barend. 'Send it to school? University perhaps? Train it to be a receptionist?'

Barend doesn't understand sarcasm, because he's such a good person, so he stared bemused at Legend for a few moments and then broke into a disarming smile.

'That's a good joke,' he said, and went forward to shake hands with Legend and then Kwanele. And that basically took the wind right out of Legend's sails.

Barend was thrilled when he heard that Legend and Kwanele were from Yamihle. Like me, he apparently also had a hero crush, but his was for them both.

'You must come into the house directly and have some tea or a brandy,' said Barend, sweetly hospitable. 'And listen, it goes without saying that you must stay for as many nights as you want.

Everyone is welcome. There is plenty of room and we can put some chops on the fire tonight.'

'We haven't come all this way for a fucking braai,' said Legend, his anger suddenly escalating. 'I've driven right across the sodding country to find out, before I fuckenwell fire her, what Alex thought she was doing by stealing that fucking baboon and absconding in the middle of the unholy shit show that she caused.'

I knew he was going to fire me, I thought. And then Jess spoke up.

'Leave her alone!' she shouted furiously. 'And maybe you can dig deep and find some adjectives other than 'fucking', you thick moron.'

We all turned to look at Jess in surprise. Basically, of the whole entire family she was the one who never ever lost her temper, and this was literally the first time I'd heard her yell at someone. Actually, she looked really beautiful, her eyes flashing and her cheeks flushed.

'And who the fuck are you?' said Legend, rounding on her.

'I'm her *sister*,' she replied. 'And you must be Legend, the famous legendary arsehole who couldn't be bothered to even give her a chance to explain and maybe you could do us all a huge favour and piss off.'

They stood staring at each other, at first with their eyes locked antagonistically, and then with quite a bit of interest. And then Legend actually went a bit red. Jess blushed, and I know this time it wasn't anger, because when she blushes her neck and chest go pink. And her ears.

'I apologise,' he said in a much milder tone and not in the least bit sarcastic. 'Profusely.'

'That's okay,' Jess said, her voice so mild it could even be interpreted as *friendly*.

They carried on looking at each other until my dad cleared his throat. 'Yes, well, I think we should all calm down and talk this through.' Which was a very lawyery thing to say, and I didn't like the sound of 'we', because I didn't want everyone listening to Legend shout at me. Plus, there were a few little things I hadn't told anyone about.

'Alex must talk to this Legend person and Kwanele on her own,' said Antoinette. 'She's an adult and it's got fokkol to do with us. We leave them now and they can go sit in the lodge lounge.'

She pointed again at Legend. 'And you, you just remember how grateful you should be to Alex for taking the trouble to help you out of your own fokken mess, okay?'

'Do you want me to come with you?' said my dad in an undertone as everyone drifted into Antoinette and Barend's house.

'No, it's totally fine,' I said, 'but thanks.'

And it actually was totally fine. Or almost. Because although Legend let me explain and listened closely and didn't shout once or say terrible things, and although he didn't fire me then and there, he also didn't mention anything about not firing me. That wasn't a surprise, though. I mean, what else could he do? Kwanele was kind but detached and supported me in a logical and unemotional way.

We spoke for about an hour and then Legend got up. 'Okay, I need that brandy now,' he said and then looked at Kwanele. 'And we need to talk to Barend about what we're gonna do about that fucking baboon. Brunelda. Christ.' He shook his head.

I was about to say that Antoinette and Barend would literally only give Brunelda up over their dead bodies, if that was on his mind, but then I found that I didn't want to. This is excellent instinct, I thought. It's your *filter* Alex. Finally.

We walked back to Antoinette and Barend's house without saying anything, and although I was glad that I'd talked to them both, I felt very, very sad about Kwanele. I had hoped he'd ask if we could talk privately. I knew that our spark was over and that it was all my fault, but I felt desperate to talk to him some more. I didn't dare ask him in case he said no.

Everyone else had gathered in Antoinette and Barend's formal lounge. No one saw us as we were about to walk in, since

Antoinette had this bead curtain covering the doorway to stop flies. We paused as we heard Saskia speaking. I could picture her sitting forward in her chair, hands clasped on her knees.

I stiffened and listened, horrified, as I realised that she was telling them all about my deepest, darkest, most awful secret. What happened at school.

'There was this one girl, Athena,' Saskia was saying, 'who was really jealous of Alex, and I suppose it was because Alex was fun to be around, and lively and gutsy and popular. It started with Athena saying stuff about her, spreading stupid rumours, and it then it spiralled. It became a sort of game – everyone made fun of her, and no one wanted to be friends with her.'

'Why didn't Alex say something to her teachers?' asked my dad. 'Surely they could have put a stop to it?'

'She did try to tell this one time. I made her do it and I went with her to the principal to make sure she told her everything. The principal asked Athena to come to her office, and then Athena made a huge scene and started crying and accused us of lying. So the whole thing was a bit pointless.

'After that, Athena stopped the bullying for a little bit, but then she started again. Only this time it was much, much worse, because she realised she could get away with it, and it became totally out of control. She and her friends started setting up stuff to humiliate Alex, and took videos, and one time they got this group of boys at a school dance to spike her drink, and ... they did loads of other horrible stuff. She couldn't even walk down a corridor without someone trying to trip her up or shove her into a wall. They just wouldn't leave her alone. They were *completely* relentless. And so Alex was on high alert all the time. She never knew when something terrible was going to happen, but she always knew it was coming.'

'She didn't say a *word* about it to us,' said Liesbet, her voice breaking as if she was going to cry.

'Well, how do you trust anybody when you're going through five years of hell? Alex barely trusted me, and she got so angry when I said she must tell you. She made me promise not to say anything, and of course now I wish I had. But we were both scared and we didn't know what to do.'

Saskia looked up and saw me standing in the doorway. Her horrified expression mirrored my own.

'Alex,' she said, 'I'm sorry, and … and I'm also not sorry. I just felt that your family needed to know what happened. And I know it looks like I'm talking behind your back, and I suppose I *am* talking behind your back, but I promise I was going to tell you about it *immediately*.'

'Please don't be upset, Alex,' said Jess. 'Dad started asking Saskia questions and then it all came out. She didn't set out to tell us. And she's right. We did need to know. And, oh God, Alex, I'm so devastated.'

I scanned their faces as they all stared at me. Pity. Compassion. Concern. I felt raw and exposed and humiliated beyond belief. I pushed between Legend and Kwanele and ran for my life.

That sounds very dramatic, but you can't actually run very far at The Plains on account of the encampments, so I headed for an area behind the lodge where guests could walk on their own. I had just reached the top of a koppie when I realised that Kwanele had followed me.

'You remind me of an impala,' he said, breathing heavily and leaning against a rock. 'Anxious and always alert and ready to run. And a really fit one, by the way. But other times you're a lioness.' He smiled. 'An interesting mixture.'

'Alex,' he continued, 'no one should have gone through what you did. I'm sorry.'

I looked away. I didn't want pity.

'Why didn't you tell anyone?'

Still staring ahead, I said, 'It was too shameful, all those years of humiliation. So I tried to pretend it hadn't happened, but I couldn't put it out of mind. And then, I don't know, I suppose I thought it was my fault, that I wasn't a likeable person. And then it became a self-fulfilling prophecy because I could feel myself almost deliberately starting to mess things up. Just to get it over and done with.'

'What do you mean? Get what over and done with?'

'People not liking me. That's how it always seemed to end up. I mean … look at how things turned out between us.'

'So you're saying that to get me to dislike you, you deliberately went off and stole a baby baboon?'

'No, obviously not!' I said, turning to look at him, and saw that he was smiling at me. Kwanele came towards me and took my hand.

'I *was* angry about it,' he said. 'But Alex, it would take a lot more than that for me not to like you. You made a mistake, but that doesn't change how I feel about you. If you'd read my messages, you'd know that. Why didn't you read them, by the way?'

'I was too scared to read them,' I explained. 'I couldn't face what I thought you'd probably say.'

'Maybe you won't like what I wrote but I can't help that. I had to be honest. And I think it's important for you to read the messages.'

'Okay,' I said, my heart sinking. I knew what the messages would say, though. Basically, that he liked me as a friend. He'd said how he felt anyway, that night at Yamihle. *You're not who I thought you were.* I knew I had turned out to be a disappointment, and so I took my hand from his, and he didn't try to keep hold of it. 'Anyway, Legend said he's going to fire me.'

He sighed. 'You must know Legend's temper by now. If he's worried, he loses it, if he's angry, he loses it, and sometimes he loses it for no reason at all. In this case he lost it because he was worried about you. He didn't actually care about the guests. And in the end, it wasn't so bad because they started getting more interested in what had happened to the baboon. He went completely off the deep end when we discovered you were missing. What I'm saying is that I don't think he's going to fire you.'

I looked down and scratched the ground with my foot. 'Well, if he can't bring himself to do that then I should resign.'

'Alex! Stop it! Are you descending into some kind of noble pity party or something?'

'No, I'm not! I just think I made a huge mess, and I can't see how anyone at Yamihle is going to trust me again.'

'Let's go back,' said Kwanele after a while. I nodded. So that was that. Kwanele and Legend would leave the next day and then it really would be all over. I didn't think I could go back to Yamihle even if Legend didn't fire me. But I'd known that for a couple of days, and I'd also known that the glimmer of possibility that had made me so happy, the chance of there being something between Kwanele and me, had been extinguished. While I felt flat and defeated as we walked back, I also began to feel a huge sense of relief that Saskia had told my family what I hadn't been able to tell them. I didn't feel like carrying that burden any longer, nor did I want the repercussions it had caused.

Barend and Antoinette had moved everyone out onto their veranda. Barend had lit a fire and was dispensing drinks from his thatched bar. He'd switched on all the fairy lights and Billy Ocean was playing in the background. Legend was sitting on a bar stool talking to Jess, who I noticed had her head tilted towards him and was playing with her hair.

Kwanele steered me right towards them, and Jess looked up, relieved to see I'd come back with him. She was about to get up when Kwanele said, 'Legend, Alex thinks you're going to fire her.'

'Why the fuck would I do that?' he said, clearly forgetting that he had said he was going to, but I decided not to point that out. 'I've only just fired that son of a bitch Dirk and I can't be short-staffed at Easter, for Christ's sake. It's just around the corner and the lodge is full.' He accepted another brandy decorated with a cocktail umbrella from Barend and grinned. 'By the way, I forgot to tell you. Dumi says you've stolen his dog.'

'Darling,' said Liesbet as she and my dad came over, 'I feel as if I need to go into therapy or something. I'll *never* get over this. I think Dad must sue the school and Athena's parents and oh God we feel so absolutely *terrible*. I've found the number of a wonderful family therapist that we can *all* go to, and the twins must come too, because bloody Charles has broken up with that lovely girl Sarah, and I'm convinced Richard made him do it.'

Liesbet had clearly had quite a bit of wine already, and my dad and I both looked alarmed at the mention of family therapy.

'So actually,' I said, 'I mean, I'm really glad that you all know and that's kind of enough for me, but we can all totally get deep and meaningful tomorrow if you want, but only for a little bit.'

My dad squeezed my hand. 'Lots to talk about,' he said, 'and just for a little bit, as you say. Let's get Liesbet another drink.'

'Where's Saskia?' I asked, looking around for her.

'She's making salads with Antoinette and Brunelda,' said Jess. 'You won't be angry with her, will you? She's so upset.'

Brunelda was watching from her cot and Jackson's nose was poking out from under the table while Saskia and Antoinette sliced aubergines.

'This recipe is really simple,' Saskia was saying. 'You roast the aubergines, and then you make a dressing with olive oil and balsamic vinegar and garlic and honey. Have you got basil? We can add that too.'

'Don't you also add toasted almonds?' I asked. I went up to her and gave her a hug.

'Oh Alex,' she said, returning the hug so fiercely that I nearly fell over. 'I'm so sorry. But ... but I think it was okay, wasn't it?'

'Yes,' I replied. 'Yes, it was. We're all having a very quick deep and meaningful tomorrow if you want to join us?'

'Send a formal request to The Mutual Protection Society. But I'm sure I can make it.'

'Roger,' I replied, 'except that he won't be there.'

She laughed, and so there was me and Saskia having a banter and smiling at each other. Like me and Marietjie. Like normal girlfriends. But it would never really be normal, and I was saving that up to tell her in the deep and meaningful the next day. It would always be a million miles better than normal, and I wanted her to know that.

'Nee, fok, Alex,' said Antoinette, 'take this Jackson outside now, he's under my feet, and get Magnus on the walkie-talkie and tell him to come over for the braai. Now, Saskia, we've put the pap on the stove for stomach lining because I can see they're getting bladdy dronk out there. Maybe we can garnish it with some parsley? Or is that too fancy?'

After I'd radioed Magnus, I went to my room and forced myself to read Kwanele's messages. At first I scanned them quickly, and then I read each one a few times, and then I slowly made my way back to the veranda.

'I promised I'd phone Marietjie to let her know how everything went,' said Kwanele when he saw me. 'The last guests left this morning, so the guides are home alone. The group we got after you left were big partiers, so I'm sure they're all pretty tired and wanting an early night.'

He propped his iPad on the bar and made a FaceTime call. It took ages for Marietjie to answer, and by now Legend had joined us. 'Oh, how lovely,' said Liesbet, coming over. 'Edward, you must meet the guides at Yamihle, they're the most wonderful bunch of professionals.' So by the time Marietjie's face eventually exploded onto the screen, everyone had gathered round, including Antoinette and Barend.

Behind Marietjie we could see the rest of the guides, and they were in the middle of a raucous party. From the state of Marietjie's face it appeared that they were playing oobly doobly. Her cheeks and forehead were liberally dotted with ash from the end of a burnt wine cork. So, for that matter, were everyone else's.

I felt Kwanele's body shake with silent laughter beside me.

'It's Alex!' shrieked Marietjie, and they all cheered. 'And look, they also got a party going on! Girlfriend, are you okay? We miss you and I got so much news but I'm gonna start with the best bit.'

Before I could reply, Dumi's face popped up. 'Alex, where's my deputy?'

'Alex, you're never gonna believe this,' said Marietjie, appearing again, 'but Legend broke up with that bladdy Bianca. My liewe vader but it was a terrible scene. She threw him with a pile of those old books your ma put on the coffee table in the lounge, and he had to hide behind the couch. Then he starts laughing so she sommer goes to the bar and starts smashing glasses. Verskriklik.'

'May I remind you, Marietjie, that I am actually standing right here, and the bloody speaker is on?' said Legend coldly.

'Oops!' she said and handed the phone to Bandile, who was wearing Bianca's Prada sunglasses.

'Good evening, stand by,' he said, speaking slowly and carefully. What looked a bit like a bread roll hit him on the side of the head, and the screen turned upside down a few times as the iPad clattered to the floor amidst shrieks of laughter.

After a while Petrus came into view. He peered beadily at us for a few moments. 'Who invited all these people? I thought we din' have no guests. They must go home.'

'They're on the screen, you big mampara,' said Marietjie, taking over again. 'Listen, Alex, are you coming back? Because I just remembered another bladdy thing. Shamilla and Gavin have booked for the Easter weekend and Julia and Mikey said they not gonna come if you and Kwanele don't guide them. And guess what? Legend's flippenwell invited Bertie and the other bokdrols because he's such a big softie. Ag shamepies, but he can bladdy guide them himself, verstaan.'

'Of course I'm coming back,' I said with a huge smile on my face. 'Where else would I go?' I could feel Kwanele tensing, and I was conscious that he had turned to look at me.

They all cheered again, and Petrus waved a bottle around.

'Jesus Christ, he's got my bottle of Chivas,' said Legend and yelled into the iPad. 'Petrus, put that fucking bottle down else I'm gonna fire the fucking lot of you.'

'Sorry, Oom, too late,' said Marietjie and ended the call.

'My word, but your ship is not tight at all,' remarked Antoinette. 'Verskriklik!'

'I think you've made a sensible decision,' said my dad, and Liesbet smiled at me.

'Yes,' I agreed. 'Only, I had been sort of thinking about staying here because I've been trying to help Antoinette and Barend. Do you remember when I phoned you about Horizon Heights? It was actually to do with them and The Plains.'

'Tell me about it,' said my dad.

And that was what we all discussed while Barend and Magnus braaied the chops and we ate, and the others ended up with Amarula in wine glasses. I was glad I didn't drink, because questions were fired at me, and I needed a clear head. I started by explaining that The Plains could possibly sustain free-roaming animals.

'We talked about this,' said Kwanele. 'But you said there wasn't enough land.' I looked at him, thinking it was a challenge, and then realised he was on my side, encouraging me.

'Yes, but there *could* be,' I replied. 'The Plains currently has twelve thousand hectares, and that's obviously not enough to sustain free-roaming animals, which is a requirement for it to be upgraded to a private game reserve. But if the owners of the surrounding farms sold their land to The Plains, and they are actually keen to do that, it would add another thirty thousand hectares, which would result in a viable and self-sustaining reserve of forty-two thousand hectares, with the Big Five.'

'How do you know they would sell the land to Barend and not Horizon Heights?' asked my dad.

I turned to Barend, who was looking bewildered. 'So, I've been to see all of them, and Magnus came with me,' I explained. 'I'm sorry, Barend, that I didn't tell you, but I wanted to find out how they felt about Horizon Heights. And it turned out that none of them want to sell to developers. They all want to sell to *you*.'

'Ja, but I told you Antoinette and me don't have the money,' said Barend shaking his head. 'That was a waste of time.'

'Just let Alex speak, man,' said Antoinette. 'Listen to what she's got to say.'

I continued. 'Oom Piet wants to go to Florida. The one in America, not in Roodepoort. And Oom Marius and his wife are looking for a house in Mossel Bay so they can fish, but they want to keep a bit of land and their house. That was Magnus' idea, and it was a really good one, because they want to keep ties with their farm and that way they can.'

'Ja, but what about Tannie Santie?' said Barend. 'She said she'd set her rottweiler on the developers if they ever came back,' he explained to the others. 'She's not selling. That farm has been in her family for generations, and I don't blame her.'

'Well, that's a good thing though,' I said. 'Because it means that she won't sell to Horizon Heights, but she also said that she would sell her land to you. But she needs to keep six hectares because … well, because she and her grandson Gert are growing cannabis.'

'A very good idea,' said Antoinette to my surprise. 'The oil is bladdy good for your skin tone.'

'It is,' agreed Jess. 'I use it in my spa and it's amazing.'

'Fucking *brilliant* idea,' said Legend enthusiastically. 'Not easy to grow, though. Wonder if it's any good?'

'I think it really is,' I replied, trying not to look at Magnus. 'Gert gave me some and you can try it later if you like. And no, I haven't tried it myself,' as Legend seemed about to view me in a new light. 'But basically, the point is, all the farmers want to sell to Barend, and so Antoinette and I were wondering about investment, but we didn't get very far on that because we don't know anything about it.'

'When Alex left,' said Antoinette, and I was really grateful she didn't say she'd fired me, 'she filled in the employee feedback form, and what she said there made me de moer in at first, and I nearly put it in the bin, but it is very close to what she's describing now.'

'Problem is the big game you've got here now,' said Legend.

'Especially the lion.'

'You had a plan about that too, didn't you?' said Kwanele.

'Yes. So, there's nothing we can really do about the lions since they've been fed all their lives and can't integrate or fend for themselves,' I replied. 'But they would stay. Their camp is currently two hectares, but we could increase it to five hectares. And the males need to be fixed so there is no more breeding. In time, the pride will die out. But lions could be introduced that are free roaming. The elephant would be fine. They've got the biggest encampment now and they could pretty much roam free from the get-go. There's lots for them to eat. They're not fussy.'

'I can see you've put a shitload lot of thought into this,' said Legend.

'I thought about it the whole time I was working at The Plains,' I explained. 'Because it always seemed to me that it could be possible. And then at Yamihle I talked about it to Kwanele, and he agreed. Besides making it a proper game reserve, it's a chance to preserve and restore the land. I don't need to tell you how incredibly special the Karoo is.'

Sometimes you can talk and talk about something you're passionate about, but no one really gets it. But sometimes there can be a sort of tipping point where everyone understands, and then they're completely on your side. My dad started asking questions about zoning and access to utilities and municipal ordinances and wondered if the accommodation at The Plains could be expanded for more guests. And Liesbet got all excited and said it could be turned into a very exclusive lodge with a massive target market because there were so few game reserves with the Big Five in the Western Cape.

Legend said it wasn't a quick fix, and that all the surrounding farmlands would need to be rehabilitated and that would take years and years, but it was totally possible. And then Jess suggested a spa, but Legend said maybe she'd consider setting one up at Yamihle, and she went all pink and said she'd love to. Saskia said maybe the food could be a kind of fusion boerekos and that she had some really good ideas. Antoinette said she didn't know what the fok 'fusion' meant but personally she would try anything once. Magnus said he'd eaten fusion food once before and it was a really good experience. While everyone spoke, Barend could hardly keep up and looked dazed and confused, but in a good way, if you know what I mean.

As I listened to everyone talking, and all the ideas that flowed, I didn't know if anything would come of it. Perhaps it was just a wave of excitement, and they had all got caught up in the moment. And maybe the next morning they'd wake up and realise that everything they had discussed was just a dream, a wonderful dream, but in the cold and sober light of day it would seem impossible. And then everyone would go their separate ways, the ideas and excitement just a memory that would dim over time. I thought of one more thing, and I told them that Horizon Heights was ready to pay deposits. My dad's left eyebrow shot up. Then I remembered I had something for Legend in my car and as I slipped away, I saw that my dad had taken out his phone and the calculator app was on his screen. And that was a very good sign.

Standing outside, I looked up at the huge and beautiful sky. It was full moon again. Just over a whole month since I'd first left The Plains. Even though the light of the moon tried to dominate, the sky was stuffed full of stars, fuzzy and magical. I thought how tiny it was, this moment in time, but so perfect, because it was mine. A cold nose touched my hand. Jackson. And of course I knew Kwanele was there too.

'Let's go back to that koppie,' he said.

'Yes,' I said, turning to face him. 'Let's just sit there and talk about stuff.'

I took his hand, and I smiled the biggest smile I could ever remember. 'But before we do, I just want to make it very clear that I *like* like you too.'

219

Acknowledgements

A HUGE THANK YOU TO Annie Olivier and everyone at Jonathan Ball for their enthusiasm and support and for basically making my biggest dream come true.

I wrote this book in Mike Nicol's Writer's Masterclass, and so it mainly owes its existence to Mike, whose sharp and incisive comments and dry wit kept me focused.

I so wish that my parents, Roy and Hettie Norman, could have read this book and shared in all the excitement of it being published. It is to them that I owe my love of reading, which ultimately resulted in my desire to write. A big thank you too to my lovely sister, Jan, for reading drafts and laughing in all the right places and encouraging outrageous scenarios.